# CHAPTER ONE

*Weston*

"**N**ICE ROCK," I said, admiring the diamond ring Donovan placed on the tabletop. I picked it up and examined the stone in the dimly lit lounge of the The Grand Havana Room, the member's-only cigar lounge we often frequented when we were together. The diamond was a big one, in a platinum setting with at least four carats between the large center jewel and the scattering of smaller diamonds surrounding it. A serious engagement ring. I wouldn't expect anything less from one of the world's most successful young billionaires.

I just had no idea Donovan was even dating anyone.

Of course, we weren't as close as we used to be. Physically, anyway. He'd been managing the Tokyo office with Cade since we'd expanded our advertising firm into that market. He rarely made it stateside, and it had been nearly a year since I'd last seen Donovan in person. When he'd shown up tonight unexpectedly asking Nate and I to meet him at the club, we'd guessed he had serious news but that it was about the business.

An engagement ring was a whole new level of serious. No wonder he wanted to do this in person.

"Who's the lucky girl?" I asked, trying not to sound bothered that this was the first I was hearing about her. A glance at Nate said it was the first he was hearing about her too.

"You're asking the wrong question," Donovan said, and bit off the end of his cigar. "The question is who's the lucky *guy?*"

I raised a brow, confused. But not surprised. Donovan was known to speak in riddles. I'd figure out what he was trying to tell me when he was ready to spill. Might as well play along in the meantime.

"Okay." I pinched the ring between two fingers and lifted it toward the nearest light source so I could see the full effect of its sparkle. "Who's the lucky guy?"

He lit the end of his cigar and puffed a couple of times before taking it out and answering. "You."

"Oh, Donovan. You shouldn't have." I clutched my hand to my chest for dramatic effect. "I don't know that we've ever said it, but I love you too. Still, I don't think I'm ready for this." I handed the ring back to him with a shake of my head.

Nate hid his smirk by taking a large swig of his imported beer.

"Very funny." Donovan carefully placed the ring back in its box. "I'm not proposing *to* you, Weston. I'm proposing *for* you."

"You are, are you?" I chuckled at his attempt at a joke. Inside my jacket pocket my phone buzzed with a text. I pulled it out and quickly skimmed the message.

*I need to see you.*

Normally I'd be all up for a booty call, but my night belonged to the guys. I deleted the message without reading who it was from, silenced my phone and put it back in my pocket.

I gave my attention back to Donovan, continuing to play along with his hoax. "Just who exactly are you proposing to *for* me?"

He puffed heavily on his cigar before removing it from his mouth to speak. "Her name is Elizabeth Dyson. She's the sole inheritor of the Dyson Empire. She's twenty-five, classy though spirited, well-bred—definitely a suitable bride. Your union is going to take our business to the next level. Once you marry her, Reach, Inc. will be the biggest advertising company in Europe."

All humor drained from my face. He was serious. Donovan never joked about business. But marriage? "You've got to be kidding me."

"Not even a little bit."

I was beginning to regret not looking at the name before I deleted that text. I'd have loved to have a reason to bail right about then.

But it was Donovan's first night back in town, I really couldn't leave him now. Not to mention, I knew him. Once he got an idea in his head, it was nearly impossible to get it out. My best chance was to listen, find the weakness in his scheme, and then propose an alternate strategy.

If that failed, I'd tell him *fuck, no*, and that would be that.

Hopefully.

Saying *fuck, no* to Donovan Kincaid was often a bit harder in reality than it seemed in theory.

If I was going to stay, I was at least going to need a stiffer drink. I signaled the waiter. "Can you bring me a shot of Fireball?" Nate nudged me. "Two shots of Fireball?"

Then I turned to Donovan. "You'd better explain this from the beginning."

He took a puff of his cigar. "It's a short explanation. Dell Dyson, founder, CEO, and majority shareholder of Dyson Media—basically France's version of Time Warner—died about eight months ago, leaving his daughter the sole inheritor to the bulk of his fortune. However, the will states she can't get her hands on any of it until she's 29—with one exception."

"Ah, I think I'm getting the picture," Nate said, taking a pull on his beer.

My brows remained wrinkled, *my* picture still unclear. "Explain it to me then," I said, turning to Nate. "Because I'm not following."

He set his bottle on the table and tilted his head toward me. "Daddy Dell was a traditionalist. The daughter inherits when she puts a ring on it."

"Oh." Understanding settled in. I screwed my face up in disgust. "That's gross."

"Completely terrible and misogynistic," Donovan agreed, not sounding terribly upset at all. "But there's nothing we can do about the unfortunate set-up of her situation, and there is something we can do to get her out of it. Something that works out in our favor. So what we need to do is focus on getting Elizabeth married to our man Weston—"

I started to protest, but Donovan rose a hand to silence me. *"Tempo-rarily* married—a couple of months is all we need for Elizabeth to claim her inheritance of Dyson Media. Once she does, she can push through the merger of Dyson's advertising subsidiary with Reach, and we'll take over as the biggest ad company in the European market."

"Just like that," I said, skeptically.

"Just like that." There was no trace of doubt in Donovan's voice.

"And what makes you think that she'd be interested in this?" I asked. "I mean why would she be interested in giving someone—giving *us*—part of the company? Not why would she be interested in me." I wasn't worried about women being into me. But I certainly wasn't into discussing it with Donovan.

Of course he had an answer for this as well. "I'm in preliminary talks with her already. And she seemed quite interested in the whole arrangement. I didn't specify who her groom would be but told her I had an eligible bachelor. She's thinking about it further. Tomorrow afternoon in the office, all four of us will have a meeting to hammer out the details. I've already cleared your schedule."

It was a good thing the shots arrived then. "You mean I have to have this all thought through and decided by tomorrow afternoon?"

"Oh, you'll agree," Donovan said, confidently.

I threw back the shot. It didn't burn half as much as Donovan's proposal.

I rolled my neck, easing the muscles in my shoulders. "I need a minute to think about this."

"Take two."

I wasn't really considering any of it, but it was an excuse to order another drink and make Donovan pay for it.

I gestured for the waiter to bring two more shots. Then I leaned back against the plush leather upholstery of the bench seat and rubbed my hand across my forehead, pretending to weigh Donovan's offer in my mind.

To be honest, I'd been restless recently. I enjoyed the benefits of my life—my rental apartment in Midtown, my sex life, the view from my office. But my twenty-ninth birthday was looming and that was so close to thirty. A milestone birthday, and what did I have to show for it?

Okay. I was one of five shareholders of Reach,Inc., one of the most successful ad agencies in the world, but everyone knew that was Donovan's brainchild.

What did I have that was purely my own?

A month ago, I'd been so caught up in the desire for clarity that, on a whim, I'd asked a girl to move to New York from LA. It wasn't the first impulsive move I'd ever made, especially not for a girl—a girl I'd been naked with all weekend, no less—but it had been the craziest.

Almost as crazy of an idea as getting married to a stranger in order to improve our business status.

Sabrina, the naked woman, had been a peer that Donovan and I had gone to Harvard with. I'd been fortunate enough to spend a magical reunion weekend with her. There was something about her—a combination of her sexy laugh, serious demeanor, and intelligent brain that struck a chord deep inside me. Our conversation had made me feel warm and interesting and I wanted to capture that. Wanted to make it last.

So much so that right there on the spot, I demanded she take the position of Director of Marketing Strategy. Who cared that there was somebody else who held the position already?

She'd turned me down, wisely, but after she'd left, when the hormones calmed down, I looked into her resume anyway. Turned out she actually deserved the position, and I'd been halfheartedly working on making the transition happen legitimately ever since.

I'd spent good time thinking about making a real go at a relationship with her, too, if I got her to take the job.

I'd even told Donovan about my plans. Had he forgotten?

"But I don't want to get married," I reminded him now. "I want to bring Sabrina Lund to New York City and find out whether or not we fit together."

"Sabrina *Lind*," he corrected, his tone peppered with annoyance.

"Isn't that what I said?" I was starting to feel the alcohol.

"Still bring her here," Nate suggested, always the reasonable one. "She can take the job, and settle in. By the time she gets the hang of things around here, you'll be through your annulment and then you're free to date her."

"That could work, I suppose." Still wasn't considering it.

"If *she's* interested, that is," Donovan scowled.

"Why would she not be interested?" I asked.

"She'll be interested," Nate assured me. "But it is hard to move into a new city and get into a new relationship all at once. Better to take it in steps. And meanwhile, you can do this thing for the company."

I could hear the subtext in his words. Subtext that said he thought maybe I owed the company a little more *doing*.

Possibly I was reading too much into it.

I slammed back my next shot and considered what other reason there might be for Nate Sinclair to take Donovan's side. He was usually Switzerland.

"You're just saying all that because you don't want to be the one to get married, aren't you?" I eyed Nate accusingly.

He averted his eyes. "I'm old enough to be her father. It's not really appropriate."

I turned my stare to Donovan. There wasn't a band on *his* finger.

"It wouldn't work," he said flatly, guessing my thoughts. "No one would ever believe I'd get married."

"I can't dispute that." It was hard for me to believe the guy had friends. And I was his *best* friend.

"You are the ideal candidate," Donovan insisted.

"Damn right I'm the ideal candidate." I grinned, giving him my full dimpled smile, because hands-down, I was the best looking of all of us. My panty collection proved it. Cade could give me a run for my money with his constant brooding—women seemed to go for that—but he was in Japan. And Dylan Locke's charming British accent only worked on girls outside the UK, and he was never leaving the London office.

So, I wasn't just the ideal candidate—I was the *only* candidate.

But I wasn't doing it. It was crazy. Stupid crazy.

I ran my hand over my face, wondering how much longer I should allow Donovan to think I could be convinced. There was a fine line between hearing him out and becoming roped in.

"Is this Elizabeth person hot?" I asked, my lips numb from the shots.

"Why?" Donovan asked suspiciously.

"If I'm stuck with her I might as well . . . you know."

"You just said that you couldn't marry her because you've found the love of your life with Sabrina . . ." I could practically see steam coming from Donovan's ears.

"I didn't say Sabrina was the love of my life. I said she *might* be the love of my life. It's too early to tell."

"Either way," Donovan said, snarling, "it's probably a good idea if you don't sleep with your fiancée."

I exchanged glances with Nate.

Donovan followed my gaze as he tapped the ash of his cigar into a tray. "That didn't sound right, but I stand behind my recommendation."

Again, Nate and I looked to each other. We maybe had less conventional sexual standards than our business partner.

Correction—we *definitely* had less conventional sexual standards. Especially Nate. Which made him a god in my book. But that was beside the point.

The point was that good ideas were for the office. In the bedroom, I preferred my ideas to be bad.

I was just messing with Donovan, anyway. I didn't need this set-up to get laid, and I most certainly didn't need this set-up to feel like I'd contributed to the company. I'd strung him along far enough.

"Well, Donovan, this is maybe the most strategic and outrageous plan you've ever come up with, also possibly the most brilliant." I patted him on the back. He did deserve credit where credit was due. "But I'm going to have to pass, brother. It's a little too crazy for me."

Donovan sat back and slung out an arm, his elbow resting on the back of the bench. He looked relaxed, far too at ease with my decision, which made *me* uneasy. He was a guy who was used to things happening his way. He didn't like it when his plans were altered. If he wasn't upset now, it meant he had something else up his sleeve.

Which meant I needed to keep my guard up.

Unfortunately, Donovan also had patience. So despite my suspicions, I'd have to wait until he was prepared to move into the next phase of his plan to find out what he was hiding.

I glanced over at Nate who shrugged again before catching the eye of a gentleman at the bar.

"Excuse me," he said, "I know that guy. I need to say hello."

I gave him a wink because there was no telling how Nate knew him—whether it was from his past crazy illegal dealings or from his current wild sexual dealings. Either way, it probably made a good story, and one I'd like to hear.

A good story that I wasn't going to get to hear because I was stuck at the table with Donovan and whatever bullshit scenario he had worked up for me now.

Before he could start in on another one of these brilliant schemes, I started a conversation of my own. "How long are you staying in town, Donovan?"

"Haven't decided yet. A few months. Longer, maybe. Cade's handling Japan for now. Meanwhile, you've been complaining about needing some help up here. So here I am."

"Well." This was awesome. Donovan and I hadn't lived in the same city for years. Our parents owned King-Kincaid Financial, and we'd spent so much time together growing up, we were practically siblings. My only sister was a decade younger, so Donovan had been the one I'd bonded with most. Only four years older than me, he was the one who had mentored me through all my significant firsts. First time drinking, first time smoking, first time sneaking out to meet a girl, first time starting a company.

"Glad to hear it. You should've told me sooner. Are you moving back into—"

"I'll wipe the loan," he said, cutting me off.

And there it was. The bit that would make my jaw drop. The offer that would make me sit up and listen.

"The *entire* loan?" My heart was thumping in my chest now, and I could hear blood gushing in my ears.

"The whole thing. Gone."

Gone. All of it. *Whoosh.* Just like that.

What a fucking relief that would be.

Donovan was the only one who knew that I hadn't put all my own money into the company when we first started up. After nearly draining my inheritance from my grandmother, I'd borrowed the rest of the seed money from him, a sizable amount that I'd slowly been paying him back with the profits earned over our five years in business.

I still owed him a million.

It was quite an amount to just write off, even for him.

The irony of it was that I had more than twenty times that in my trust fund. I could've wiped the loan out myself years ago. If I'd wanted to.

Again, Donovan was the only one who knew why I chose not to borrow from that sizable fund.

And so, since Reach had begun with Donovan and I—and since we had pledged the most start-up money—when he covered my portion, he also got the advantage.

It was one of the reasons why the company always felt like it was more Donovan's than mine.

And it was a reason I often bent to his will, even when I'd rather not.

"Why is this merger so important to you?" I asked, unsure what to make of this offer. It wasn't like Donovan held the loan over me all the time. It wasn't like he wasn't generous. He would give me the shirt off his back if it was the last thing he owned.

But he also knew about integrity, and he understood that I wanted to be a self-made man. And he respected that.

I respected him for getting me.

So if this was that important to him, then I really needed to be listening. Because I would give Donovan the shirt off my back too.

"Number one in Europe, Weston," he said with a gleam in his eye. "We've only been open five years, and it would take a long time to get that title any other way. It's been far more difficult than I'd hoped to crack that market the way we have here."

I always knew the guy was competitive, but this really took the cake.

"And it's just a fake marriage then? Just a sham?"

*Dammit.* I couldn't believe I was actually considering this.

"A complete farce. You'd start right away, fake a whirlwind romance and engagement. Have the whole thing done in four, five months tops. But the benefits to Reach would last a lifetime. Think of it as your legacy, Weston."

I drummed my fingers on the table top. "This is fucking insane."

"You *like* insane," he said, leaning in close, knowing exactly which words would push my buttons.

How did he do this every time? He really was a mastermind. Able to wield the strings of all the puppets, controlling everyone, getting them to do his bidding. Not that I resented him for it. I admired him, truthfully.

And there was that something in my life that was missing.

Not that a fake wedding was going to fix it, but maybe the chance to contribute could make a difference. The chance to leave a legacy.

And to be able to give something back to Donovan after all the things he'd given me—well, that was something I couldn't take lightly.

Plus the end of that loan. To be my own man. Finally.

"Ah, fuck it. I got nothing better to do with my life. Let's be number one in Europe." Actually, that did have a pretty decent ring to it.

The corner of his lip lifted. "You know how to talk dirty to me." He reached into his pocket, where he'd deposited the ring back into its velvet box earlier, and handed it over before taking a long, satisfied sip of his drink.

I dropped it inside my jacket. The small square shape felt like a lead weight against my chest.

I wondered how heavy its contents were going to feel when it was on Elizabeth Dyson's hand.

# CHAPTER
# TWO

*Elizabeth*

I DROPPED MY sunglasses and my Louis Vuitton purse on the table in the entryway of my mother's condo and headed inside, searching for her. Since it was July and the sun was out, I knew exactly where I'd find her—on the deck outside the living room, sunning.

"Mom," I whined, bursting out onto the balcony. "Did you hear what Darrell's done now?" I dropped the printout from my computer in her lap. Then I headed over to the table where Marie, my mother's assistant and friend, had set out lemonade and poured myself a glass, gulping it down in four huge swallows.

I slammed the glass down on the table and turned back to face my mother. She sat stretched out on her lounge chair, her fingers bright with freshly applied nail polish. Marie was now working on her toes. She ignored the paper in her lap, which made sense—it was written in French and my mother didn't read French very well.

Honestly, I'd only printed it up for dramatic effect.

"Good morning to you too, darling," she said, lifting her chin up to present her cheek for a kiss.

"I'm too worked up for pleasantries right now," I said in a huff. But that wasn't fair to Marie, so I turned to her. "Hello, Marie. The lemonade is perfect today, by the way."

"Thank you," she said, looking up from my mother's left big toe.

Or rather, just looking over at *my* feet. "Your shoes are fantastic. Jimmy Choo?"

"Valentino. I bought them to go with this pantsuit. I think they just—" I stopped. Fashion was not what I was here to discuss. And if I got onto the topic of beauty with my mother and her assistant, I was going to be off track all day long.

"That's not important. Darrell—" I threw my hands up in the air. Honestly, my father's cousin was going to be the death of me. I was only twenty-five. I was not ready to be planning my own death.

"Settle yourself down, dear. You're going to break a sweat. Then tell me what it is that Darrell has done to get you in such a tizzy." My mother nodded to the lounge chair next to her.

I was entirely too upset to sit down, but I did try to rein it in a bit.

"He's selling off the children's network. *The children's network.*" I said again, when neither my mother nor Marie reacted with enough exasperation to satisfy me. "After last quarter's suggestion that they sell off some of the news stations—" It was a sentence I could barely stand to think through to the end. "By the time I get my hands on this company, there's going to be nothing left!"

My mother looked to Marie, who gave an encouraging smile. "Maybe it will just mean less to manage when you take over," the dark-haired assistant, who was more family than staff at this point, suggested.

"Less to manage?" I couldn't believe I was hearing this.

I stomped back over to the lemonade and poured some more, wishing it was laced with vodka. I sipped this time, trying to remember the words of my therapist. *You cannot let your day run you. You run your day. You cannot let your day run you. You run your day.* I repeated the mantra a few more times and then turned back to my audience.

"The company is only as good as the sum of its parts," I explained, as calmly as I could manage. "Dyson Media is everything put together. Darrell wants to slice off bits and pieces, and sell them to the highest bidder so that he can collect money and profit while the company is still his. That means that when I take over, it will be nothing but crumbs. Don't you see? There won't *be* a Dyson Media anymore."

Not to mention that without the company, how on earth would I ever be able to make up for the wrongs of my father? By the time I stood in his place, I wouldn't have any power, any platform. My cousin's pockets would be lined with my legacy, while I was left to clean up the leftover rubbish.

I didn't expect them to truly understand. My mother had never been interested in business, and she'd hired Marie to help her do her makeup and go shopping with her.

Marie *was* really good at shopping, I had to admit. I learned everything I knew about clothing from her, and I was really good with clothing.

But looking good was not going to save the Dyson empire. And neither was waiting four goddamned years to take over. "I have to fix this. I have to do something drastic."

"But what exactly can you do, honey? That lawyer told you that appealing was a lost cause, and Darrell isn't about to let you into the company before he has to. I swear, though," she said, shielding her eyes from the sun as she looked up at me. "If your father weren't already dead, I'd kill him myself for the shit he pulled with the terms of this inheritance. Such an asshole. Treating his only child like this. I can't believe I stayed with him as long as I did."

She'd stayed just ten years. I'd been born after two. She wasn't his first wife, and neither of us were clear on whether he'd even been divorced when she met him. He'd gotten another wife soon after he left Mom, too. But I was the only kid out of all three of his marriages. A daughter. Maybe he would've been more attentive and loving and *there* if I'd been another gender.

I'd never know.

At least he hadn't left us penniless. The divorce had left us with more than enough money. My mother never had to work another day in her life and was still able to live the lifestyle she'd gotten used to. I'd been able to go to the best schools and had the best opportunities. The best toys. The best cars. I never lacked for anything—besides a father.

My bank account meant I could turn a blind eye and let Darrell do whatever the hell he wanted with the company. I could let it go. I didn't need Dyson Media. I didn't need my father's legacy.

But I *did* need it too. For reasons I couldn't explain to anyone but myself.

"You're right. I can't appeal," I said. I'd spoken to a lawyer extensively. Three lawyers, in fact, to make sure I had absolutely no ground on which to fight to get my company earlier than my twenty-ninth birthday. "But there is something else I can do."

"And what's that?"

I watched as she removed the papers I'd left on her lap with the palms of her hands, careful not to touch them with her fingernails, and drop them on the empty lounge chair next to her. She was a nice bronze color already, her skin golden with rich yellow undertones that I lacked.

I took after my father with my fair skin and red hair. She was all Italian and Mediterranean and blond. When I was a kid, and we'd go to the beach, she would soak up every ray while I practically had to wear a full wetsuit just so I wouldn't get burnt.

We were different in so many ways, and I hesitated, wondering how she would react to my decision.

When I didn't respond, she looked up at me expectantly. "Honey?"

"I can get married." It hadn't been the first time we'd discussed it, so it wasn't exactly out of the blue.

"But I thought you said that wouldn't work either. You haven't been dating anyone, and anyone that you brought into this affair would be a stranger. How could you trust them?"

I walked around the table to the chair on the other side and plopped into it, trying to hide from the sun by sitting under the umbrella.

"I still have my concerns," I said hesitantly, "but Donovan Kincaid has approached me with a business transaction that might work."

Honestly, when Donovan had first asked for a meeting, I'd thought perhaps he was working for his father and wanted to sell me on their financial trusts. When he suggested his idea, it was so absurd I nearly walked out of the room.

But there was something about the man that intrigued me. Something about him that *spoke* to me. He was manipulative and scheming and also brilliant. He was passionate about his work and the things that he thought we could accomplish. I was attracted to it—not in a sexual way, though he was an attractive and sexy man. It was more like he reminded me of who I wanted to be.

And perhaps he reminded me of who my father could've been had my father actually been a decent man.

When I left, I'd told him I would think about it, although I hadn't really meant it. But after waking up this morning to the news that Darrell was selling the children's network I was actually thinking about it.

"Donovan Kincaid of King-Kincaid Financial?" my mother asked. I supposed my mother *did* pay attention to some business affairs, or at least the lifestyle pages.

"That's his father. Donovan has his own advertising agency, and he's come up with an agreement where I could marry someone from the firm. It would look genuine, and no one would be the wiser."

"And what would Mr. Kincaid want in return?" she asked, peering at me with that cut-the-bullshit look. She'd been a trophy wife. She knew how these things worked.

Or she thought she did.

The women in our family had come a long way in a generation—I had more than my body to sell. "He wants to merge his company with Dyson's advertising subsidiary. It wouldn't be an outrageous loss. Dyson barely does anything in advertising. Most of their market share and focus is in television. It would be a small price to pay for control of the company."

I hoped, anyway. I really didn't know that much about Dyson's advertising firm.

I really didn't know that much about Dyson Media at all, to be honest.

I didn't know that much about business in general, if I was laying it all out on the table.

Gah! What the hell was I *doing*?

I was being ridiculous, jumping in too fast, dreaming too big. I stood and walked to the edge of the roof and looked out over the street below.

"It's a dumb idea," I said now, all my confidence from earlier suddenly gone. "I have a meeting with Donovan this afternoon. I was going to turn his offer down when we met, but then I saw what Darrel was doing, and . . . I don't know. I guess I thought I should do something . . . for some reason."

I heard the scrape of the lounge chair against the deck and knew my mother was coming over to me. A moment later, I felt her hand around my waist.

"You thought you should do something because you knew you could," she said, her warm voice dripping like honey.

I sighed at her.

"Elizabeth, if the company is that important to you, you should take whatever risk you need to in order to get your hands on it. I'm sorry I'm not a better advocate for you. I mean to be. I do. The problem is that you are your father's daughter."

I cringed, hating it when she said that.

"Don't look at me like that. You are. And it's wonderful that you are. Because if you were only *my* daughter you wouldn't be even considering something like this. And I think it's amazing and wonderful that you want to do something so bold and grand. But your father never got things done by doubting himself. He certainly didn't get where he was by dismissing his own ideas as dumb. If this is what it takes to make you happy, I think you should take the chance. And if it's not with Donovan Kincaid, then keep searching."

"You mean it?" I glanced over at her and this time I held her stare, searching for every bit of reassurance. With her encouraging me, the plan didn't seem quite so dumb after all.

"Yeah, I mean it. Go in there confident. Show them you have your father's balls." She pulled me into a tight hug that was quickly followed by an exclamation of, "My nails, my nails!"

I let her go so she could examine her manicure and make sure that it had come out unscathed. Just then, the old grandfather clock chimed the hour from inside the apartment.

"It's one already?" I checked my wrist watch, needing the double verification. "Shit. I have to get going if I'm going to get to Midtown by one thirty. So much for grabbing lunch first. Thanks, Mom, for the advice and for listening." I bent in and kissed her cheek then walked over to Marie.

"There's chicken sandwiches in the fridge," she said, standing to give me a side hug. "Take one on your way."

"Thanks. I will." I started inside.

"Elizabeth," my mother called after me. She waited until I turned to give her my full attention. "Are you going to go through with this plan, then?"

I shrugged. "I don't know yet. Maybe. Yes. Probably. I haven't met the groom. I won't agree if the guy's lame. It's a fake marriage, but I *do* have standards. My name is riding on this."

"Maybe you'll get lucky, and he'll be good looking! Wouldn't it be nice if a woman got to have a trophy spouse for once?"

I laughed, but I wasn't holding my breath. I was taking her advice to heart, though. If Donovan Kincaid's plan was going to be a real option, he couldn't know I didn't know what the hell I was doing. I had to be confident and self-assured, like my father would have been. I had to show the men of Reach that I had balls.

I had to prove I could own that meeting and every man in it.

# CHAPTER
# THREE

*Weston*

"**W**ESTON, QUIT PACING and sit the fuck down," Donovan said—correction, *demanded*—from his seat on the couch at one-thirty the next day. "You're making me dizzy."

It was easy enough for him to sit calmly, enjoying his after-lunch scotch since he didn't have a hangover and a fifty-pound ring in his breast pocket.

I ran a hand through my hair, ignoring his instructions to move to the couch. "I don't know how you talked me into this. You laced my drink with something?" Drinks. Many drinks. There had been so many drinks.

"You were still rather sober when you agreed, as I recall."

I looked out the window over the city. Our offices occupied the top floors of the King-Kincaid building we rented, and the view was spectacular. We'd designed the space so all of us had floor-to-ceiling windows, and the lounge where we entertained all incoming clients had the best views of all.

Usually, looking out over the small specks on the sidewalks below made me feel powerful and confident, gave me a bit of the backbone that Donovan had naturally. But today I just felt agitated and nervous, like all the people below were priceless pawns in a chess game, and somehow I was going to squish them with my bad behavior.

"Nate really could do this," I said, turning to look at Donovan now. "Twenty years difference . . . What does that mean these days? It's a fake marriage anyway. Who's going to care?"

"It's important this marriage *looks* like it's real. Those running the business aren't going to want to relinquish power, so they need to be convinced that the two of you are in love if they're not going to contest. Nathan doesn't even give the vibe of a groom."

"And *I* give the vibe of a—?" My sentiment was cut off by the opening of the lounge doors.

Speak of the devil, Nate came bounding in and glanced around the room. "Good, I'm not late."

No, he was late. But so was the Dyson girl.

"I was arguing shades of green with one of the design teams. I swear half the staff we've hired is color blind."

"You look fantastic. Are you not even a little bit hungover?" I had watched him drink at least as much as I had. How was it even possible?

Nate paused his stride on the way to the mini-bar, his forehead wrinkled in confusion. "Hungover? No." As though the idea were ludicrous. As though he'd never been hungover in his life.

Maybe he hadn't. Now that I thought about it, I'd never been around to see him if he had.

He really was a god.

"Hey, Nate, I was just telling Donovan that we really haven't given as much consideration to your candidacy as bridegroom as we—"

"No," he said with finality.

Donovan shrugged as if to say, *what did you expect?*

"This is bullshit. I shouldn't be the one condemned to—" Once again, I was interrupted by the opening of the lounge doors. This time, Roxie, my amazing and faithful assistant, stood there, gesturing for the woman behind her to come inside.

I moved my gaze to the stranger as she entered the room. She was sharply dressed in heels and a designer pantsuit. The royal blue color showcased her creamy skin and long red hair, which bounced with natural wave. The tailored pants were business and attitude while the satin cowl-neck softened her and gave just a hint of cleavage, so the outfit managed to make her appear both professional and feminine at the same time.

She was a knockout. Put together and made of money. She held her shoulders back and her neck high. She knew how to carry herself.

She was the kind of woman who could carry the world.

"Here you are," Roxie said in her Hungarian accent. "Gentlemen, Elizabeth Dyson here to see you."

Donovan immediately jumped up to greet her. Nate followed suit.

And I forgot words.

What words meant, how to say them, how to translate what they meant when other people said them around me.

The thing was this—I was not particular when it came to which women I took to bed. Tall, short, plump, thin. I liked them blond or brunette. I liked them of all racial and religious varieties. I liked them moody or sporty. I liked cougars. I liked them barely legal. It didn't matter. I liked women. Period.

But I did have a type.

Smart.

That was my weakness. If she had a fantastic body to match, I was a goner. Sabrina Lind, for example. She was that kind of girl. She had everything going on upstairs plus everything going on outside.

And dammit, so did Elizabeth Dyson.

She had yet to open her mouth, and I could tell that she was one of the smartest women I'd ever met. I could spot a hot brain a mile away. I had a sense for it. It was something about the way a woman carried herself. The way she wore her clothes. The way she did her hair, the way she held her lips. A smart woman wore her brain everywhere on her body.

Fuck if Elizabeth Dyson's hot brain wasn't on full display.

"Weston?" The tone in Donovan's voice made it sound like he'd said my name more than once before I heard it.

I shook myself and stepped forward with my hand out in greeting. "Hi, Weston King."

"As Donovan just said," Elizabeth Dyson remarked, her hand closing around mine. Her shake was as firm as her voice, and both were stiff. Neither were as stiff as my cock was threatening to be in my pants if I couldn't keep it down.

I focused just past her, not meeting her gaze, in an attempt to settle myself.

"It's a pleasure to meet you." She included all of us in her appraising look, not lingering on anyone. It was a much-needed reminder that this was an arrangement. There was going to be no flirting, no "player" me, as Donovan had said the night before.

Though, for the life of me, I couldn't quite remember why.

"Let's get started, shall we?" Donovan said, gesturing for all of us to sit down. He dominated most rooms without even trying, and I expected this one to be no different.

Except as we headed toward the couches to take our seats, Elizabeth surprised me.

"Donovan, just a moment," she said, and even though he hadn't been talking, it felt like an interruption. "I'm sure you have things to say, but I have a few things I'd like to say first."

She was still standing, and so the rest of us didn't know what to do—whether we should take a seat, or stand as well. It was common courtesy to wait until the guest took a seat before we did, and here she was still erect.

Shouldn't have thought the word erect. It was a bad mistake on my part. I had to think of unsexy things very quickly. *Zombies killing people. Zombies eating their flesh.*

"Go ahead and take a seat," she said, looking mostly at Donovan.

And that's when it was completely clear. She'd taken over. She'd taken *charge*.

She was dominating Donovan.

And something about that was fucking hot. I tried to think unsexy thoughts.

*Zombies eating Donovan's flesh.*

We sat. Everyone did. Including Elizabeth. Including Donovan.

"Would you care for something to drink?" Nate asked.

"No, thank you. I'd rather just get to the point." She crossed one long leg over the other and set her hands in her lap. Then she leaned back ever so slightly, shifting her gaze from one of us to the next, meeting each of our eyes.

I leaned forward, the anticipation built up so much that I was near the edge of my seat.

"Now. I haven't decided yet if I'd like to take you up on this very interesting offer, but I have considered it very thoroughly. And if I do, there will be even more to take into consideration."

She was a witch. She had to be. Only moments ago, I'd been doubting this arrangement, but now that she was potentially taking it away, I was already starting a mental litany of reasons why she shouldn't.

Which was stupid. I didn't really want to do this. No matter how hot she was topping Donovan.

"I'm guessing that everyone in the room is caught up on the situation I'm in?" she went on.

"Yes, everyone here is aware of the predicament you're in, and of the offer Reach has made you. But don't worry," Donovan continued, predicting her unease. "No one here has said anything to anyone else. And of course, anything that's said in this room will stay in this room."

"That's actually the first thing that we need to discuss," Elizabeth said. "This arrangement would have to be kept fully under wraps. Though it's headquartered in Europe, you all know Dyson Media is a genuine world empire. I hate to bring numbers and figures into it, but it's safe to say that my father's company is well above the net worth of anybody else in this room. Even when we put you all together."

That comment alone should have killed my boner. It was rather emasculating to be reduced to a relative bank account value.

But instead of being turned off by it, I wanted to pull Elizabeth Dyson across my lap and spank that smug grin off her face. Spank her and then . . .

"That is safe to say," Donovan affirmed regarding our net worths, and he was the one who would know. He had the most money of all of us, and I was certainly no pauper. "And we do recognize what is on the line, Elizabeth," he added. "I promise you that."

"Yes," she said, that sly uptick of a smile bordering on condescending. "I'm sure you do. The point is, so does my cousin. Darrell is currently in charge of the Dyson empire and does not want to give up that position before he has to. He'll do anything he can to prove that any marriage of mine is a false one. If I'm going to get married in an attempt to inherit my company earlier, it has to be a relationship that appears entirely legitimate.

"I can't run away to Vegas. There can't be a small ceremony at City Hall. There would have to be a ring of truth to it, which means there will have to be a wedding of somewhat large proportions. The kind that would be expected of a woman of my wealth and stature. As soon as I announce an engagement, Darrell will likely investigate to make sure I was dating that person beforehand. Even though he's in Paris, he'll watch over every step of my engagement. I don't assume he'll take anything at face value. To be blunt, my groom will have to be both a convincing choice and invested for the long haul."

"How many months are you talking about here?" I braced myself, afraid that she was going to say that years were required for this game.

"I don't want to be ridiculous, as this *is* a sham relationship. But I do also understand that in order for it to look real, it can't be quite as much of a whirlwind as we'd prefer. So if we announce the engagement fairly soon . . . perhaps seven months? Give or take."

I almost choked. Seven months? Seven months with my ring on someone else's finger?

I needed a drink.

I stood up and headed over to the bar, pouring myself a gin and tonic. Donovan side-eyed me, but fuck Donovan. It's not like he was the one going through with it; he was just directing the play, as always.

"Seven months does seem fairly reasonable," Donovan traitorously agreed. "A wedding in December and then a month or two to finalize your takeover. And I don't see any reason why annulment couldn't happen soon after."

"I think it would need to be a divorce," Elizabeth said. "Darrell will believe the whole thing was a ruse in the first place. I wouldn't want him to come back in retrospect and re-take over the company. Or try to appeal the decision."

"Divorce?" I directed this at Donovan. I had not intended to have a divorce on my record. I drank my gin and tonic in four gulps and then started to make another one.

"Weston, sit down."

I scowled, cursing under my breath. Donovan was right. This wasn't a good first impression to make, and for some reason I did want to make a good first impression on Elizabeth Dyson.

I abandoned my drink and slunk back over to the sofa to listen to other people plan my future.

"I know a lot of people who could pull off a spectacular wedding in a short amount of time," Nate mused. "With our connections we could book a fantastic hotel with a ballroom—"

"I can handle catering with my restaurant," Donovan offered.

"I'm friends with the Pierce's, Donovan," Nate said. "Mirabelle's has amazing wedding gowns, and I can arrange an appointment. Lee-Ann Gregori, the wedding planner, is an acquaintance as well. She can arrange the rest."

Jesus, it was like I wasn't even in the room.

"And you are perfectly okay with a pretend relationship lasting that long? There would have to be dates and public outings. We'd have to be seen together. Is that going to be a problem?" Her eyes darted from one of us to the next.

It occurred to me then that Elizabeth didn't even realize who she was supposed to be addressing, didn't know who was supposed to be her fiancé.

I could still throw Donovan under the bus if I wanted. If this whole arrangement was so easy to take care of—by *them*—then it was only fair that one of them should be the nominee.

But, honestly, that wasn't what I wanted, either. Nate didn't look right next to her, and the thought of Donovan pretending to be her lover made my gut twist in some weird strange way that I couldn't understand. Didn't want to understand.

"Weston?" Donovan asked. "Are those expectations going to be a problem?"

I looked to Elizabeth, watched her features as she realized that I was the suggested candidate and tried to discern if she was disappointed or intrigued.

But her face showed no emotion at all except the lift of one brow. "Oh," she said as if it should've been obvious. "It's you."

Something in that indifferent stare of hers made me want to eat her up. Tear her apart. Find her heart and see what made it beat faster. I didn't know if it was a sexual attraction or an angry kind of attraction.

At the very least, I needed to stop thinking about zombies while around beautiful women.

But it was more than that; I felt insulted for the second time in as many minutes.

Women didn't ever toss me aside easily. Women didn't look at me with an indifferent stare. And they never made me doubt myself. She should be appraising me with her gaze. At least to flatter me, if nothing else. After all, I was the one doing everyone—including her—a favor.

I had never been as competitive as Donovan about anything. Except for winning the hearts of women, but only because I didn't really have to do very much to try to win them. In Elizabeth Dyson, I was suddenly sensing a challenge, the kind I'd never truly experienced before.

And if she was going to be so stoic about our arrangement, hell yeah, I was into this game. That's why I was called a player, after all.

"I don't see a problem with it," I said, holding her stare.

"Then perhaps this will work out." She pursed her lips and tapped a finger on them as she considered her next move. "I am surprised you didn't choose yourself to be the groom, Donovan."

"We'd never get along," he scoffed. "And who would be the alpha?"

The two of them laughed, and I did too until I realized that the joke was at my expense.

Instead of growling, the instinctive method of showing off my own alpha skills, I took control with more civilized means—steering the conversation in another direction. "And what are you planning to do with the company when you take over, Elizabeth, since Darrell's the current CEO?"

"Not as CEO, but as an officer. I'll have to fire Darrell and everyone on the board, since they are all his followers. They were loyal to my father as well. I'll need a fresh start."

"Um." I looked to my fellow businessmen in the room. Was she for real? "You're going to fire everyone who knows what they're doing and then lead the company to greatness with a board full of newbies?" I knew she was young, but this was Business 101.

Her confidence wavered, her forehead knit into little wrinkles of concern. "Oh. Good point. I'll start by hiring just a CEO then, one who can lead them in another direction."

I couldn't believe it. She had no plan. No direction.

I was going to stake our company's future in Europe on this girl? What on earth was Donovan thinking?

I laughed out loud. I couldn't help it—she was insane. "Do you have someone in mind already for this position?" Finding that kind of talent, someone willing to take over a board of disgruntled officers . . . ? That wasn't a role I'd want to play.

"Are you laughing at me?" she bristled.

"I'm just saying the idea needs some work. Where did you go to college anyway?" I was curious now. More than curious. I'd found an opening in which to press my advantage, to show her that I wasn't just an inferior bank account, an interchangeable fake husband. Besides, I would have to know this stuff if we were getting married, right?

"Penn." She threw her shoulders back, announcing her alma mater proudly.

"And they taught you nothing at the University of Pennsylvania?" I was being a dick. Sometimes that happened. People around me learned to live with it.

"I didn't major in business," she said coldly.

"You have your MBA though, right?" Lots of people got their bachelor's degree in something else before they got a masters in business.

But Elizabeth shook her head.

*Jesus.* I was afraid to ask, but now I had to know. "What did you major in?"

"Poli-sci," she said timidly.

"You've got to be fucking kidding me, Donovan." How did he find her? A twenty-five-year-old spoiled little brat, planning to take over the Dyson empire with a political science degree? I couldn't have laughed harder.

Turned out there was a good reason dear old dad had been keeping the reins of the company from her. She needed to grow up before she even thought about playing with the big boys.

"I'm sorry, honey, but this is ridiculous," I told her. "We might be able to convince the world, we might be able to convince your cousin. But you will take over that company and it will fall apart in five seconds flat. Is that really what you want to put seven months worth of fraud into achieving?"

"Weston," Donovan warned.

"I'm sorry, D. I'm just being honest here." What a shame—she would have looked so good in a boardroom, too.

"I'm grateful for your honesty, Weston." Elizabeth shifted to face my partner. "He's right, Donovan. This won't work. I don't need your help after all. I was wrong in thinking that I did." She stood, and smoothly picked up the purse that she'd dropped on the floor beside her, pulling the strap onto her shoulder as she held her hand out to shake Nate's.

"It was nice to meet you, Nathan." She nodded to Donovan, "And good to see you again, Donovan. And you, Mr. King. I'm grateful to have escaped marrying you." She smiled brightly. "Good afternoon."

She spun on her heels and that was that. My engagement over and done with before it began.

Which was a good thing, I reminded myself.

The door had barely shut behind her when Donovan roared in my direction. "*Weston.*"

"I am not wrong here," I protested. Surely they could see that. "Everything that she'd just laid out is—"

"I don't *care*, Weston. She will make this takeover happen with you or without you. With Reach or without Reach. We want to be there when it happens so that we can at least benefit from the fallout. *Fix it.*" He pointed a long demanding arm toward the door.

I glanced at Nate, who shrugged, but his expression said that he was firmly on Donovan's side on this one. Which made sense. I'd been kind of a prick. I looked around the room, but that was it. It was just us, and I'd been given my marching orders.

Yes, there was nothing left to do but suck this one up and fix it.

# CHAPTER
# FOUR

*Elizabeth*

I HURRIED OUT of the lounge so quickly that I got myself turned around in the offices of Reach, Inc. The open floor space brought lots of outside light in and all the glass front offices looked the same. I passed several people sitting at desks who looked up at me as I walked by, but I was so near to tears that I didn't want any of them to ask if I needed help. I wouldn't have been able to hold it together.

So I threw my shoulders back and put my chin up and walked past, even though that just made me even more lost. Weston's statement, *this is ridiculous,* kept replaying in my mind, but I heard it in my father's voice. *This is ridiculous. You can't do this. Who do you think you are?*

He never said it to my face, my father, but he hadn't needed to. He'd said it by never letting me into his life. He'd said it by giving his company to his nephew instead of his own daughter. He'd said it loudest by thinking that whatever man I married would be more worthy of running his empire than me.

And wasn't he right? Wasn't Weston King right?

I was no one and I didn't know anything. I was just a spoiled girl with a lot of money. I might have a good head on my shoulders, but I didn't know the first thing about business.

I was such a fool to have thought I could walk into that meeting and take control.

I wiped a stray tear from my cheek as I turned down the hall and the elevators came into sight.

Thank God. Escape.

But then I heard the rush-and-click of shoes running toward me across the marble floor. I turned, expecting to see Donovan. He was the one who'd wanted this scheme to work out the most, and he was the one who would care enough to come after me, but instead . . . Weston?

I sucked in a breath and willed my emotions to hide inside me, in the deep-seated place that I buried most every feeling of mine that mattered. I'd rather it have been Donovan who'd come after me. It would have been easier to remain stoic and confident in front of him, because while he was admittedly good looking and sexy as hell, he didn't make my knees weak and my palms sweat in the way that Weston did.

Weston, with that killer face and those panty-melting dimples. With that wicked grin and a body that wore a suit better than any other man in the room. When I'd realized he was the one who was volunteering to be my groom, I didn't know if I was overjoyed or in over my head. It had taken everything I had to give him my coolest look while inside I was drowning in butterflies.

To be honest, although I'd decided to approach the meeting with backbone, it was Weston who'd given me the added boost of confidence I'd needed when I'd first walked in the room. His electric blue eyes had sparked energy in me, evoked passion that I knew I owned but hadn't been able to wield until his gaze first crossed mine. He looked at me and made me feel not just like I was beautiful, but that I was worthy of being listened to. He looked at me like I deserved to be there.

How ironic that he was the same man who made me realize that I didn't belong.

Based on everything he'd said, I was pretty sure he hated me even though he was coming down the hallway after me. Even though he was now calling out my name, asking me to wait.

I reached out and hit the button for the elevator anyway.

"Just give me a few minutes," he said, slowing his trot to a walk as he neared. "I know I don't deserve it, but I'm only asking for two minutes. Please."

I scowled, wishing the doors would open. I might have been wrong about the meeting, might have been wrong about what I would do with the company, but I wasn't wrong to try.

And I wasn't going to let him make me feel like it again.

It hurt too much coming from a man I inexplicably wanted to impress.

"I don't need you," I repeated. "I don't need Reach."

"You don't. You definitely don't." His left hand went behind his neck, rubbing the muscles there. "Honestly, we don't really need you either. Which is why there's nothing on the line right now if you'll just come talk to me for a minute. Let me show you something."

He was right again. Reach really didn't need me. Sure, they wanted my advertising company—Darrell's advertising company—but they were doing fine without it. Reach still had massive holdings even without the merger. They would be just fine even if they didn't go after this one market. They didn't need me, and his remark was more than a bruise to my ego.

Because it meant I really wasn't holding any cards.

It was further proof I was clueless and out of my league.

The elevator doors opened with a *ding*. I closed my eyes momentarily and let out a low, quiet breath.

Then I opened them again, and turned to meet Weston's piercing blues.

"I'll give you five minutes," I conceded. Because I was curious. Because I had nothing to lose. Because he was so goddamn cute with that half-smile and that dimple.

"Come this way." His grin had widened, the dimple deepening. He walked backward to make sure I was following him, then, when he was certain, he turned around and retreated into the office space. This time he didn't lead me to the lounge, but toward the opposite corner.

We passed the desk of the woman who had escorted me in—Roxie, she'd said her name when she introduced herself, and then we were inside a corner office that I could only assume was his own. He shut the door behind me and I tensed slightly.

He didn't notice.

How lucky for men to not have the constant worry about being in close rooms with the opposite sex, but I needn't have worried either because the walls to his office were glass and anyone could see in.

But then he moved behind his desk and pushed a button, and suddenly the transparent glass went opaque, and we could no longer see out. And, I assumed, no one could see in.

"Wait a minute," I said hesitantly. "I just met you." Ironic, considering I had been about to marry him.

He raised a brow in question, not understanding my meaning.

Then both brows raised as he got my drift. "Don't worry. The door isn't locked—go ahead and check."

I did so and found he was telling the truth.

I remained by the door and watched him, as next he walked over to the cabinets that ran along the side wall and opened two up. They were the kind that usually hid a TV screen behind them or a safe. When he opened them, I was shocked to discover a dartboard waited behind.

And stapled to the middle of the dartboard was a black-and-white printout of a man's face.

I squinted and took a couple steps forward, examining the face. "Is that . . . Nash King?"

I didn't know a lot about business, but everyone knew who Nash King and Raymond Kincaid were. Anyone who had any sizable investments had a relationship with Weston and Donovan's fathers in some form or another. Nash was one of the financial kings—har har, the pun—of the United States. He and Kincaid owned so many banks that together they were one of the leading financial institutions of the world.

Why was Weston throwing darts at a picture of his father's face?

I turned to look at my almost-groom. His hands were shoved casually in his pockets and his eyes were cast down, embarrassed.

He shrugged. "It's kind of an old picture now," he said. "I just printed something from the internet. It would have been even more awesome if I'd brought in an actual portrait, but I'm lazy."

I felt the whisper of a smile on my lips. "Weston King. Do you have daddy issues?" Was *that* what he'd brought me here to show me?

"I didn't say I had daddy issues," he said defensively. Evasively. "But it blows off a lot of steam to throw a dart at people's faces every now and then. I'm not going to say that I have or haven't occasionally placed Donovan's face in that spot, but I *am* telling you that it works. Hold on."

Suddenly, he was in motion. He jiggled the mouse on his computer to wake it up, and then typed something on the keypad. He pushed a few buttons and a moment later, I heard the printer spitting out a piece of paper.

He ran over to it to retrieve the document, and then, snatching up his stapler, he walked back to the dartboard and pinned a new picture up over the one of Nash King.

When he stepped back, we were looking at the famous profile picture of Dell Dyson. It was on his website, on his Wikipedia page, on the book he'd written, on any sort of byline. He'd always thought it made him look powerful, but I only ever saw his arrogance in that expression, in the tilt of his head. I had hoped to see it next as I removed it from the wall of *my* new office, but here it was.

*This* was what Weston meant to show me.

Oh, boy.

Weston stepped back from the cabinet and held both his hands out to display the dartboard, Vanna White style. "Go ahead."

"No way," I scoffed, but I did spin around, surveying the room for something to throw. "I don't even have any darts."

He was already scurrying back to his desk. "What was I thinking?" A moment later he'd pulled a handful of darts from his top drawer and was handing them over to me.

I laughed, a small chuckle, mostly to myself as I regarded his offering. Talk about ridiculous.

But then, there I was, taking a red dart from his palm and setting up my stance, lining up my aim. It wasn't a fantasy I'd ever had, but the second it showed up before me, I couldn't imagine why I hadn't tried it myself.

I'd never thrown darts before. That was probably reason number one. I'd taken archery in school, though, and been fairly good at it. Still, nothing, not even that class, had ever made me feel quite as much like I was Robin Hood taking an arrow from Little John as I did right now.

I pulled my body back, rocked forward, let the dart go, and watched it smack right into Dell Dyson's tie. It quivered directly in the middle of his perfect Windsor knot.

Man, did it feel good.

"Wasn't that fantastic?" Weston whispered, as though he knew that admitting it might feel dangerous. "Do another."

This one didn't take any encouraging at all. I grabbed a green one.

I drew back and let it go. It sailed with a whoosh and landed in the corner of the paper, not hitting any of his face or body at all.

"Ah. Shit throw. Try again," Weston encouraged.

I did. Again and again. A yellow dart and blue and another red. Another blue. Each time thinking of a new offense. *This one is for the company that completely blocked women from holding executive positions—including your own daughter. This one for the seven consecutive years you landed on the worst places to work list for people with families. This one for the thirty-seven percent difference in pay rates between men and women that exists at Dyson Media.*

*This one for the summer that you invited me to stay with you in Paris and then left me alone with the nanny, while you entertained at your other houses.*

*This one for every birthday you forgot.*

*This one for every Christmas gift that was picked out by your secretary.*

*And this one for every time that you said you would visit, that you said that you would show up, that you said that you wanted to be there, and you never, ever were.*

I was shaking when all the darts were gone.

"Bullseye," Weston said beside me, oblivious to the ragged state of my emotions. "Literally. Bull's-eye, as in, you got that one right in between the eyes."

He went to gather the darts off of the board, and while I was staring at his long, lean backside, perfectly sewn into his tailored suit, I found words spilling out that I never meant to confess. "I thought I had more time," I said quietly.

"Huh?" Weston seemed appropriately confused. "Oh, you can go again after I get them all. I don't own that many." He turned back to pulling out the rest of the darts.

But I didn't mean what he thought I did.

I swallowed and strengthened my voice this time. "I thought I had more time," I said again. "I thought that it would be years before my father died. I traveled after college. I spent time in Europe. I was enjoying my youth. I didn't know he would have a heart attack in the middle of the night. He was only sixty-one and was fairly healthy—or so everyone thought. Nobody expected him to . . ."

I trailed off, remembering how I'd found out he'd been rushed to the hospital by hearing it on CNN. I'd reached his secretary easily enough, who informed me that I'd been "on the list," but "further down," and she just hadn't gotten to calling me yet.

I was in the air flying to France to be with him when he'd officially died.

I shook off the memories of his death and funeral, a whirlwind of commotion where I'd been made to feel insignificant and inadequate at every turn. The memories were still too fresh and unprocessed, too near the surface to think about without turning into a sobbing mess. Truly, they might always be.

"I was already registered for a Masters degree this fall in business at the University of New York. I had planned to learn . . ." My voice trembled. I swallowed again before going on. "It just took me by surprise."

Weston had gathered all the darts by then, but he stood frozen, listening to me, as though he didn't dare to turn around, as though afraid any movement might break my monologue, and the honest truth was, it might.

I would have never said any of this to Donovan. I would probably never have said any of this to Weston if he were facing me. If those blue eyes were boring into me, I'd have assumed he could already see into my soul.

But while his back was turned, right here in this moment, the truth continued to pour out. And even though he was just a stranger politely listening, it felt good to lay everything out.

So I went on.

"I took poli-sci as my undergrad because it doesn't matter what your bachelor degree is before you get your MBA, and I thought a background in politics could be helpful. And I *like* politics. But now I'm woefully unprepared, and I'm watching Darrell run, and systematically dismantle, this company. I could let this go. I could take the next four years to become the best business leader possible, to find out everything that I need to know to lead an empire of this extent."

I took a step toward him.

"But if I wait, it would be selfish. It would be because *I* don't feel ready. Because *I'm* scared. Meanwhile, there are hundreds of thousands of other people depending on that company to be their livelihood, and others depending on it to be the place they look to for quality entertainment and programming. If I have a chance to change the lives of the people, the *women* who work for him, if I have a chance to change the lives of the people who watch entertainment put out by Dyson Media, and if that chance makes those lives better . . . Weston, I feel like I have to take that chance. Whether I'm ready or not."

I turned away with a sigh. I'd said everything, and now I felt dumb. Too dumb to even be able to face his backside.

Behind me, I could hear the rustle and shuffle of movement. He stopped a foot or two behind me, close enough that I could feel the heat radiating off his body, smell his cologne. It made me flushed and dizzy and my heart started to race.

"I could teach you," he said quietly.

"What?" I turned to face him, not understanding what he meant.

"I'll teach you about business while we're together." He tossed the darts back onto his desk and jammed his hands back into his pockets, admittedly a very arresting look. "A tailored, condensed MBA. Everything you need to know to find the right people to run the company. Everything you need to know to make sure you're not being taken advantage of. The Weston King Crash Course in Business."

My skin felt itchy and my insides were fluttering.

Too many times, though, I'd gotten excited by promises from my father, promises he didn't ever keep. I'd listened to my mother ask what the quid pro quo was so many times.

I'd learned from both parents. I'd learned to be circumspect.

I tilted my head, my mouth parted slightly. "And why would you do that, exactly? My advertising company can't possibly be worth that much to you."

Weston threw his head back in a way that said he wasn't really sure why he'd made the offer.

But then he said, "Let's just say I have a soft spot for companies that are vulnerable. And Donovan wants it. And I owe Donovan. We'll leave it at that."

I studied him for another moment. It didn't *feel* like a bad idea, but I also knew that you weren't supposed to use feelings in business—I wasn't completely ignorant in the field. I couldn't see a downside, though, either, anyway I looked at it.

And I really wanted my father's company. The more obstacles I faced—the more everyone else told me that I couldn't—the more I needed to do it, if only to prove I could to myself.

"Okay," I said, such a little word to begin such a big arrangement. But all mighty things started out small. Even the Mississippi River started in some little puddle of bubbling water somewhere.

Weston nodded once, taking it in. Then he drew in a breath, and I could see he was *really* taking it in, maybe even kind of regretting it.

My stomach dropped.

Then his expression changed as he suddenly had an idea. "Let's do this right." He reached into his suit pocket, and I wrinkled my nose as I tried to peer over and see what he was doing. A second later, he pulled out a small box and set it in the palm of his hand.

Immediately, I started giggling.

"Stop giggling," he said, practically laughing himself. "We have to be serious about this. This is a very serious moment between us."

"I can't help it! I'm a giggler."

"First rule of business," he said, "if you want people to take you seriously, you can't giggle."

I sucked in my cheeks, making probably the silliest expression I'd ever made. Weston tamped down his smile as well, though not all the way. I kind of wondered if that half-smile was permanently on his lips, wondered if he even noticed it. It was fitting for the occasion, the tiny upturn of his lips as he opened the black velvet box and pulled out the gorgeous platinum ring with tiny diamonds surrounding a large one that had to be at least four carats.

I could almost believe he meant this. Could almost believe he was enjoying it.

"Give me your hand," he said, taking it before I'd actually given it to him. Goosebumps sprouted up my arm at his touch, or maybe just because I was so thrilled that this was finally happening, I was *that* much closer to my dream.

Yeah, definitely that.

He slipped the ring over my knuckle to put it into place. It fit perfectly, which made me certain that Donovan had had a hand in it.

"Elizabeth Dyson, will you do me the honor," he said in a very warm tone, as he dropped to a knee, "of becoming my bride."

Part of me wondered if he should've added the word fake in there, because that's what this was. It was fake, it wasn't real. Even though this moment was beginning to feel very, very real.

But on the other hand, it *would* be a real wedding. We would have real marriage certificates. It would really be on file in the state of New York, and when we got divorced, that would really be on our record, too. We would have to file taxes together.

There wasn't really anything fake about this fake wedding at all.

So maybe how he'd asked was appropriate indeed. And there was only one appropriate answer for him.

"Yes, Weston King, I will."

# CHAPTER
# FIVE

*Weston*

ELIZABETH CRANED HER neck to look past me out the car window.

"This is where you like to hang out?" she asked when she saw where the car had stopped. "There's a line a mile long."

It had been two days since we'd decided to get engaged, and we were putting the scheme into action. She'd taken the ring off her finger for now, figuring it best to wait to announce the engagement until after we'd had a few public sightings. This would be our first, but so far, she'd complained from the minute she'd picked me up, and if she kept it up, I was going to have to . . .

Well, I wasn't sure what I was going to have to do, but I knew what I wanted to do. Especially with her wearing that black and white striped sundress with the kind of skirt that bounced up just the way I liked—it was simple and elegant and not at all what most women her age would wear on a date that involved a nightclub, but somehow, with those strappy high designer fuck-me shoes, she pulled it off.

Problem was, it also made me want to do just that—strap her high on my waist and fuck her.

But I wanted to do that with most girls I spent any time with. Elizabeth Dyson might be my favorite brand of sexy, but she wasn't special. I could fuck her once or twice, but eventually I'd get bored with her, like I always did, and then I'd still be stuck with her through our arrangement. It would feel like a real relationship, and I had zero interest in that.

Besides, I was about ninety-nine point nine percent sure that Elizabeth was not the type to fuck around for fun.

That point one percent of doubt was what my cock kept twitching about.

"The line wouldn't have formed yet if we had come straight here instead of going to dinner first," I said, with an edge of complaint of my own. "I never take my dates to dinner."

"That's exactly why we had to go. I'm not supposed to be like all your other girls. I'm the woman you're going to choose to marry." It wasn't the first time she'd explained this tonight, and it showed in her tone.

"Right, right." Except if I ever *did* get married, I was still sure I'd never let the woman drag me to the French frou frou place Elizabeth had insisted on going to.

Thank God that part of the night was behind us. Now we were on to the fun. Since she'd said that we would need to be seen out on the town, and since she didn't have any regular haunts, I'd recommended the place *I* frequented.

That meant The Sky Launch.

"Anyway, don't worry," I assured her as I pulled her out of the backseat, feeling oddly comforted by the contact of her hand. "The line isn't for us."

It was a Friday night so the club was busy, even though it wasn't yet ten o'clock. I was known here, so I pulled her to the front desk where the bouncer let us in with a nod. We were halfway up the entrance ramp when Gwen, one of the managers, approached and gave me a hug.

I felt Elizabeth stiffen at my side, and so, simply to rile her up more, I kissed Gwen on the cheek, something I didn't normally do because she was happily married with children.

Sometimes I'm a dick just because it's fun.

"It's been a few weeks since you've been here," Gwen said, prying.

"I've been . . . preoccupied," I said, making it sound like the things that had kept me busy had been sexy things.

They hadn't been. Not recently. The office really had grown too big to manage with just Nate and I. But it wasn't cool to admit to being a workaholic. Plus, I liked the way it made Elizabeth silently fret.

As though prompted by my thoughts, the woman at my side cleared her throat.

"Gwen, I'd like you to meet my girlfriend, Elizabeth Dyson."

Gwen's brow arched in surprise. "Did you say . . . *girlfriend?*"

I had almost tripped over the word myself. I wasn't sure I'd ever actually used the word in reference to anyone connected to me in the whole time I'd been alive.

"I did. I did say girlfriend." I was saying it again, just to get used to the sound. *Girlfriend.* It wasn't that terrifying, really. Girl. Friend. Nothing to it.

"This must be serious then." Gwen turned to Elizabeth and shook her hand, then held it with both of hers. "I've known Weston for quite some time now, and he's yet to have introduced me to anyone as his *girlfriend*. It's a real pleasure to meet you."

Elizabeth's eyes wandered over to the wedding ring on Gwen's finger and I saw her expression relax just a bit.

There went that fun.

"It's been a whirlwind of a romance," Elizabeth said, and I had to look down at my shoes so that no one saw how utterly disgusted I was with her phrasing. *Whirlwind of a romance* didn't sound convincing; it sounded like a bad Hallmark movie.

I needed to remember to tell her that later.

"I'm delighted to finally meet some of Weston's . . . friends?" Elizabeth said *friends* with a bit of a question in her tone, as though she wasn't sure how to refer to Gwen.

"Gwen is one of the managers here at The Sky Launch," I said, taking pity on my *girlfriend*—the more I thought the word, the easier it came out. "She knows how to take care of us. Is my regular spot available?"

"Of course," Gwen assured me. "I had a bubble room saved the minute you called and said you were coming. Right this way."

We followed Gwen across the dance floor and up the stairs to the second floor of the nightclub, and though I held Elizabeth's hand in mine as we walked across the dancefloor, I made sure to keep my eyes on Gwen's behind.

I was a player; it was to be expected, and I liked the way it made Elizabeth bristle and fume. Plus, it was important she knew early on that although she was marrying me, my eyes could still wander.

It *was* a fake marriage. I still got to look.

In fact, I still got to fool around—discreetly, of course.

On the second floor, Gwen handed us off to the waitress who showed us to our bubble room, one of several that overlooked the dance floor below. These rooms were the highlight of The Sky Launch, the reason that I loved this club so much. The tables were enclosed in a private setting, but the wall around them was glass so that you could see out and everyone could see in.

It combined the perks of VIP with all the exhibitionism I could want.

"This is interesting," Elizabeth said with what sounded like disdain in her tone, once she was seated at the table and the waitress had left.

I unbuttoned my sports jacket and threw her a glare. I couldn't imagine the places that she hung out.

Actually, I could. Boring places. Coffee places. Places that only served wine. Places that required you to wear a tux.

Places I sincerely hoped I wouldn't be forced to frequent as part of this charade.

"If you hate it so much, make sure we're seen here tonight, and we don't have to come back again." I picked up my drink menu even though I knew what I was going to get, just so I didn't have to look at her for a minute. Looking at her confused me too much.

It was hard to correlate that rockin' body with the things that came out of her mouth.

"I didn't say that it was terrible. I said it was interesting. I haven't been here long enough to find out if it's terrible." She looked out at the dance floor beneath us, gazing at the sea of sweaty bodies pulsing to the steady beat. "I like that you can have a conversation in here. While the music's going. That's nice."

The hint couldn't have been stronger. I set my menu down and gave her my attention. "Let me guess, you have something you want to talk about."

"There *is* something I think that we should go over. I hadn't thought that we needed to talk about it as soon as tonight, but I realize now that we do." She was talking fast and not looking at me, and I could sense she was maybe nervous, which intrigued me to no end.

"Go on."

"You *do* know you can't see other women while we're engaged, right?" She looked up at me now, and met my eyes. Her irises were startlingly blue, almost as startlingly blue as my balls were going to be from what she just said.

Except that she was wrong.

So I corrected her. "You mean no one can *find out* that I'm sleeping with anyone." She couldn't actually be suggesting I wouldn't sleep with anybody. For seven months? I couldn't remember the last time I went seven days. It wasn't going to happen.

She sighed, a great big heavy sigh that brought her whole upper body to rest on the table between us, drawing my eyes to the way her breasts peeked over the neckline of her dress. "No, Weston. I mean, you can't sleep with anyone. Even discreetly. It's too big of a risk."

I laughed. Then I started scanning the ceiling for hidden cameras. "Is there a film crew in here somewhere? Because there's no way you're serious."

"I knew this wasn't going to work. You can't keep it in your pants for even a minute, can you?" She picked up her phone and started to text somebody. "There's just too much on the line for me here. Donovan should've been the one to volunteer; he would have been able to go seven months."

"Are you texting *Donovan*?" I wasn't sure if it bothered me more that she was texting Donovan while she was on a date with me, or that she'd suggested Donovan had the strength to do *anything* longer than I did.

Either way, I was bothered. A lot.

"Stop," I said. "Don't text him. There's no need. I just didn't know.

We hadn't discussed it yet. That's all." I ran a hand down my thigh back and forth, back and forth. Fuck, was I really, actually, agreeing to discuss this?

"I already texted him," she said smugly, setting the phone down. "It's too late."

I rolled my eyes. "We don't need his input. Let's discuss this, just you and I."

"It's just you and I right now. Go for it." Her tone wasn't angry or unreasonable. She was simply meeting the obstacle head on.

Which was admirable.

I owed it to her to be admirable as well.

I stretched my neck, trying to get rid of the kink that had suddenly shown up, and thought quickly. "You know," I said, leaning forward, "A lot of guys get married, and it doesn't mean they stop fooling around."

God, that sounded terrible. I didn't know if I'd ever get married for real, but if I did, I didn't want to be the kind of guy who fooled around on his woman.

But I wasn't getting married for real. So it was okay to play an asshole in *this* marriage. Hell, maybe it could even give us fuel for our divorce.

I was about to suggest that, but she spoke before I could.

"I'm sure that's acceptable among *some people*." She sneered as she emphasized 'some people.' I didn't know who some people were, but if some people were the kind that fooled around on their fiancées she'd had every right to sneer. "But I can't be engaged to that. I wouldn't tolerate it. Weston King would bring his girlfriend to this club, so we're here. Elizabeth Dyson wouldn't stand for a fiancé fucking around behind her back—"

"This wouldn't exactly be behind your back." Maybe it wasn't the right time for a joke.

"And she *definitely* wouldn't stand for it in front of her face."

I wracked my brain trying to figure out where all of this was coming from. Certainly the evening hadn't gone that badly. Had it? "Is this about the hostess at the restaurant?"

"I came out of the bathroom, and she was at our table giving you her phone number." She'd lowered her voice as if even letting me know that a girl had been flirting with me might be telling too many people.

I knew it!

I took a breath so I wouldn't get too eager in my explanation. "First of all, she was not giving me her number." I'd known Lexie from somewhere or other and she'd come over to show me pics of her new clit piercing. Elizabeth must have seen me take Lexie's cell phone and assumed we were exchanging numbers.

Now that I thought about it, the real explanation didn't sound any better.

"It doesn't matter what *really* happened," Elizabeth said now, her volume rising. "It matters what it *looked* like. And it looked like she was trying to hook up with you while you were on a date with me."

Her nostrils flared, and angry splotches of red appeared on the creamy skin below her collarbone.

She was cute like that, all flustered and worked up. I could imagine that blush creeping up her neck and flooding her face when she was lost in a fit of passion. Part of me wanted to see her like that. All frantic and unnerved because she was squirming underneath me . . .

Whoa. Hold on there.

We had to change the topic. "Fine. We'll be monogamous. Or not sexual. Whatever. I was just throwing the idea out there. We were talking about making it look real and everything." Good God, I hoped she knew what she was asking of me.

The doors opened to the room, and I realized we didn't have the privacy setting on. It was the waitress coming to take our drink order. I chose the house gin specialty, a martini made with house-infused spirits and a Meyer lemon-rosemary simple syrup. Elizabeth ordered—surprise, surprise—a glass of Merlot. The waitress left and Elizabeth's phone shook with the vibration of an incoming text.

She picked it up and I tried not to look like I cared about what it said, but I wasn't fooling anyone.

"Donovan says there's already a pool going to see how long you can make it." She typed something in response and threw her phone into her purse.

I wrinkled my brows. "A pool? Betting how long I can go without sex? That's ludicrous." Though it wasn't really that ludicrous because I was already having withdrawal and I hadn't even gone without sex yet.

I was also more than a little annoyed with Donovan for turning my sacrifice into office amusement. "Who's in on this pool? What did you respond with?"

"I put in a wager for two weeks."

I laughed, a real, hearty, from-the-belly laugh. That was not at all what I had expected her to say. "That doesn't serve you well if I fail within two weeks. You need me to stay celibate for seven months."

"I do need you to stay celibate for seven months, but at least I get *something* if you fail as soon as I think you're going to fail at this rate." She was annoyed.

"At this rate? I've been a perfect gentleman all evening. What makes you so certain I'm going to fail?"

"You can't even keep your eyes off the waitress."

I'd been checking out the waitress? It was so natural I hadn't noticed it. I couldn't even remember what she'd been wearing, or whether her hair had been long or short.

Honestly, the only woman I'd been thinking about all evening was the one sitting across from me, the one in the dress with the tight top that molded against her full, round breasts. The one with the mouth that curved naturally down into a kissable pout. The one whose hair lay in perfect cascades down her shoulders.

"Well, fuck you all. I can make it the whole goddamn seven months. You'll see."

And of course, that's what Donovan had meant to do by having a pool in the first place. He knew it would just get me all up in arms. Get me all pissed and want to prove everyone wrong. He wasn't even here, and he still knew just what to say to push my buttons.

I could never decide if he was an outrageous asshole or a giant I could never measure up to. Maybe he was both combined—an outrageously giant asshole.

"Then it's settled?" she asked, with that snotty look on her face and just the smallest touch of doubt. The littlest hint of vulnerability.

It was that hint that made her so soft when she was trying to be so hard. That hint that made me want to reach across the table and touch her, even just take her hand in mine.

But I didn't.

I had to remember that she was also the woman putting a chastity belt on my lower regions for more than half of the year. Just thinking about it made my balls ache.

"It's settled." Thank fucking God for porn and my left hand.

"Then I'll cancel my wager."

"You aren't doing me any favors," I said, maybe a bit too harshly. "But thank you."

We were silent then, the conversation killed by abstinence. Sure there were still things to say, things to work out, but I wasn't in the mood to get into wedding details and I sure as hell wasn't getting into business now. The Sky Launch was sacred. This was not a place for business.

Elizabeth took the silence as something else. "I'm sorry, Weston. I really am. I imagine that a healthy sex life is important to—"

"Don't apologize." I didn't want to hear Elizabeth Dyson discussing my overactive dick. I couldn't control my hard-on already.

We fell back into the quiet. The waitress came in, left our drinks on the table along with the tab.

A romper. Long auburn hair.

That's what the waitress was wearing, that's what she looked like. I made sure to notice this time. Truth is, there was a time I would have noticed earlier.

Hell, maybe it was time for a cleanse. I had been bored lately. Maybe a sex break would solve that. Not that I wanted to find out, but since I didn't really have a choice . . .

The waitress left, and I hit the privacy button out of habit. Elizabeth and I sipped our drinks silently. She looked out again over the dance floor, then studied the buttons along the length of the table that operated the glass window. She pushed the one that turned the glass opaque.

"Clear it," I ordered.

She looked up at me, startled. Then she pushed the button to make the glass clear again. "You have lots of glass in your office too. You like being seen?"

If she thought I was a dirty oversexed player before, she couldn't handle all the things I was really into.

Of course, that made me all the more eager to tell her. Something about her prissiness made the idea of shocking her a turn-on.

"Yeah. I do."

She pursed her lips, considering. She peeked out the window again, this time looking out to the other bubble rooms. Most held parties of people gathered around the circular bench enjoying their dinners and their drinks in a place where they could talk. A couple, though, were opaque.

She turned her gaze back to me. "What exactly do you do with girls when you bring them here?"

God, I felt like I was on Secret Confessions. "Do you really want to know?"

She took a swallow of her wine and licked the little drop of Merlot that lingered on her lip. "I wouldn't have asked if I didn't want to know. I'm supposed to be one of those girls. Remember?"

Of course, she could never really be one of those girls. One of *those* girls would've had her panties off already. That was too crass to tell her outright.

But there was a whole Internet that could tell her for me. "Pull up YouTube. Search my name and Sky Launch."

She hesitated a moment before she pulled her phone back out of her purse. Then she swiped the screen, entered her password, and searched as I'd told her to. I didn't look to see what she was watching—I kept my gaze only on her face as she played first one video, then the next. Then a third.

I watched her eyes widen. I watched her pupils dilate. I watched her lips part and her breathing get heavy. I could only imagine what she was seeing.

Random footage from people on the dance floor taking film with their phones of the most eligible bachelor in New York caught once again at his favorite nightclub with the flavor of the week. I'd watched plenty of those videos. I'd whacked off to a few of them. They didn't usually show very much of me, but they often showcased a topless girl, sometimes more than one. Always in a bubble room. There was no mistaking what was going on in here.

The window was always clear.

And I always made them come.

Elizabeth's face was red by the time she put her phone back in her purse, the same red color that I'd imagined earlier.

I really needed to stop imagining that.

"Wow." She swallowed and I watched her throat as it delicately bobbed. "People really do watch you up here."

I almost laughed. *That* was her takeaway? "Yes, people really do watch."

"And you . . . like that." I couldn't tell if there was judgment in her voice or not. But of course she was judging me.

"Hey, before you get all high and mighty—"

"I'm not." She said it so emphatically that I stopped speaking. "I'm not," she said again. "I'm just saying that—if that's what you like, and if that's what you bring girls here to do . . . and if I am supposed to be your girlfriend, and if we're supposed to make it convincing . . ."

She paused and took a deep breath, and I thought I knew where she was going, but that really couldn't be where she was going, could it?

"Then we have to make it believable, too."

My dick perked up. She'd said exactly the words I'd hoped against hope to hear come out of her mouth.

Well, how about that? Elizabeth Dyson might be a fun girl after all.

# CHAPTER
# SIX

*Elizabeth*

HOLY SHIT, I was in over my head.

How on earth had I not seen it coming?

It wasn't like I hadn't prepared for our date. I'd researched Weston the minute I'd left the Reach offices and learned the essentials. Turned out the man used those panty-melting dimples to get women. A lot of women. But I could have guessed that just from the short time I'd spent in his presence. Sex emanated from him like cologne. As though he'd put it on with his aftershave and pomade.

So I'd chosen the restaurant, I'd chosen my clothing, I'd provided the driver—all of it so that I would feel that I had some sort of an ounce of control on my first outing with this stranger. The stranger I was about to pledge myself to in legal matrimony. I'd thought maybe that would put me on some sort of an even playing field.

But it had only taken a few hours to realize that nothing could put me on an even playing field with Weston King.

What I'd failed to realize, was that it wasn't Weston I needed to compete with—it was his women.

And they were at every turn. Beautiful, strong, smart women. Women he knew, yes, but the ones he didn't know seemed to notice him and swarmed as though they were bees, and he was the hive.

He was just as attentive. Whatever it was they said or did, or however it was they smiled or walked, they knew how to catch his eye, because he checked out every damn one of them. Or it felt like he did.

And here I was next to them, plain and insecure, a little bit awkward and a whole lot inexperienced. And somehow, I was supposed to capture him the same way all these women before me had. Keep his eyes on me and off of them for the duration of our time together.

I'd only had three steady boyfriends. My mother was the one who knew how to handle men like Weston. She was the one who knew how to flirt and flaunt. She was the one who knew how to be sexy and desired. Who knew how to be confident in her skin, to bring men to their knees.

She was the one who men stared at in the way that Weston was staring at me now.

And he was only staring at me because he thought I was one of those girls, because I'd just suggested that maybe I should pretend to be one.

He did realize I'd meant pretend, didn't he?

"I'm not suggesting that we actually *do* anything," I clarified. "But we need to make it seem like we're doing the same things you do with other girls up here. Stage it."

"Right." He grinned.

And I had to hold back a shiver. That dimple was pure sin. It was distracting and unnerving and just plain rude. I was trying to be practical and salvage this whole sham while he acted like he was looking forward to this. I wasn't even sure what *this* was yet. There were several variations of sex shows in those videos I'd watched. I was bendy enough. Years of ballet gave me experience in physical performance. The trick was figuring out which position was the easiest to fake.

I looked around our set, weighing our options. "If I stand on the bench with my hands on the window with you behind me . . ."

"Come over here," he ordered as though I hadn't even spoken.

My heart skipped a beat at the subtle edge to his command. "Why?"

"If we're going to make this believable, you're going to have to be closer. Come over here and sit in my lap. Straddle me."

Now my pulse raced inside my chest. Of all the positions we had as options, straddling his lap was definitely the most intimate.

I scooted tentatively around the bench and then turned so I was on my knees facing out the window. I paused when I was next to him, not quite sure how to do the next part. I'd never done this before. Never straddled a guy. Not to trick people into thinking I was fooling around, certainly. Not even because I was actually fooling around.

I took a deep breath, gathering my nerves, but before I'd gotten it together, he grabbed my elbow and tugged me so that I fell across his lap.

Well, hello.

"There you are," he said.

His body was warm, and I instantly had the urge to curl into him. I fought against it, sitting back on his thighs, away from his pelvis so that it wouldn't be too weird. Too intimate. Still, we were close, our faces only inches from each other. I could smell his cologne and his shampoo and the faint scent of sweat underneath—a scent that was pure Weston. And, shit, he was even more gorgeous close-up. His skin, flawless. His eyes, deep pools of blue.

I swallowed, suddenly nervous.

Weston seemed to sense my anxiety because next thing I knew he was reassuring me. "I'm keeping my hands on the bench next to me. Okay? You can lean on my shoulders to give yourself some balance, if you want. And then anything that happens here? It's all up to you. You run the show."

I ran my tongue across my lips in a circle and nodded. "Okay." My voice sounded unusually high and shaky, and my palms felt sweaty as I settled them on his shoulders to balance myself. I shifted my hips, trying to get comfortable.

And accidentally slid forward, my pelvis hitting his.

Whoops.

My cheeks went red as Weston let out a low chuckle. I was sitting on his lap. With nothing between my crotch and his except a pair of panties and his pants. And whatever he had on underneath his pants.

And now I was thinking about what he had on underneath his pants.

I looked at the windows past him, trying to distract myself. Lights flashed and swirled around the dance floor in time to the beat, the only part of the music which made it into the sanctuary of the bubble room. I could tell it was crowded, but I couldn't make out faces the way they could probably make out ours. "I don't know if anyone's looking," I said.

"Don't worry about them. Just focus on what you're doing."

Easy for him to say. He wasn't facing them. He was only looking at me.

Nope. I couldn't think about that either. Just had to focus on the task at hand.

I closed my eyes. "So just pretend that I . . . That we are . . . That under my dress . . ." I couldn't even say it.

Weston leaned forward and murmured near my ear. "Yes, pretend that under your dress you are not wearing any panties. I have my dick out. I'm working you, and you are showing me exactly how you like it. Now go."

Just like that, my panties were damp.

I didn't know if he was saying those things to loosen me up or to get a rise out of me, either was possible.

Whatever his intent, it did the trick. He set the scene. I felt my face flush like the women in the videos as I imagined him rubbing his crown against my slit before nudging his tip inside and then burying himself to the hilt.

I opened my mouth in a silent gasp, acting out how I was sure it would feel. *Good. It would feel so good.*

This was so . . . weird. So hot and sexy and arousing and weird.

I wondered if he was feeling it too, feeling turned on, or if it was just me. It wasn't like I could ask though, and knowing probably wouldn't help my performance anyway.

So I concentrated on me. Focused on the task.

"Do I move or something?" I bucked my hips forward and felt the friction against my crotch as it rubbed the fly of his pants.

*Mmm.*

"Yeah," he said breathlessly. "That's good. That motion. Just like that."

"Okay. Okay." I rocked against him again, and again, my hips tilting back and forth, my clit brushing against his fly. Every time, stroking and kindling a fire in a fireplace I hadn't had cleaned for some time. I spread my thighs a little wider and braced my knees against the bench so I could swing my pelvis all the way forward, in and out, in and . . .

Oh.

I froze. "Is that—?" But I didn't have to ask. There was most definitely a fat, thick ridge pressed against the crotch panel of my panties. I guess that answered the question of whether he was feeling it too.

My eyes flew open. "Oh my God!"

"Look," he said, ready to defend himself. "There's an extremely attractive woman sitting on my lap. I cannot help what happens to my cock. It has a mind of its own."

A really *big* mind of its own.

"Just pretend it's not there," he said at the same time I said, "I'm pretending it's not there."

Like hell I could pretend it wasn't there. I wasn't even sure I wanted to.

Our eyes met momentarily. His were lit up and crazed, mirrors to how I felt inside.

I rocked forward again, without even thinking that I wanted to, and I had to bite my lip because it felt so incredible rubbing my pussy along the outline of his cock.

"That's great," he hissed. "Pretend it's not there just like that, and you're great."

That was exactly what I planned to do. Glad we were on the same page.

Though *plan* wasn't quite the right word for what was going on with me at the moment. My body was just moving on its own, rocking steadily, trying to ease the ache between my legs, trying to rub against the firm thickness anchored beneath me.

But nothing was enough.

I twisted and circled my hips. I writhed. I let go of his shoulder and grabbed my breast with one hand, brushing across my nipple with my thumb. Everything I did only made the buzz louder, the hum in my veins more intense.

I'd forgotten about the glass windows and the crowds below. The performance was no longer for anyone but me. The end goal wasn't about looking like one of Weston's girls—it was about *becoming* one of them.

But I was aimless and an amateur, and I needed help.

"Tell me what you're doing to me," I begged. "Tell me what you would be doing to me right now."

"I'm so deep inside you," he said without any hesitation. "I'm balls deep, my dick is touching the very end of you." His hips bucked up, and I wondered if he knew he was even doing it. "I have my hand under your skirt and I'm rubbing your clit in tight circles, and it's driving you insane. You're so wet that my thumb keeps sliding off your nub." His voice was strained as he talked, and I could hear his fingernails digging into the bench on either side of us, clawing into the upholstery.

God I wanted him to touch me. If he touched me I'd explode. I was already so close.

"Then I grab your ass to pull you closer, so I can fuck you even deeper, and you tilt your hips up slightly. I tell you to touch yourself because you're on the edge and I want you to come for me. I want you to come when I tell you. Come all over my goddamn cock until you're shuddering and writhing and gasping for air. Do it, Elizabeth. Come all over me. Do it now."

I closed my eyes, but all I could see was light behind my lids, bright starbursts sprayed across the darkness. My hand fell back to his shoulder in an attempt to steady myself as a torpedo strength orgasm ripped through me, splitting my insides, leaving me shaking and trembling and moaning out in ecstasy.

I threw my head back and called his name once before falling forward, limp and spent.

*What the fuck just happened?*

I hadn't even caught my breath yet when I flung my head up again, shock and horror surely written all over my face. Fortunately I found only another full dimple smile on his.

"I didn't mean to do that," I said.

"It's okay. Really. You were great."

I scrambled up to my feet and smoothed my dress down as if I could hide my entire being with the movement. I couldn't help it. My eyes wandered down to his pants that were still straining at the zipper. His eyes followed mine to the wet spot that now darkened the material. A wet spot I had clearly left behind.

If it were possible to die from humiliation, I would have right about now.

"You know what? That's hot." The rasp in Weston's voice suggested that he wouldn't mind if I got more of him wet.

And even having just finished coming down from the best orgasm of my life, there was a part of me that wouldn't mind getting more of him wet myself.

I met his eyes. There was no way he wasn't thinking the same thing I was thinking. We were already here. We were already about to be engaged. We were obviously into each other.

"It wouldn't be a good idea," I said, yet for the life of me I couldn't think of any reason why it wouldn't. Sure, I'd never fooled around with a man just for the fun of it, but that didn't mean I couldn't start now. The words were already out of my mouth though, so now all I could do was wait and see how he reacted.

"Right," he agreed. "It would be a terrible idea."

"Because it would just complicate things," I said.

"Exactly. We're stuck together for the better part of a year. If we crossed this line now, we couldn't go back. And that would be a long time to have to be around each other afterward. As you said, it would complicate things."

"Right. Glad you see it the way I do." I swallowed, grateful that my voice hadn't caught. I understood what he was saying, but it sounded a lot like an excuse. A nice way of saying I'm not really *that* interested.

My throat suddenly felt tight and my eyes began to sting. This was the downside of being one of Weston's girls, I realized. Any night of fun would end in being casually dismissed.

How did his usual dates handle it so gracefully?

Probably they always knew it was coming, which I should've known too, but where rejection was concerned, I was already a bruise that refused to heal. I'd been overlooked too much of my life by the only man who'd ever really been important to me. My father had wounded me, and any other rejection felt like fingers pressing against purple and black skin, and I recoiled from the pain.

Also, I was a little bit angry at Weston now that I thought about it. How was this behavior supposed to sell me as a businesswoman? It had been my idea to give the performance, but Weston had been the one to say I needed to do a better job of selling myself as a smart, competent woman, one worthy of running the Dyson empire. How could he let me do *this* with him? Slutting it up only justified my father's points. And now I was going to be all over the Internet, and the headlines weren't going to convince anyone of anything except that Weston King gave good orgasms.

I had to keep my head in the game. The *long* game. Proving our relationship would be pointless if I didn't prove myself first.

Which was why I couldn't have sex with Weston. *That* was the reason.

It was also why nothing like this could ever happen again. Not even for the show. It shouldn't need to now anyway. If we were truly dating, we might have engaged in the same behavior he had with women of the past in our earlier days, but as I'd told him, *I* was supposed to be different. I was the girl he married—not the girl he fucked in a bubble room then never called again.

It was time for me to take charge.

I lifted my chin and cleared my throat. "Hopefully that display was convincing. Because we're not doing that again. We'll come back to The Sky Launch every Friday night, since it's your hangout. We'll let ourselves be seen here, but when we get to this room we'll turn the privacy windows on." I stared him head-on to make sure he understood what I was saying. "Once we are engaged, the world doesn't need to know what we are doing in here anyway."

"Uh, okay," he said, obviously caught off guard. He shifted in his seat, reminding me he was still . . . uncomfortable. "You just want to come have drinks every week?"

"You can use that time to teach me the business like you promised," I said coldly. I didn't give him a chance to disagree. "I'm going to go to the restroom now and clean up. That will give you some time to take care of your little . . . problem."

I turned before he could say anything and headed for the exit, but I heard him call after me, "It's not little!"

I could tell it wasn't, just from the shape I'd rubbed against. Weston was packing, there was no doubt about that.

But I wasn't in the mood to give him any less rejection than what I'd felt. I swiveled my head in his direction, tossing my hair over my shoulder. "I guess I'll never know, will I?"

With those parting words, I left the bubble room.

# CHAPTER
# SEVEN

*Weston*

"**Y**OU GOING TO tell me what you're moping about today?"

I glanced up at Donovan who was flipping through LeeAnn Gregori's portfolio while we waited for Elizabeth to arrive for our meeting with the famed wedding planner.

What the hell did he mean by moping? I glanced down at my body language—my arms folded, my shoulders hunched.

My frown deepened.

I was irritated, that's what I was. And I had been for the last several weeks, the source of my irritation none other than my bride-to-be. For the last month we'd played the fake courting game, going to lunch at least once a week, where we usually ended up bickering about restaurants or menu items, and attending the symphony where I always fell asleep before intermission.

Then every Friday night we'd returned to The Sky Launch where she'd sat so perfectly innocent beside me, asking questions about mergers and stock options while her lids fluttered as she thought. And each time I was forced to give her knowledgeable answers when all I could think about was pulling her back onto my lap. Making her hips grind against my dick the way they had that first night, when she was putting on a show. I wanted to make her grind against my dick for real.

I hadn't changed my mind about what I'd said—fucking was a bad idea. It would make things messy, and I didn't do messy. She'd already proven that she couldn't mix sex with business by how she'd acted immediately after. One orgasm and she'd turned cold and snide, shoving her nose up as though what we'd done was dirty or beneath her. Imagine how she would have reacted if I'd treated her to a night at the Weston Inn. Dirt and filth were the house specialty—money back guaranteed.

But it didn't change the fact that I was still attracted to her, that I still thought about her pouty lips and perky round breasts, that I could still remember the scent of her arousal drifting in the air as she pressed her pussy against my straining cock. Fuck, if I didn't hear those breathy little moans in my sleep, and the way her face twisted in pleasure as she called out my name haunted me when I sat at my desk trying to concentrate on marketing conversion rates. My hand was getting such a workout from the memories that I wouldn't be surprised if I got carpal tunnel before our marriage was through.

None of this was anything I was going to admit to Donovan, though, because that asshole was the reason I was in this shitty situation in the first place. I was starting to believe my misery was his form of entertainment, and I wasn't giving him anything I didn't have to.

"I'm not moping." Shit, even I could hear the scowl in my tone.

"Good. Brooding looks much better on me than it does on you." Donovan shut the portfolio and crossed one leg over the other at the knee.

I clenched my fist, but took a breath so I wouldn't be tempted to punch him.

"She's late," I said, when I was calm. We'd been waiting in the lounge for ten minutes, but Donovan knew I was speaking about Elizabeth and not LeeAnn Gregori, though technically she was late as well.

"She's probably in traffic. It's rush hour in New York City. No one's on time."

That was Donovan, always making excuses for her. "You really should've been the one to marry her," I grumbled, the thought making my stomach turn in weird strange ways.

He shook his head and opened his mouth, but before he could give me his usual spiel, I added, "People would have bought it."

"I was about to say that I don't really care for the girl."

My jaw dropped, and I stammered wordlessly for several seconds. "What?" I finally managed. "What does that have to do with anything?" As if *I* cared for the girl.

He narrowed his eyes in my direction. "Do you really want me to prove that *you* like her more than *I* do?"

I hesitated. Because . . . could he? Prove it?

Of course he couldn't prove it. He was bluffing, as always. I *didn't* like her better. I barely liked her at all.

But Donovan was good with his propaganda. So it was best not to let him speak, best to drop it.

Except I didn't want him thinking I actually *liked* Elizabeth.

Which made it a good time to tell him my other news.

I sat forward and rested my elbows on my thighs. "I officially offered the marketing job to Sabrina Lind today," I announced.

His chin tilted up ever so slightly. "Oh?"

"I should have done it a long time ago. Robbie will be leaving for London in three weeks, and we need the spot filled. I've just been busy, I guess." Busy playing boyfriend to Elizabeth. Spending all my time focused on her had made it difficult to remember why I'd wanted Sabrina to transfer to New York so badly in the first place.

"What did she say?" Donovan asked, seeming only slightly interested. It was a rather important position in the firm, though, so he was surely cataloguing it somewhere in his brain.

"She said yes. We have to work out the transfer package and help her find a place to live. She'll be here in a month."

"I'll take care of it," he said quickly. Then he changed the subject abruptly. "I have news as well."

"Oh?" I tilted my head back toward him.

"I've decided I'm staying. Cade has a handle on the Tokyo office. New York City seems to need me. I'll stay and take on operations."

That was so Donovan. Making all the decisions for the firm without asking anyone else's opinion. Not that I wasn't glad to have him here.

The work had grown to be too much for Nate and I, and I really didn't give a fuck about operations. Just, it would be nice to have a say in things every once in awhile.

I pretended it didn't bother me. "Great. Glad you decided to stay."

Before anything else could be said about it, the doors opened to the waiting room. We both looked up expectantly, hoping to see Elizabeth, but in walked a middle-aged woman with blond hair streaked with gray, skin freckled from too much sun, and the purplest eyeshadow I'd ever seen on someone not in drag. She was dressed in business casual, which still meant lots of bling, and platform heels covered in rhinestones. Apparently this was LeeAnn Gregori.

"Gentlemen!" she exclaimed, and then her brows furrowed. "I'm sorry," she looked down at the tablet she was carrying. "I had noted that I was meeting with a bride and groom. Not a groom and groom."

"The bride's not here yet," I said as quickly as I could. Not that there was anything wrong with a groom and groom getting married, but there was no way anyone was groom and grooming me with Donovan. I had my manhood to defend.

"I see. Well, in that case," she took a step forward, her hand out, "I'm LeeAnn."

"I'm Donovan Kincaid," he said, rushing in before I could introduce myself. "This is Weston King, the groom. Elizabeth Dyson is the bride. She's running late. Also, as we mentioned on the phone with you, this wedding is on a very tight deadline. We are looking at a December date, but it will be a very large affair. Money is not an issue, we're quite prepared to pay whatever is needed. Tell us what we can do in that amount of time."

"Yes, yes, we can do something spectacular in that amount of time. . . . Tell me again what your relationship is to this wedding, Mr. Kincaid?"

I bit back a smile. It was always a highlight of my day to watch Donovan get questioned on his authority. It actually brightened my mood quite a bit.

Just then, Elizabeth burst in. She was out of breath and her face was flushed from rushing. My cock jumped in my pants, remembering that she'd looked that way when she'd come on my lap, tempting me into another fantasy of putting that look on her face in other ways.

"Hello, I'm sorry I'm so late. I'm Elizabeth Dyson." She held her hand out to LeeAnn. "You must be the wedding planner. I've heard so much about you. You're quite famous among my mother's friends."

"A pleasure to meet you, Ms. Dyson. I'm honored to work with someone so notable as well. We were just discussing what Mr. Kincaid's involvement was in your wedding to Mr. King?" LeeAnn shifted her eyes from Elizabeth to me.

Elizabeth slipped in between me and Donovan, looping an arm around me as she placed a hand on my partner's arm. "Oh, Donovan is my life coach. I don't do anything without his say-so. I invited him here to advise us. I hope that's not going to be a problem?"

I couldn't decide if I was impressed at how easily Elizabeth could act on her feet, or if I was annoyed at how eagerly she covered for Donovan.

And why *was* Donovan here anyway? Didn't he think we could handle this on our own? Or did he just insist on having his fingers in every pie?

Though I had to admit, it was really nice to have somebody else handle all the big details of a wedding I didn't give a shit about. Almost as nice as watching his face as it registered with him that he'd just been demoted from Fortune 500 company owner to life coach.

"Not a problem at all," LeeAnn said congenially. "If everyone is here, let's sit down and start planning, shall we?"

We sat down and LeeAnn filled out a few initial details about us in her tablet. Then we jumped right into making arrangements.

Immediately, we hit a snag.

"I do not think we should have the engagement party at The Sky Launch," Elizabeth said patronizingly.

"What's wrong with The Sky Launch? It's our place, honey." I made my voice sticky sweet, playing the part of fiancé. "We're there every week, after all."

Her eyes narrowed. "It's *your* place. How many other women have you taken there? Need I remind you of all the videos on YouTube? Half our guests will be attending and remembering their own trysts with you!"

I rolled my eyes and looked to Donovan, then to LeeAnn. "It's not like I'm actually inviting ex-girlfriends to the engagement party." Well, I'd slept with so many women, it was kind of impossible not to invite a few. Or, okay, a lot. "There won't be *that* many of them," I amended.

"I would tend to agree with Elizabeth on this one," LeeAnn, the traitor, began, "but unfortunately on such short notice, there aren't many other available places that will hold four hundred to five hundred guests. Unless you want to book the Marriott, I could maybe get—"

"Ew, no. Not the Marriott." It was Elizabeth's turn to look to Donovan.

"Considering the circumstances, Elizabeth," his subtext was clear—fake arranged marriage was the circumstance, "I think The Sky Launch is a perfect venue for the engagement party."

"Fine," she huffed. "But I want to be in charge of the music."

LeeAnn interjected before I had a chance to give my opinion on the matter. "I think that's a fair compromise. Moving on."

And so it went. We argued about everything. Every venue, every arrangement. Everything from catering to clothing to wedding-day events to photographers to whether or not we would be throwing a joint engagement shower (I put my foot down with an emphatic no). There was absolutely nothing we could agree on, which was insane because none of it even mattered. I swore half the time it felt like she was arguing just for the sake of arguing. I knew I certainly was.

There was one thing I did feel strongly about, though. "I don't want my parents involved," I said.

"Do they . . . do they know about me?" Elizabeth asked, and I realized I hadn't informed her yet that I wasn't planning to tell them anything other than that I was getting married.

"Of course, sweetheart," I said, careful of my audience. "They're excited to meet you. I haven't told them *everything* about us. Don't worry about that." I winked and met her eyes to make sure she understood what I was saying.

She nodded once, but her brow furrowed. "And you don't want

them involved."

"That's correct."

She continued staring at me, her mouth open in that cute little annoying way that said she wanted to say something, and so help me if she did, I wasn't sure what I was going to do.

"No parents. Got it." LeeAnn entered the information in her tablet.

"No, my mom will be involved," Elizabeth clarified. She opened her mouth to say more, then shut it. Then opened it again. Then shut it.

*Good girl,* I thought. *Leave it alone.*

But then she turned abruptly to me. "You really need to include your parents, Weston," she said, her lips set in a smug line that made me want to draw her across my lap and spank it off of her.

"No, actually, I don't."

"Why?" She stared at me, her blue eyes looking inside me as though she could see through my walls. As though she thought I would divulge my reasons to her here, of all places.

"It's none of—" *your business,* I started to say, but Donovan cleared his throat and I caught myself in time. "Our life is none of their business," I said, instead.

"It's their *son's wedding.* And what about your sister?"

Shit. I hadn't thought about Noelle. "We can involve my sister somehow. What can an eighteen-year old girl do as part of the wedding?" I directed this last part to LeeAnn.

"She could greet people as they arrive, and since you've decided against a receiving line, you'll want to have a guest book. She could manage that."

"Great. Have her do that," I said.

"Awesome. Stick a teenager behind a table all night when she'd rather be mingling and dancing," Elizabeth muttered.

I glared, but otherwise ignored her. "As for my parents, they don't need to be seated at any special time, they don't need to have any special recognition, and they certainly don't need to pay for anything. And that's final." I looked over at Donovan, because he was the one person in the room who would understand.

But he didn't say anything to either back me or refute me.

"Okay, then. You heard him. He doesn't want his parents," Elizabeth said in obvious disagreement. She leaned toward our planner. "Make sure that if anyone asks, it's clear that was Weston's decision, and not mine."

God. Sometimes she was a real bitch.

A gorgeous bitch that made my pants feel too tight every time I looked at her too long, or thought about her just right, but a bitch all the same.

"At the wedding itself," the gorgeous bitch continued, "We should probably have a large family picture taken, with all the extended family. I have a cousin that would really like to be in that portrait." She looked at Donovan and I to see if we understood, and we did. She wanted to make sure that her cousin Darrell was invited to be in that photograph. That he was part of one piece of the wedding, so he would feel like the whole thing was real.

"Good idea, Elizabeth," Donovan said, and she beamed.

"We'll send him an invitation to the engagement party too, though I'm sure he won't tear himself away from work to attend." Again she sounded bitter, and this time, when the bitterness wasn't directed at me, I felt a tinge of sympathy for her. That she had to play this charade in the first place, for a piece-of-shit asshole who didn't give a damn about her personally.

Not that I was about to let her know.

"And your bridal parties? Do you have ideas of who you'd like to have in your line?" LeeAnn went on, marking each of our requests in her tablet.

"There are several people I could choose. I have some good friends from college . . ." Eliza-bitch chewed on her lip as she considered.

Donovan shook his head. "Make it simple. One attendant each. Don't you think?"

"Yeah, one attendant is good," I agreed. The simpler the better. Having fittings and rehearsals for something that wasn't going to last was a waste of time, not only for us, but for these friends of ours as well.

"You're right," Elizabeth said. "I'll pick my friend Melissa from college."

"If we're going with old friends, I guess that's you, Donovan," I said.

LeeAnn looked confused. "I thought you said he was your life coach?"

"Donovan is my life coach. He's Weston's best friend. He's a lot of things to a lot of different people," Elizabeth explained.

"I see," LeeAnn said, though it didn't really look like she did see.

Donovan side-eyed me. "Do you really think that *I* would be the best choice for planning your bachelor party? And writing the speech about true love to toast you with at your reception?"

I rubbed two fingers along my forehead. A bachelor party from Donovan actually might be fun. It would be all cigars and scotch, but I would probably regret everything that happened afterwards. And weren't those the best kinds of nights? But any speech he wrote on true love would be so depressing half the audience would grow suicidal.

"Brett Larrabee," Donovan and I said in unison. Brett was a roommate from college, a guy I still kept up with pretty well. He was extroverted, charismatic, a good speaker, the life of most parties and a decent friend. Most of all, he wouldn't mind being the best man for a night, even if he found out later on that the whole thing was a farce.

"I'll give him a call," I said.

"Great," LeeAnn said, relieved that at least one item had been ticked off without a fight. She had to be wondering why on Earth we were marrying at all. "We have that settled."

We managed to continue without any brawling through the next few items, but then we got to the details of the actual ceremony and hit a doozy of a bump.

"I hate traditional vows," Elizabeth said, her jaw tight. "I do not want to read traditional vows at our wedding."

"LeeAnn just gave us seventeen different options. We don't have to use any of the ones that say 'obey and honor.' We can use one of the more modern ones. But we definitely don't need to write our own!"

Because of course she wanted us to write our own vows. For our not-real wedding. For our not-real relationship. Was the girl insane?

"It's not just that they are old-fashioned and outdated. Yes, some of them are more modern," Elizabeth flipped through the booklet of vows LeeAnn had given us to look through, "but they're just so standard. So conformist. So trite and overdone."

*Fake wedding.* I said it really loudly in my head, zooming it toward her, hoping that she would hear me. *Fake wedding, Elizabeth. Overdone is okay for a fake wedding.*

But apparently she didn't hear my thoughts, because she continued to speak her side. "I really think we should write our own."

I was going to murder her. I'd actually tried to get along with her for the most part. It had been hard, especially with how close she was sitting to me. Every time she moved her scent would drift toward me—a combination of tropical body wash and expensive perfume, a smell so purely *her* that it made me want to bury my head in her neck and breathe her in until I was high. And every time her skin brushed against mine, my dick perked up. And every time she argued I wanted to choke her or fuck her or both.

God, I was so fucking horny and blue balled.

And I was not going to sit there and listen to her try and twist me around her pretty little finger one more goddamned minute.

"Excuse me, LeeAnn. Donovan, may I please speak to my lovely fiancée alone for just a moment?" *So that I can wring her lovely neck.*

"Of course. Donovan, why don't you come in the other room. I can show you those examples I have of invitation vellum." She stood and he followed, giving us a warning glance before he disappeared behind the closed doors.

As soon as we were alone, Elizabeth turned to me. "It's my wedding."

"It's a *fake* wedding."

"Nobody else knows that. I'm going to be judged on this. Everyone will look at me and say, 'Elizabeth Dyson, boring, unoriginal.' I need to have original vows."

"Then we will pick the most original pre-written vows there are. But we are not writing our own. I refuse."

She drew her lips into a tight line and folded her arms across her chest, the action showcasing her tits, not that I noticed. "Why don't you want your parents involved?"

"Maybe I don't think it's fair to bring them out just so you can play fantasy wedding." Ouch. I went there.

But she didn't flinch. "That's not why. You have another reason."

"And I'm not telling you what it is."

She took a deep breath in, her breasts heaving and expanding. "Fine. I'll drop it."

"We're still not writing our own vows."

I swear she growled. My dick jumped at the sound. "This is stupid. You can't write your own vows because you can't think of something nice and genuine to say about me?"

Honestly, I could think of a *lot* of nice and genuine things to say about her. Things a man who had no real interest in a woman probably shouldn't say to that woman. Things that a woman like her might be scandalized by hearing. "No. I can't."

"You're an asshole." But she'd taken a step closer to me.

"You're a bitch." I noticed our bodies were only inches apart now, her mouth was tilted up towards mine, her eyes pinned on my lips.

And suddenly all I could think about was kissing her. I couldn't give a fuck about vows or parents or secrets or anything but finding out what her lips tasted like, what they felt like against mine. If they stayed pressed shut until I worked them open or if they eagerly parted for my tongue.

I bent closer, leaned toward her—

And suddenly the doors burst open again.

"We found your invitation material," LeeAnn said with a boastful grin. "You'll be quite pleased, it matches everything else you selected. Have you sorted out the vows?"

Elizabeth jumped back the minute we were interrupted, putting as much space between me and her as she could in as little time as she had.

"It's settled," she said, before I could even remember what the disagreement had been. "We'll do pre-written vows. A version of the traditional. Minus the honor and obey."

LeeAnn raised a brow. "Oh. So the groom won this round."

"Yeah." I glanced over at Elizabeth but she wasn't looking at me. "I guess I did."

Why then, did it feel like I'd lost?

# CHAPTER
# EIGHT

*Elizabeth*

"OH NO, OH no! What did you do?" Weston's anguished voice came from behind me.

It was the night of our engagement party, and we'd been bickering for weeks. Since the meeting with our wedding planner, to be precise, and *bickering* was maybe too light a word. Outright arguing might have been more like it. The only time we hadn't been arguing was that strange moment when I thought he was going to kiss me, where everything calmed down except the beat of my pulse and the flutter in my tummy, and the noise between us finally hushed.

But the moment had passed, our lips never met, and the calm turned out to be only the eye in a hurricane of constant tension.

I expected tonight to be more of the same. Luckily, I'd arrived at The Sky Launch first, having only managed to do that by telling him our meeting time was a full hour later than it was. I turned from the florist, prepared for another battle but when I caught sight of him, I nearly lost all the air in my lungs.

I'd seen pictures of him in a tux before. My Internet search had turned up quite a few of him in various versions of Armani and Tom Ford. I couldn't say that I hadn't lingered over one or two of them. The man did photograph so well.

Turned out pictures didn't tell half the story.

His jacket was custom-fit, tightening in at his hips, making the broad stretch of his shoulders accentuate his muscles. He spun, surveying the night club, and I caught sight of his backside, which was equally stunning. His jacket was tailored in just the right spots and hit perfectly below his ass, hinting at the treasure underneath. He was breathtaking. When most men wore tuxedos, they blended in. Weston King wore one, and all heads turned.

Fortunately he didn't see me gawking, because he was too busy gaping at the dance floor.

I strode over to him. "Exactly what is it that I did?" Because there was no doubt in my mind it was me he was yelling at.

"The music. The jazz? The flowers. This isn't a nightclub anymore. It's like a banquet before a symphony." He turned to face me at the end of his sentence, and I didn't miss the slight look of shock when he saw me.

I stood up taller. I'd chosen a rather conservative gown for the evening—a white halter top dress that went all the way to my feet. But it was a mermaid shape that hugged every curve of my breasts and my hips. I'd watched every last gram of carbohydrates I'd put in my mouth for a week to make sure it fit me like a glove.

I knew I looked good, with my hair off my neck and my shoulders bare, but I hadn't gone extravagant. I'd left that for my mother, who would most likely be wearing glitter, decked out from head to toe. Lee-Ann Gregori would be her only competition for bling queen.

But Weston looked at me like I was wearing the most beautiful gown at Bergman's—or like I was wearing nothing at all—and it made my stomach do a slow roll.

Then he shook it off. "What did you do to *my* Sky Launch?" he demanded again, even more enraged than he was a second before.

"It's an engagement party! We're not here for dancing. We're here for mingling and meeting our guests. And you said I could be in charge of the music."

"I wasn't expecting it to sound like Muzak. Plus I see we're only serving champagne? At this rate, everybody's going to be asleep."

I crossed my arms over my chest, shifting my weight to one hip.

"Well then, good. Then maybe they won't realize the set for all those video files of you fucking random girls was up in those bubble rooms."

"Darlings, darlings," LeeAnn said, showing up out of what felt like nowhere. "I know that all this wedding stuff can be so tense, but you lovebirds really should kiss and make up before your guests get here, which will be any moment now. Smile. Enjoy yourselves! This is your night!"

Before either of us could react to her, she was off to attend to some other aspect of the party.

Weston opened his mouth, probably to say something else smart, when Gwen strolled up to us.

"Hello, you two," she said, a gift bag tucked under her arm. She hugged first Weston, then me, then stepped back to admire us both. "You look beautiful tonight, Elizabeth. That dress is absolutely gorgeous! You've really found yourself quite a catch, Weston."

His cheek muscle twitched, but then he gave his dazzling dimpled grin. "Didn't I?" He said it so smoothly that even I almost believed him. "I already know she's going to be the most beautiful woman in the room, and I haven't even seen any of the other guests yet."

Goddamn, he was a charmer. And if he kept looking at me the way he was now? At least people would believe he was smitten with me. I'd just have to ignore the dampness in my panties.

"He's good," Gwen said to me.

I bit back a laugh. "You have no idea."

"I hope you aren't nervous about anything," Gwen said, now in business mode. "We have everything under control. The food, of course the alcohol, the music. And I have a gift here. It's from all of us. Our manager, Alayna, wanted to wish you well in person, but she's still at home on maternity leave with the twins. I'll just set this on the gift table. Have a great night!"

She took off in the direction of the bar, which was where the gifts were being collected, and I swiveled to thank Weston for his believable performance, but when I met his gaze again his smile had disappeared, and he was back to the frown that I'd seen going on four weeks straight.

"Congratulations on one person fooled," he said, beating me to the punch. "Now, just four hundred more to go."

Yes. Four hundred more to go.

I took a deep breath, rubbed my lips together to make sure that I still had gloss on them, and turned in time to see that our first guests had been led into the club.

Fortunately it was just my mother, dressed in a bright purple gown with a slit up to her thigh and rhinestones embroidered over the net mesh that—barely—covered the skin between her breasts.

I tried not to roll my eyes. "Where's Marie?" I asked, searching over her shoulder as I hugged her.

"Parking the car. You look beautiful, baby. Everything going okay?"

*Thank God.* Someone I could bitch to.

I started to answer her, but just as I opened my mouth she noticed my groom-to-be.

"Weston! You're adorable." Her voice was sticky sweet, her pose suggestive with her hips sticking out.

I recognized that tone of voice. I recognized that pose.

"Mother! You're hitting on him?"

She shrugged. "You didn't tell me how good-looking he was. I'm Angela." Weston took her hand but somehow she turned the handshake into a hug—classic move of my mother's.

"He's my *fiancé*," I snarled.

She looked back at me, her eyes fluttering. "*Fake* fiancé."

"The fiancé part is very real. I *am* marrying him." I stuck my hand out with the engagement ring and wiggled it. "We are getting married, and this is my engagement party to prove it." I didn't know why it bothered me so much to see her flirting with him. It wasn't the first time my mother had flirted with a man in front of me, nor the first time my mother had flirted with one of my boyfriends. Not that Weston was my boyfriend or that our relationship was even real, but still.

My mother stepped away from the hug, but her arm remained around Weston. Her eyes grazed his backside. "The marriage will end soon enough," she said with a smile.

Weston latched his arm through hers. "It's nice to meet you, Mom."

My mother faked a shiver. "Ooo, I love the way that sounds when you say it."

"You two are the worst." I slapped Weston's arm with the back of my hand. "Keep it in your pants—both of you—during this party. And Mom, I know you can't help yourself, but please try not to be such a MILF for the next few hours, okay?"

Then with the brightest smile I'd ever put on my lips, I swiveled toward the door, ready for yet another performance at The Sky Launch. Hopefully this one would fall under the genre of art film rather than porno.

For the next while, I discovered it wasn't too hard to feign enthusiasm for my betrothed. Most of the initial guests were people that I knew quite well—my friends, my bridesmaid, people I'd gone to high school with. Even though I had to pretend that I was madly in love with Weston, their energy and excitement was easy to act off of, and both of us could make it a game. There were too many people to spend much quality time with any one person, but good conversations were had and it was entertaining to try and embarrass Weston in front of his work associates. Of course the payback was him trying to embarrass me in front of my friends.

Despite the underlying current of friction between me and my betrothed, the party was going quite well.

Until his parents arrived.

I'd wanted to meet them, especially since finding out Weston wasn't letting them in on the truth behind our relationship. I'd tried more than once to ask why he wouldn't be honest with them, but each time he'd been just as elusive as he'd been in front of our wedding planner. His secrecy only made me more intrigued.

"Weston!" his mother exclaimed. "And you must be Elizabeth!"

I put my hand out to shake hers.

She frowned and pulled me into a hug. "We're going to be family. No handshakes for us."

Her voice was sweet, her perfume light and lavender. She was pretty, but her makeup was age-appropriate—*mother* appropriate—her clothes as well—a long mauve gown with a beaded jacket. Her hair was coiffed perfectly, and her French manicured nails were filed to a reasonable length. Her blond hair and blue eyes matched her son's, and even though I was sure she had a dye job—it was unlikely she'd reached her age without any gray hairs—it still looked natural. Unlike my mother, whose platinum locks definitely came from a bottle.

She seemed warm, put together, and genuine. For some reason, maybe because of Weston's insistence to not include her in the wedding, I'd expected she'd be terrible.

It was nice to be surprised. "It's wonderful to finally meet you, Mrs. King."

"It's Maggie, please." She even had a nice laugh. A polite one that didn't sound gregarious or overbearing.

Maggie turned to hug her son, who let her begrudgingly, so I swiveled toward Nash King. While I could see that Weston took mostly after his mother, there were some characteristics that he shared with his father. The dimple, for instance. Both of them had that crazy dimple. He also wore a tuxedo well. Not Weston King-well, but better than most.

"Dad, this is Elizabeth, obviously," Weston said without a lot of emotion, and it was Nash's turn to pull me into his arms and embrace me in a welcome hug.

"I'm delighted to meet you. Weston hasn't told us much about you, but from what we've heard, you seem like the right person for him. We've always wanted more children. And I look forward to having another daughter. I hope you'll call me Dad."

My gut dropped. I hadn't considered what it would mean to play this charade for Weston's parents. What fooling them would feel like. It was one thing to fool acquaintances and associates. Quite another to be welcomed into his family. To be invited to call his father my own.

I hadn't been prepared for that.

My throat was suddenly tight, and I was grateful that Weston was there to interrupt so I didn't have to say anything.

He slipped his hand around my waist, his touch sending an unexpected shock through my body, and pulled me to him. Putting on the act. "Don't get all clingy on day one, Dad. She's mine, not yours."

Somehow, despite the dizzying effect of his proximity, his words didn't make me feel any better. Because I *wasn't* his. And that was sort of the whole problem.

Nash put his hands in his tux pockets, looking so much like his son in that manner if not in his physical characteristics. "We'd just be happy if you shared her a little, son. Bring her by for dinner sometime."

"We'd love to!" I answered, caught up in the need to feel at ease about the situation with them in whatever way possible.

However, my fiancé responded at the same time. "We'll pass."

"Weston," I chided, sure that he was kidding. But one look at his tense jaw and stiff shoulders said that he was absolutely serious. "Surely we can make time for one meal . . ."

"Please do!" Maggie's smile had slipped, her eyes bright with hope.

"We can't," her son insisted, ending the conversation.

I bit back the desire to argue further, though inside, a funnel cloud of rage was stirring. "I'm sorry," I said, trying to smooth things over with the Kings. "We're just so busy between now and the wedding. I'm sure Weston has a better memory for our calendar than I do."

"It's not a calendar issue," Weston said.

My face went hot. "I'm so sorry . . ." I trailed off, not knowing how else to make excuses for my groom-to-be.

"Don't worry about it, honey," Maggie said, clearly hurt. "We aren't new to his life. We were hoping you'd make things better, but I see that's not how things are going to be."

Make things better? What things? How could Weston have a bad relationship with these people who obviously cared very much about him?

Whatever the problems were between them, Weston seemed to think we'd engaged enough for the evening. "Thanks for coming, Mom and Dad. We have to see to our other guests." With his hand still at my waist, he steered me away from them and into the crowd.

"What the hell was that?" I hissed so only he could hear.

"I don't know what you're talking about."

"You know exactly what I'm talking about. Your parents were nice and warm and caring." I was so frustrated and worked up that I was having trouble getting words out. "And you were so . . . mean! You should be respectful. A fiancé of mine would be respectful."

How could he be like that? Did he have parental baggage of some kind? Did his dad work too hard? Not pay enough attention to him? His dad was *here*. Whatever he thought his folks had done, he couldn't possibly understand what real parental baggage was.

Weston stopped and turned to look at me, his eyes harder than I'd ever seen them. "You know what? You don't know the first thing about it. I give respect to those who deserve it. I've known them my whole life. You've known them for five minutes. Grow up."

I felt like I'd been slapped. My eyes stung and my face burned, and the worst part was that I'd deserved it. Everything he'd said was true. I was in the dark on this subject, but only because Weston had left me there.

Maybe that's what hurt most—that he didn't *want* to let me in.

And wasn't that a dick move to keep it from me and then get angry when I didn't understand? He knew how important this union was, what the stakes were. How believable was it for a bride to not know much about the relationship of her husband-to-be and his own parents?

"You're right," I said, thrusting my chin forward. "I don't know the first thing about it. Because you've been too much of an asshole to *tell me*."

His eyes sparked and he began to say something in response, probably the kind of thing that shouldn't be said in the middle of our engagement party, but before he got the words out, someone nearby sang out our names. "Weston, Elizabeth. The stars of the show."

We turned to see Donovan with a woman I didn't know.

Without missing a beat, Weston slipped his arm in mine and directed us toward them, likely eager to escape the heated conversation. A smart decision, while admittedly unfulfilling.

Once again, I put on my smile.

"Elizabeth, you know Donovan," Weston said, sarcastically. "And this is Sabrina Lind, our new director of marketing strategy."

"Delightful to meet you. It's so fascinating to see how my love—" as I spoke, Weston glanced covertly around us, and when he seemed to be satisfied with what he saw, he cut me off.

"No one's watching. And Sabrina knows."

"Oh thank God." I dropped Weston's arm with a huge sigh of relief. "If I have to gush about him a minute longer I might have to throw up."

Donovan flashed a sly grin in my direction. "Elizabeth, I think you and I might get along better than I once thought."

Even among people who were part of the farce, the tension between Weston and me felt thick and taut, and I desperately needed a reprieve.

I cozied up beside Donovan, hoping he might be a balm. "I told you, Kincaid, this deal was really better suited for you and me. I can't believe you turned down the offer."

Not that I really wanted to marry the man. He was too ambitious for my taste. Even for a fictional marriage.

I shared a smile with Donovan then turned my eyes to Sabrina. She was pretty. Prettier than pretty—she was probably the most attractive women in the room with her dark hair and dark eyes and legs that went for miles. And she had a respectable position at Reach. All that beauty plus brains too. Good for her.

Good for *Donovan*.

"You were up for the nomination of groom?" she asked cautiously.

"No one would ever believe I'd get married," Donovan said dismissively. "Besides, Weston looks much better on Elizabeth's arm."

I didn't miss Weston shooting daggers in Donovan's direction.

And I absolutely didn't miss Weston saying, "Sabrina, you're absolutely stunning."

She thanked him, and I felt my insides ruffle. "She is gorgeous, Kincaid," I said, subtly reminding Weston that this woman belonged to someone else. "You make quite an attractive couple."

"We're not a couple," Sabrina said at the same time that Weston said, "They're not a couple."

And then I realized.

My insides sank like an elevator with the cable cut, but somehow I managed to keep my voice from shaking as I asked Donovan, "You're here alone?"

"I'm not," he said.

But he wasn't here with Sabrina. And Sabrina knew about our sham, which meant . . .

"Sabrina is from Weston's stable," Donovan said, and now my suspicions were confirmed.

"You are a fucking asshole," Weston scowled.

"Ah." Jealousy spiked through my veins with the sharp sting of everclear in the punch at prom. "Recent?"

"The most recent, I believe," Donovan said, trying to be helpful, or stir the shit—the latter was more likely. "Last girl he spent any significant time with before you, anyway."

Sabrina's face went red, a mixture of anger and embarrassment, if I had to guess. It was the color that I felt, even though I was pretty confident I'd managed to keep it from showing on my skin.

And who else knew about her? Was I the laughing stock of the town right now? Letting my groom parade his ex-girlfriend under my nose.

The way they kept exchanging glances, I couldn't actually be sure she was an ex.

"Huh. I might want in on that pool after all," I said, spitefully. "What were the terms?"

Weston ran a hand through his hair, which made him look ridiculously sexy. "For fuck's sake, I'm not going to fuck around."

I wanted to trust him, but the compliment he'd given her, the fact she worked in his office, the way they kept looking at each other . . . The scale was tilting against him.

I winked at Donovan. "We'll talk later."

"Fuck off," Weston muttered in Donovan's direction. He scanned the room again. "People are watching us. Better play cozy." He took my hand without looking at me, and the lie of his fingers in mine burned my skin. Because he'd probably rather be holding hers.

"Is it you who wants to fuck around?" he asked suddenly. "Is that why you keep bringing up concerns about me?"

I rolled my eyes, hoping to hide my stupid confusing emotions. "It was just a joke. You're so sensitive about everything I say."

"Everything you say is a criticism."

"Everything you do is stupid." Good one, Elizabeth.

He swung his head toward me. "Anyone told you lately you're a bitch?"

God I wanted to claw his eyes out, stomp on his feet, and then grab him by the lapels and kiss him hard.

What the fuck was wrong with me?

"Not since the last time you told me, which was, I think, oh, twenty minutes ago."

From a few feet away, I heard an older gentleman exclaim, "There's the happy couple!"

"That's us," I said with a big grin, looking over to see who was calling us. "Mr. Jennings!" The loan officer from my mother's bank. If he pinched my cheeks like he usually did, I was going to have to dig my fingernails into Weston's arm so that I didn't reflexively punch him.

At least I wouldn't have to worry about Weston checking out his cleavage.

After visiting with Mr. Jennings, Weston and I did another round of the room to make sure we'd seen everyone, which proved to be a true test of our acting skills. By then, I was tired and miserable, my feet and my spirit hurt. The contention between Weston and I was worse than ever, but I didn't have any energy left to give to our arguing.

Finally, after what seemed like decades, it was time for us to wrap things up and make our formal speech. I'd volunteered to be the one who spoke, not trusting that Weston's remarks would be either on point or appropriate.

I took my place at the microphone and welcomed all our guests once again. "It's so lovely to have all of you here to celebrate Weston and I, and our future together. There isn't anything we'd like more than to share our happiness with those that we hold most dear, and that's all of you." Even though I could only name a third of the people in the room. "Please make sure to finish off the hors d'oeuvres and the champagne, there's plenty to go around and we're not taking any home with us."

There was the expected round of applause and cheering.

And then it happened. The thing I should have been prepared for. Why hadn't I been prepared? Someone—was that Nate Sinclair?—heckled us to kiss.

Then it was several people heckling for us to kiss. "Kiss her," came from Weston's assistant, Roxie, clear as day.

And my bridesmaid, Melissa, "We want to see you kiss!"

Soon it was the whole dance floor cheering in unison, "Kiss, kiss, kiss, kiss."

Weston, better at improv than I—or at least this kind of improv— already had his hand at the small of my back, drawing me to him, away from the microphones. "I guess we better give them what they want."

Hell, it was only a kiss. With someone I was truly beginning to think I might hate. Why did I suddenly feel so nervous? So terrified? So absolutely weak in the knees?

"We should have practiced this," I whispered. My belly fluttered as I met his blue, blue eyes.

He dimpled, leaning closer. "Just let me lead, for once."

I parted my lips, my tongue running nervously around them before his mouth brushed softly against mine, testing me. Tasting me. Then, when I tilted my chin up for more, his lips pressed firmly and eagerly, sending heat through my body like a fever, unraveling the knots of tension in my shoulders and back and winding a different kind of tension in the pit of my belly.

I threw my arms around his neck, without even thinking as I did. Thank God he was holding me, because I wouldn't have been able to keep standing on my own, the way that his kiss spread through my body. I could feel it everywhere. In my toes. My knees. In my belly button. I felt it at the bottom of my spine and behind my eyelids, which were closed, and underneath my toes. I felt it in my mouth. In the places where his tongue searched and explored, and I for sure felt it in the deepest core of me, spiking arousal that I hadn't felt in—well, maybe ever.

It was just a kiss and I felt like he was undressing me. Just a kiss, and I felt like he was discovering things about me that I didn't even know about myself. Just a kiss, and I never wanted him to stop kissing me.

Then the kiss was over, and I was out of breath and dazed, confused by the applause.

"You okay?" Weston asked, quietly. Smugly.

I was still clutching him, and I let go quickly, then pretended that I'd done it just to straighten my dress. "I'm fine."

I spun toward our audience and smiled once again. They clapped some more, and as soon as possible I made an excuse, and escaped to the restroom.

Alone outside the ladies' room, I put a hand to my chest and attempted to get control of my breathing. I was a wreck from that crazy, incredible moment. From the dizzying lust that Weston sent spiraling in me with just a simple kiss. And also from the herd of other emotions taking residence inside. Hurt by the secrets Weston had chosen to keep from me. Anger because they threatened my whole end goal. Shame for what these lies did to his family. The sharp prongs of jealousy for a woman I'd just met because she probably knew more about the man I was going to marry than I did. Confusion because all of these feelings wrapped around a guy who wasn't supposed to be anything but a stepping stone to what was next. Inferior because . . . well, I didn't even know how to pinpoint the source of that particular feeling.

And then that kiss . . .

Shaking my head, I slipped into the restroom to fix my lipstick and freshen up. In front of the mirror I reminded myself that tonight wasn't about Weston. It was about me. It was about me moving in the right direction, toward the target—Dyson Media. The party had gone practically flawlessly, in that regard. We'd sold ourselves as a couple, and I needed to feel good about that.

I did feel good about it. Really good.

Feeling confident after my mental pep talk, I came back out of the restroom to find someone else in the hall. Someone whom I'd invited, but hadn't expected to show up.

"Darrell," I exclaimed. My heart rate sped up again, and this time it wasn't because of Weston or because of kisses that had knocked the wind out of me, but because the person who could ruin my whole scheme was standing in front of me. "I didn't know you were coming. I'm so glad to see you." I stepped forward to give him a kiss on the cheek.

He took it brusquely, then looked me over. "I wouldn't have missed this for the world." He straightened his tie and brushed a wisp of orange hair out of his face.

"Did you just get here? I should introduce you to Weston." I was talking too fast, eager to make sure he saw everything he needed to validate my betrothal as real.

He shook his head. "No need. I've been here for a bit. Saw that speech and kiss of yours." He paused, studying me. "That's some act you have going on there."

"Act? I don't know what you're talking about." How could he know? *How could he know?* We'd been careful in our setup, spending time together, being seen. We'd been attached to each other all night. Our chemistry was good.

"You and the King boy. You think I'm going to buy that you're suddenly engaged to such a perfect candidate for husband? Of course I was going to come and check this whole thing out. The relationship screams sham, and I intend to prove it. It shouldn't be too hard. You're not capable of pulling off a scheme like this."

"That's ridiculous," I said, breathlessly. "We're in love." It sounded so weak, so trite.

"Right," Darrell sneered. "Love. I bet you think that YouTube footage proves it too."

He'd seen the video. My face went red with shame. Well, wasn't that what I'd wanted?

But then it hadn't been what I'd wanted, and by then it had been too late.

Darrell snickered. "That video does prove one thing: how slutty you are. Your mother spread her legs for money too, and how did that work out? She didn't end up with anything except a measly trust fund. And that's what I'll make sure you get too because you're *not* getting your hands on my company."

And the feeling that I'd had, the feeling that, just maybe, Weston and I could survive this crazy scheme after all, it left with a whoosh.

As I watched Darrell stalk back down the hall, unable to think of a parting shot to offer, I realized he was right about one thing—I had no idea in hell what I was doing.

# CHAPTER NINE

*Weston*

THAT KISS.

God, that kiss.

It was Monday, two days after the engagement party and all I could think about was that goddamned kiss. My balls ached from it. My stomach twisted inside from it. It kept me up nights, kept me distracted through work all morning, made my dick sore from all the jerking off I'd done in the shower, and *still* it wouldn't leave my mind.

And it was stupid, because I really was starting to think I might hate the girl—the girl being my fiancée, of course.

By the end of Monday I'd thought about her so much—thought about wringing her neck while I led the weekly executive meeting, thought about scratching her up while I walked Sabrina through her new duties, thought about spanking her ass while Donovan gave me the rundown on the latest financial goals—that I'd even put Elizabeth's picture on my dartboard and thrown darts at her. Then I'd felt so guilty about marring her gorgeous face, I'd immediately printed another and slapped it over the autographed copy of Watchmen that I had in a frame on my shelf. A guy should have a pic of his bride-to-be on his desk, right?

So now I had to hate her and stare at her and fight my dick for having a mind of its own for the better part of the afternoon.

She was driving me insane.

I had to remember why I was in this predicament in the first place, why I was still participating in this stupid farce. There were a million and one reasons why I should just quit the whole thing and walk away.

But there were also reasons why I shouldn't. Good reasons.

I'd told Elizabeth I would help her, for one. And I'd told Donovan. And also because of the money. Mostly, of course, it was the money. I didn't know why I listed that last.

And to remind myself further, I decided to make a phone call that I normally made monthly but had neglected the last couple of months in all the Elizabitch hubub. I sat back in my chair and dialed the number that I knew by heart.

When the female voice answered, an easy smile spread over my lips. "Hello, Mrs. Clemmons, it's me. Weston."

"Weston, it's so good to hear from you. It seems like it's been ages. How are you? And you know I told you to call me Nicole." She was always cheery, no matter what time of day I caught her, no matter what the circumstances were in her life. But there was no way I was ever calling her Nicole. I'd known her and her husband since I was five years old. Remembered climbing onto her lap at company picnics. Her twins were the age of Noelle, my little sister.

"I'm good, I'm good. How are you, though? Did you get my latest check?" I hated always bringing it back to the money, but it was the reason I was calling. The reason I always called.

"Yes. Thank you. I did. I can't tell you enough how much I appreciate it."

I ran a hand through my hair. "Good. I'm glad. I wish I could do more. And how are the twins?"

"Well, some days are better than others. Eva is trying a job outside the home now with this great program that works with autistic kids. Zach, though . . ." She trailed off, and I understood. Zach would probably never be able to work in the traditional sense. His outbursts and tantrums hadn't been managed, and his speaking skills were still at an elementary school level.

"I understand. You're still getting good home help though, right?

Because if you're not, I will—"

She cut me off. "Our help is fine. The money you send is perfect. It covers everything we need. It really is more than enough, Weston."

"Good." I sounded like a broken record, I'd said that over and over again. *Good. Good.* What else was there to say?

A beat went by.

Then I asked the question I hated asking the most. "And how's Daniel?"

She sighed, but when she spoke she sounded bright. "He only has thirteen more months on his sentence. And the lawyer says he might be able to get parole soon. So we're looking forward to that."

My door opened, and I looked up with a scowl. I'd had it closed for a reason. Nate walked in, and he didn't know anything about this phone call, which meant I needed to wrap it up. "Well, that's great. I hope that goes well. Just let me know if you need anything on that front. I'm happy to help out."

"I will."

"Great, then. I'll be talking to you later. Have a great night." With my vocabulary of adjectives reduced to the word great, I got off the line so fast I barely heard her say goodbye. Which made me feel guilty—more guilty than I already felt—but I wasn't about to entertain questions from Nathan, and if I'd stayed on the phone with her much longer I was certain to face interrogation.

As it was, Nate was eying me. He'd slumped in the seat opposite my desk, an ankle crossed over the other leg at the knee, and laced his hands behind his head. I waited a few nervous seconds while he stared at me then remembered that I had a bone to pick with him.

"You're the one who started the kiss chant at the party on Saturday night, aren't you." I didn't put a question into my accusation.

His grin gave him away. "And that was some solid entertainment. Thank you, Weston."

"You're a giant fuckwaffle."

"Damn," Nate said in awe. "Fuckwaffle is usually reserved for people who really offend you. I'm surprised. If the tables had been turned, you would have been catcalling *me* to kiss Elizabeth."

I frowned for a number of reasons, not the least of which was that the tables never would have been turned, because Nate had absolutely refused to put himself in this position. Also, the idea of him kissing Elizabeth made me want to vomit and punch him all at once.

But he was right—under different circumstances, I would have been the guy in the crowd stirring the shit.

Just.

That kiss.

"It wasn't cool," I said. "You know the circumstances. A lot is riding on this, and it was bullshit to put us on the spot like that. This isn't a fucking game."

Nate barely blinked. "You're in a foul mood. What broomstick is up your ass?"

The broomstick of a very feisty red-headed witch, that was what.

I stood up from my seat, walked over to my printer to get the Opportunity Analysis I'd printed earlier, and forced myself to pull my shit together. There was an opportunity here, somewhere, I had to remember that. Had to hold onto it. With that in mind, I took a deep breath that did nothing to calm me down, walked back over to my desk and threw the document down without sitting myself. "I'm under a lot of pressure, okay?"

"Or, rather, you're *filled* with a lot of pressure. You need to get laid."

I leaned a palm on the desk and glared at him. "What makes you think that I haven't?" Fuck him for even thinking he knew anything about it. Even if he was right, he was only guessing. "I know you guys have a pool and everything, but how are you going to know if you win?"

"Oh, we'll know," Nate said, laughing. "But seriously, what's your damage?"

I rolled my eyes and sat back down in my chair. "Your vernacular is dating you." Sometimes it was hard to remember that Nate was fourteen years older than me. He was just so cool most of the time. Then he went and said something like that, something that came right out of the eighties.

But while he was here, and since he was so cool, I actually would be dumb not to take him up on some advice.

I placed my other palm on the desk so I was leaning evenly on both hands. "You want to know what my deal is? Here's my deal. I'm engaged to a woman I don't like. Can't even be in the same room with her without getting in an argument. And what's more, I'm stuck with her for the next several months. But the worst part, the abso-fucking-lutely worst part, is that despite how much I can barely stand her, and how much she's taking up all my time with this wedding planning and this fiancé shit, and how much she's messing with my head, and getting into my business, I still want to rip off her clothes and give her the best orgasms of her life. Like how can she be so insanely attractive and a total bitch all at once? I can't even figure it out."

Nate nodded, taking everything in. "That doesn't really sound like a bad problem to have."

"What the fuck are you talking about? It's the worst problem of my life!" Okay, I'd lived a privileged life. "Even with the help of porn, I have blue balls every single minute of the day. How the hell am I supposed to get her out of my head?"

Nate put his hands out in the air like the answer was obvious. "Simple. You fuck her and get it over with."

I threw my head back. "Did you miss the part where I said I hate her?"

"So hate-fuck her. Your cock will be happy."

I shook my head. Nate obviously didn't understand, which was weird, because he was a god with these things. Didn't he have the answer to every sexual problem? "I can't fuck her."

"Why?"

"Because—" I trailed off, not quite remembering why I couldn't, besides my personal feelings toward her. "Because Donovan said I couldn't."

Nate laughed. "Oh, well then. If Daddy said you can't."

"Shut up." But now I was really wondering . . . Why couldn't I fuck her?

Oh yeah. The part that came after. "Because I still have to be engaged to her for several months. See the problem?"

Nate raised an eyebrow. "Have you *never* seen a girl again after you slept with her?"

"Of course I have." I couldn't think of a single one that I'd seen on purpose, but whatever. Then I straightened and pointed at him excitedly. "Sabrina! I've seen Sabrina! I even *work* with her."

"So what's the problem? And you're so confused about why you'd want to give a qualified woman *that you slept with* a job, that you've decided you must want to have some sort of relationship with her in the future. Have you ever banged a woman and not been weird about it after? Do you not know how to do casual sex?"

"Never mind," I growled. "Forget I brought it up. What did you come in here for, anyway?"

"There's a showing tonight at a gallery I used to deal with. Want to come? I know women are off-limits to touch, but you could always . . . watch."

Shit. Watching Nate in action was a dream come true.

Strangely, I wasn't as disappointed as I thought I might be to have to turn him down. "Wish I could, man." I checked the clock on my computer. I had to get going. "But Elizabeth wants to have dinner to discuss our current living arrangements."

Nate's eyes rolled. "Sounds like a fun time. Sad I'll miss it."

"You should take Donovan. Or—better yet—Sabrina, who I am *not* confused about, asswipe. She's new here. Someone should entertain her." She'd only been in town a week, and I knew I should feel guilty for throwing her into the city without being available to guide her around.

"I can't ask either of them," Nate said as we stood up together. "They're having dinner."

"Ah," I said, only half listening. We headed out of my office where I paused to hit the lights and lock the door behind me. "Wait. They're having dinner *together?*"

"It seems so."

"Huh." I took off toward the elevators, wondering if I should be jealous. Though Nate couldn't understand, Sabrina was the girl I was planning to actually have a relationship with later, after all. Probably. Maybe.

But of course I shouldn't be jealous. Donovan knew my plans, and he'd known Sabrina from Harvard as well. He was likely being a good friend to both of us by taking her out when I couldn't.

Besides, I couldn't really muster up any animosity toward Donovan. I was too plagued with animosity toward Elizabeth. Just like how I couldn't muster lustful thoughts for Sabrina lately because I was too consumed by lust for my fiancée.

I'd let Elizabeth think otherwise at the engagement party, of course. Just to piss her off. Sometimes it was too easy.

Unfortunately, where Elizabeth Dyson was concerned, I was beginning to find that I was even easier.

⌒๏

"NOPE. NO WAY. Not happening." I was trying to make it clear that there was no way in hell I was moving out of my apartment.

Elizabeth's eyelid twitched. "It's only for the rest of our engagement. I'm not asking you to give it up permanently."

"I don't care. I'm not moving my stuff. I'm not living in your West Side overpriced snobby-ass apartment. I'm not doing it."

"What do you have against the West Side?" she hissed in a quieter voice as a waiter walked by, in case somebody might overhear us.

"Well, for one thing, it's twice as far from the office as my place. That's a lot of time I would waste every morning on unnecessary travel. You don't work, so you don't understand. That's not something you have to worry about."

"But that's not the Upper West Side's fault. And don't say that I don't work with that snide tone of yours." The corners of her mouth turned down like she was offended, hurt even. "It's not like I do nothing with my days. I'm studying. Working on all the information you give me to learn."

"And you can learn just as easily in my place." Not that I wanted a woman living in my apartment either. Though the idea of having her there, in my space, somehow didn't bother me as much as I thought it might. She'd take the extra bedroom, of course, but just having her close by . . .

"Your place is probably a pigsty." She raised her voice just enough, causing a nearby patron to look over at us.

"No, it's not." For the record, it's really not. Totally not a pigsty. I just didn't spend the money on those fancy maids like Miss Moneybags did. I cleaned the old-fashioned way—with my own two hands. When I got around to it, that was.

"I don't know why you thought we would ever agree on any of this." I took a swig of my beer. "We couldn't even agree on what appetizers to order."

She shook her head and chewed her lip. I'd watched many other women do that in my day—come on, it was one of the sexiest things women could do. But the way Elizabeth chewed on her lip was unique. She pulled her bottom lip to the side so it puckered out, like a sideways fish-face. It was actually kind of funny looking, and not exactly attractive, and yet whenever she did it, my dick leapt like a dog at a bone. I wanted to bite her lip for her. Wanted to tug her into my lap and gnaw on her like a puppy.

She was a witch, I tell you. A witch.

"I was afraid of this, so I came prepared. We're going to have to make a schedule, and that's all there is to it." She reached into her purse and pulled out a notepad and a pen. It was somehow charming that she had both in this day and age of electronics. She'd clearly carried them since way before we started our lessons at The Sky Launch, and I knew it, but I never failed to be charmed by it.

"What do you mean when you say schedule?" I asked suspiciously, rubbing the back of my neck with my hand. I didn't like schedules. I barely liked the schedule that I kept for myself.

"Look," she said, meeting my eyes, and I had to take a moment to catch my breath. Every time I met her startling blues, I found they had that effect on me. "Darrell was very serious when he told me that he's going to do everything he can to rip us apart. We *have* to make it look like we're a real couple. In real life, a modern couple would be living together in some shape or form at this point in time in their engagement.

If we're not going to agree to live in one place, we've got to be sharing both of our apartments. Going back and forth. You know, make it look like we're spending time together. Like we're . . ."

"Like we're fucking each other on a regular basis," I said and immediately regretted it. Just letting my mind go there for even half a second gave me a semi.

"Yes, that."

I was beginning to see her plan. "So you're saying we need to start sleeping at each other's houses. All right. I got it now." I thought about it for a minute. That couldn't be so bad, could it? Move a few essentials over to her place, make sure to only be there on the weekends so the travel wasn't too far to work. Have her near me so much more of the time than I already do . . . Have that much more temptation . . .

Yeah, what could go wrong?

"Fine. I want to be at my place as much as possible during the week. I'll clear out the guest room for you, and give you a key. I'm guessing you'll do the same for me?"

"I'll email you a schedule then. Don't bring over too much at once or it will look obvious." She jotted down the notes that I'd given her. I watched her pretty cursive handwriting. *His place on weekdays. Exchange keys. Clear out guestroom. Hire him maid.*

"Hey, you don't need to be hiring me—"

"If I have to live there, there *is* going to be a maid."

I leaned forward. "The thing is, sweetheart, you don't have to live there. So there will not be a maid." I held her stare, but I realized now that she was bent forward too, and that it would only take just a little bit more movement on either of our parts for our lips to meet, and suddenly all I was thinking about was that damn fucking kiss again.

Shit, she was in my head. She was under my skin. She was about to be in my apartment. The one place she wasn't was in my pants, and I was beginning to really wish otherwise.

The stare-off was some sort of game of chicken, and I should have been the one to lose because of the way she was making me feel—all twisted inside—but somehow she was the one who backed down.

"Fine." She crossed *hire a maid* off her notepad.

When she looked up again, she didn't look quite at me, but straight past. Her eyes narrowed, and then widened in surprise.

"Clarence?" she asked after a minute.

I frowned in confusion and then followed her gaze to find she was looking at some guy behind me.

She stood up out of her chair and said it again. "Clarence. It *is* you!"

One of the guys at the next table got up and came over to us. "Elizabeth Dyson. How are you? You look great."

He hugged her and my entire body went stiff. Who was this freaking dude? My eyes darted from him to her with eager curiosity. The funny thing was, the Clarence dude looked familiar, but I couldn't quite place him.

Their embrace ended, and he stood back, but not back far enough for my taste. Only far enough so that he could look her over again. Slowly, this time.

I recognized that look. The one that was already eating her up, undressing her with his eyes, mentally dragging her off to the bedroom—

I stood up so quickly that my chair shook and almost toppled over. "Hi," I said, my hand outstretched so he was forced to shake it, making him move away from Elizabeth. "I'm Weston. Have we met?"

The Clarence guy looked quizzically at Elizabeth—my fiancée—then back to me. "I don't think so. Clarence Sheridan." He shook my hand, but there still wasn't enough distance between him and my girl for my comfort.

My *fake* girl, I reminded myself, but my inner caveman didn't hear any distinction.

When I was done shaking Clarence's hand, I put my arm around Elizabeth, drawing her next to me. She gasped quietly as I did, but her body was pliable, and she melted into the curve of my arm easily enough.

"Sheridan," I asked. "Any relation to Theodore?" I'd gone to school with a Theodore. That was who this guy looked like.

"He's my older brother. How do you know him?" he asked, almost suspiciously.

"We went to Harvard together. Small world." I turned to Elizabeth. "Honey, have you told me about Clarence? I don't remember you mentioning him. At all." God, I was such a dick.

"It was so long ago, Weston. Clarence and I went to high school together. We haven't seen each other in years." She looked flustered.

Suddenly, all I could think about was whether or not she'd fucked him.

"You're going to invite him, aren't you, honey?" I poured on the honey, extra thick, and pulled her closer to me, possessively. "To the *wedding*?" Yeah, I emphasized the word wedding. Because she was mine, not his.

Well, she wasn't his.

Her cheeks burned.

"Wedding?" Clarence said, catching on. "You two are getting married. That's great! Congratulations."

"Yes! Married. That's right," she said, as though she'd just remembered, and by God I wanted to spank her so she'd never forget again. Or kiss her. Or both.

"Yes, of course. If you want to come to my wedding, that is," she stammered. She'd totally fucked him.

Did she want to fuck him again?

My ribs ached with the question.

"I wouldn't miss your wedding for the world," the douchebag said. Douchebag was a more fitting name than Clarence, I'd decided.

"Oh," Elizabeth sounded surprised. And a little disappointed. "I guess I should get your current address." She looked toward the table. Then at me, her eyes blinking as if she'd forgotten I was there. "Sweetheart, can you hand me my purse so I can get Clarence's phone number?"

No fucking way I was letting her get his number. I pulled out my phone from my pocket, sure to keep my other arm still around Elizabeth. "Here. You can put your digits in here." I handed my cell over.

While Douchebag was putting his numbers in, Elizabeth jabbed me with her elbow and sent darts at me with her eyes.

She could send darts all she wanted. I was the one who fucking taught her how to shoot darts in the first place. And no fiancée of mine was going to have some other dude's number in her phone. Not some dude that she used to fuck, anyway.

When the asshole was done, he handed the phone back to me, and I put it in my pocket. "Got it. We'll send you an invite. It will be great to have you there. Now if you'll excuse us, our food is getting cold."

Elizabeth jabbed me again. I'd have a bruise in my side from all her jabbing, but it would be worth it.

"Of course. Sorry to interrupt. But when I saw Elizabeth, I had to come over and say hi. Hey, I texted myself, so I've got your number now, too." Douchebag grinned at me, smug. Then again at her—but if I were giving an objective, very non-gay evaluation, I'd have to say he did not have a smile anywhere near as stirring as mine. He leaned in to hug her again or kiss her cheek or something intimate, which was awkward since I was still holding on to her tightly, but somehow they managed a half-embrace thing, and then he went on his way. Finally. Thank God.

As soon as he was seated again, only a table away from us, Elizabeth turned to me with her full wrath. Some dark little part of me was starting to really enjoy her anger. It was the only time she ever let herself get passionate, since our night in the bubble room.

"What the fuck was that?" she hissed.

"I was just playing the part," I said. "And be careful, he's not very far away. We need to *keep* playing the part, don't you think?"

I pulled her seat out for her, and this time when I sat down, I scooted close to her and dropped my arm along the back of her chair. Then, not feeling it was enough, I let my hand slide down to her shoulder.

"What are you doing?" she asked. As if it wasn't obvious.

"I already told you. Playing the part. He's going keep looking at you. Ex-boyfriends tend to look at their ex-girlfriends a lot." I snuck a glance at Douchebag myself, and sure enough, he was peeking over at us.

"How do you even know he's my ex?"

"Oh, it's quite clear. And if you don't want him to know what's up—"

"Do you really think it matters if an ex is in the know? It seems you don't, since Sabrina is in on it."

Sabrina? Sabrina only knew because I hadn't wanted her to have a wrong idea when she'd taken the job. And because Donovan had told her.

But for some reason I didn't want to explain that to Elizabeth. Maybe because I liked the way she was so worked up about Sabrina. Because it was kind of cute. Kind of sweet. Kind of gave me an upper hand. Made me a little less upset about Douchebag.

"Sabrina is another story," I said, brushing her off. My fingers grazed against the bare skin at her neck, and maybe it was accidental the first time, but her flesh felt so warm and silky, I couldn't stop my fingers from running back and forth, over and over again.

She swallowed, her eyes down, but I didn't have to wonder if she was reacting to my touch, because goosebumps sprouted down her arms.

Still, her next words came out cold and tight. "If you get to make decisions about the people close to you who know the truth, then I get to make the same decisions about the people close to me." She turned her eyes up at me, shocking my fingers still with her piercing stare. "And that means ex-boyfriends. That means Clarence. If I want Clarence to know that this isn't real, that's my call. Not yours."

We didn't say anything more, just ate in silence.

But I kept my arm where it was, kept my fingers rubbing her skin, her satiny-smooth skin, and I was left again to wonder which version of Elizabeth was real—the one who snapped at me and wanted to reserve Douchebag for when we were over?

Or the one who shivered, leaned in close, and reacted like crazy to my touch?

# CHAPTER TEN

*Elizabeth*

"DON'T THROW AWAY the Pad Thai," Weston said from behind me.

I peered over my shoulder at him, surprised I hadn't heard him come in, before going back to the takeout. I opened the container and sniffed at the ingredients, making a face at the awful stench before throwing it in the trash. "It's three days old," I told him.

I walked over to the sink and washed my hands, noting the time on the microwave clock. It was 9:00 p.m., and Weston was coming home late for the second night in a row.

He squeezed by me to open the refrigerator door, and I tried to ignore his eyes on me in my short nightgown. We'd been living together for a month, and goosebumps still sprouted on my skin whenever his gaze traveled down my body.

"You threw out the Chinese too?" he asked, obviously irritated.

"It was even older." I flicked the water droplets off my fingers into the sink, then grabbed the washrag to scrub at the stain that I'd just spotted on the counter.

"Jesus, there's nothing in here but your stuff. Yogurt, fruit. Hummus. What am I supposed to eat?" I heard the clank of a beer bottle, then the shutting of the door.

I glanced behind me to find him leaning against the refrigerator. His suit jacket was off, his sleeves rolled up, his tie loose, and his hair scruffy like he'd run his hand through it several times. Or like *someone* had run a hand through it. Was he late because he'd been messing around?

I cared because I didn't want him jeopardizing our plans, of course.

I wished that was the only reason I cared.

"You have a box of shrimp Cup of Noodles from Amazon that came today. I left it in the coat closet. Just heat up some water and you can have that." So juvenile. It was true what they said about bachelors—they were just overgrown boys.

"You opened my mail?" Again, he wasn't happy.

"I thought it was me who it was addressed to?" He brushed past me to toss the bottle cap into the sink, sending tingles down my spine from the contact.

"I guess I didn't," I said, grabbing the bottle cap out of the sink and tossing it into the trash can. Where it belonged. "Is it really that big of a deal that I opened your mail? Are you expecting something you don't want me to know about?"

"I don't know. Maybe. Don't you think you're taking this couple thing a little too far?" He mumbled the last part, but I still heard him.

I threw the washrag into the sink and nudged him out of the way so I could open the dishwasher and load the few dishes—*his* dishes that were still sitting there from breakfast.

"I suppose I kind of am. Since I'm the one cleaning up after you like a wife." I shook my head, cursing that I was once again doing housework because of him. "You need a maid, Weston. You live like a pig." I honestly didn't know why he didn't have one. Who had a penthouse in Manhattan and didn't have a housekeeper come in at least once a week? I thought the whole cleaning profession thrived on serving his particular demographic—single, rich, male.

"Maybe I don't like spending money on things I can get someone to do for me for free." His tone of voice, matched with that half smile of his, made the statement sound dirty.

My knees swayed and my pulse ticked up. He was standing too close, and I was intoxicated, as always, by his swagger.

Intoxicated and disgusted.

"You're so full of yourself," I said, walking into the main room. I needed distance. More distance than I could find in his two bedroom apartment, but I'd take what I could get. I discovered he'd left his shoes, briefcase, and jacket in a pile on the floor. I picked them all up and carried them to his bedroom door and left them there, then walked to his bookcase and found a glass that had been neglected and left there since who knew when. I picked it up, intending to take it back to the dishwasher, except I noticed the shelf was filthy.

"When was the last time you took a duster to any of this?" I brushed a layer of dust off with my hand.

"Are you a germaphobe or something? Are you seeing someone for that?"

Ignoring him, I pulled some of his books from the bookshelf. "Your comics are covered with the stuff. Doesn't this bother you?"

"They're not comics. They're graphic novels. Don't touch them." He ran over to me to grab the comics—er, graphic novels—out of my hand, and replaced them on the shelf. With his sleeve, he wiped the shelf clean.

I shook my head again. "A maid, Weston. Hire one or I'll hire one for you."

"A little dust never killed anyone. And I'm not getting a maid. I'll clean it when my schedule eases up, okay?"

Right, he didn't have time because he was too busy working. He was working a *lot* lately. He claimed they had a lot of big accounts, but the other thing that I knew he'd been spending time on was training his new hire—Sabrina.

I tried not to let it bother me, tried not to imagine him with her all day, late into the evenings, having dinner together. Sharing a drink. Sharing more than a drink.

"You don't have to tell me again," I said, insolently. "You have to work. I've heard it before." I cringed internally. I could hear what I was saying and how I was saying it. I sounded like a nag. Shit, maybe I really *was* taking the couple thing too far.

But it was a compulsion—the nagging, the wondering. The needing to know. The harder I tried to stop, the more I couldn't stop. Even now I didn't want to ask, and yet here I was asking anyway, "With Sabrina?"

He leaned against the arm of the sofa and crossed his legs at the ankle. "That was last night. Tonight we were pitching to a big client. Phoenix Technology. We sealed the deal, if you were interested."

"Congratulations. Glad to hear all your *hard work* pays off." I tugged at the hem of my nightgown, rolling it around my finger absentmindedly.

"Thank you." He took another pull of his beer. "I'm still not getting a maid."

"Of course you're not. Because you're cheap." I crossed to load the glass in the dishwasher.

As I put the gel pack in and started the cycle, I watched him from behind the kitchen counter. He made me so confused and riled up every time I was with him. Every interaction felt unsatisfying, even if I'd won the argument. I still wanted to poke more, wanted *him* to give me more, though, if he asked me, I couldn't tell him what.

I poked at him now. "Maybe I should let you fuck a maid. At least we could have a clean apartment."

"*Let* me? Look, I don't know where you got the idea that you're the boss of my dick, but you are absolutely not. My abstinence is a fucking favor, not an obligation."

"Really? How about *my* abstinence?" I challenged. "Is that a requirement to this deal?"

His brows rose. "You're the one who said we needed to be chaste, babe. If you're getting your pipes cleaned, then you sure as hell better let me off the chain."

I rolled my eyes. Nothing was getting cleaned around here that I wasn't cleaning myself, especially my pipes. "I'm not the one who is going to fuck this up, Weston. But if you're fucking this up, then I don't want to be held on a leash, either."

"Meaning?"

I bunched my hands into fists and rested them on my hips. "Meaning—give me Clarence Sheridan's phone number." I didn't even really want to call him. I'd barely thought about him since we'd bumped into him that night at dinner a month ago. He was an ex from high school. My first real boyfriend, yes. The guy who'd taken my virginity, but we'd broken up seven years ago now. Seeing him again had knocked the wind out of me because it had been so long, not because I still felt anything for him.

But I'd use any weapon in my war against Weston King. If he got to have an ex to fire me up with, I got to have one too.

His lips settled into a flat line, his face going hard. "My phone's dead. I'll give it to you later."

"Figures," I mumbled. Either it was to piss me off or it was because he really thought I wanted to hook up with Clarence.

And if Weston thought I wanted to hook up with my ex, wasn't it logical to assume that it was because *he* wanted to hook up with *his*?

Or because he already had.

I came around the kitchen island and crossed my arms over my chest. Unless we had a date to be seen together at some event, this was usually the time of night that I slunk off to my bedroom. It was where I should be headed now, but the tension between us was particularly taut, and I felt especially unsettled with our evening's conversation.

He stared at me, drinking his beer, and I swore he could see into me, could see how crazy he made me. He stared as if he knew I needed something, and he was just waiting to hear me say it. He kept staring until I began to shift my weight uncomfortably from foot to foot.

"Go ahead. Ask what you want to ask," he said, finally.

*Do you want me?* echoed through my mind. It hadn't been what I was thinking, but now that I had, I couldn't stop. My arousal hummed up a pitch. My nipples furled into tight beads.

I leaned forward slightly at my torso, wishing, wondering—if I asked him that, what would he say? Would I be satisfied with his answer or would it feel like another rejection?

I didn't dare take the risk.

"What happened at the meeting with Sabrina?" I asked instead, hating myself as I did.

"What happened with Sabrina?" he asked with a sharp mocking

tone, as if to say, *how dare you even ask* but also *I'm so glad that you did.* "Let me tell you."

I didn't want him to, not really. How could I enjoy this, hearing about the woman I was in a silent competition with? How could I not? I had this sick compulsion to know everything about what they'd done together, to somehow make her pleasure mine.

He set his finished beer down on the coffee table and took a step toward me. "She came into my office after everyone else was gone, when it was dark, so we were alone. She had that look on her face, you know what look I'm talking about. The look that said she was thinking about my cock. Remembering the way that I'd been with her. Remembering how good I'd been to her. She was biting her lip, kind of like you're biting your lip now."

I let go of my lip, and felt my face redden, having been completely unaware that I'd been biting it in the first place.

"She was probably remembering that ride in the taxi. We'd gone to dinner and she wasn't wearing any panties so I put my fingers up her skirt, played with her. Stroked her until her clit was nice and plump and she was writhing in the seat. I could tell she was about to explode. The way she kept gasping, moaning and begging, calling my name. But I wouldn't let her come. Not during the car ride. We got to my apartment, somehow made it across the lobby and into the elevator. When the doors closed. I lifted her up against the wall, and put my mouth to her pussy. It only took a couple strokes of my tongue before she was coming all over my face. The look on her face said that's what she was thinking about as she came over to my desk and leaned over with those nice tits of hers showing."

I was breathing so hard, enraptured with his sexy, dirty story. A story that I shouldn't want to hear at all, and I *didn't*, yet I couldn't stop listening, needing to hear every detail of his past, and of what happened next. Even though I knew when I I thought about it later, it was going to hurt like hell. But right now all I could feel was the buzz between my legs, my panties going damp, the thrum of my want pulsing through my veins.

"She looked up at me with those big doe eyes," Weston continued, taking another step toward me. "Fluttered those eyelashes, licked her luscious lips. And said, 'Weston, can you please help me go over this report one more time before you present it to Phoenix tomorrow?'"

I swallowed as an odd form of betrayal started to rise up inside me, double-crossed by both Weston and my own body, which leaned forward and heated with his coarse words.

Weston let out a laugh. "You should see your face."

"Fuck you."

"I know, right? It was a good time we had back there in May, Sabrina and I. I'm hard just recalling it." He rubbed at the crotch of his pants, and I could see that he was at least semi-aroused.

The want that was simmering inside, just barely staying tethered, pulled and strained, screaming to be released. I took a shaky breath. I could feel his eyes on me, could feel them watching my throat and my mouth and the movement of my eyes.

He took another step toward me, and I wanted to walk away and toward him all at once. "You want to help me with this, Elizabeth?" And I couldn't tell anymore if he was taunting me or inviting me. Couldn't remember if I should be offended either way.

An alarm bell rang in my head, a warning that this was wrong for some reason or every reason or maybe there was no reason at all, but I was scared, and so I repeated what I'd said before. "Fuck you. I'm going to bed."

I managed to restrain myself so that I walked rather than ran to my bedroom and quietly shut the door behind me.

Forty-five minutes later I was still tossing and turning, still twisted inside from my interaction with Weston. I couldn't stop thinking about him. About Sabrina and him, and me and him, and his cock, the way he rubbed at his pants, the way it felt underneath me all those weeks and weeks ago now at The Sky Launch. He was such a player that even when he wasn't playing with other women, he was playing with me. Even if he didn't mean to, even if he didn't know he was doing it, I felt like I was always part of his game, always being shuffled around, never knowing which side of the deck I was on.

The apartment was quiet and I was sure he'd gone to bed too, but I needed to get out of my room. Just needed to be free for a moment, escape from the oppression of that closed door, anything to free myself from my thoughts. I opened the door and slipped into the darkness, quietly heading into the living room and then stopped short when I realized that I wasn't alone.

Weston was still out there, sitting on his modern armchair by the windows that ran floor-to-ceiling like they did in his office, like they did in the bubble room. He hadn't seen me, because he was facing out, looking into the city night. The lights were off, but the moonlight was streaming in, and I could see him clearly, could see the bottle of lube on the table next to him.

And, in his hand, was his fully erect cock.

His pants were open just enough so that he could hold it, and he was stroking himself, not too slow, not too fast. Just fast enough that he could enjoy it. And I could tell that he was enjoying it because his face screwed up into an expression of tension and release, tension and release, with each stroke. I could hear it, too. Hear the sound of his hand moving quickly over the thick shaft. The sound as the lube spread up and down underneath the palm of his hand. I could hear him grunt. The fall between the fast breaths while he worked to bring himself to climax.

I was fascinated and mortified. I couldn't look away. I didn't want to look away. I wanted to watch him, wanted to imagine that it was my hand rubbing along with his, my hand brushing across the top of his crown and down the other side of his shaft, up again and across the top and down and faster, faster and faster. I wanted it to be my mouth. I wanted it to be my body. I wanted to be riding him. Wanted him to make those moans and grunts. While my thighs slapped against his.

I could imagine it so clearly that I felt my pussy clench on the verge of an orgasm. What would he do if I joined him now? He couldn't turn me away, could he?

I took a hesitant step forward.

Just then, his breathing changed, his body stiffened. His hand froze and he shook as liquid squirted from the top of his dick all over his hand

and glistened in the moonlight. A long guttural low sound escaped from his throat, accompanying his release. A sound that ended in a single word. A name. "Sabrina."

I turned around and ran back to my room and closed the door. I crawled under the covers and pulled them up high, pulled my knees up to my chest, pressed my legs together, hoping it would calm the buzz between my thighs. I could put my hand between them and rub it away, like I had so many times thinking about him in the last several months. It would ease the ache between my legs.

But nothing I could do would rub away the ache in my heart.

# CHAPTER
# ELEVEN

*Weston*

I WOKE UP the next morning with a hangover of shame and regret. I'd been so angry, so irritated, so annoyed.

The worst part was that I hadn't just been upset with Elizabeth—I'd also been upset with myself. Because as every terrible thing had come out of her mouth, with every word she'd said, all I could think about was her pretty lips and her curved hips and wonder what the feel of her skin was like at the base of her spine. Wonder what sounds she'd make if she was under me.

Of all the women I could fantasize about, why did it have to be her that turned me on? It was bad enough to be celibate, bad enough to have to go months without getting my dick wet. But then for her to be the object of my horny daydreams, with her gorgeous face and her curvy body and her tight ass—even her arrogant personality showed up in my fantasies, as she argued with me and tried to boss me around while I made her come over and over again around my cock.

Whatever I'd done to piss off the universe, karma was a cruel bitch.

So when I'd finally found myself alone, I couldn't take it anymore. All that stress and tension between us left me wound tight and needing a release in the worst way. In hindsight, I should have gone to my room to, uh, work out my frustration, but I was tired and lazy and still adjusting to living with another person. Maybe part of me even liked the idea of whacking it while she was next door sleeping. It felt defiant and provocative.

And, damn, was it a turn on to feel like I was provoking Elizabeth.

I was already thinking about her, imagining what it would be like to sink between her creamy thighs and slip inside her, wondering if she was as hot and fiery inside as she was outside when I looked up and caught movement in the glass in front of me.

When I realized it was her reflection in the window, that she was watching me, I almost came right then.

I'd thought I was an expert in what's-hot-to-spank-to. Nothing I'd ever thought up was as erotic as that moment. Not even close.

I'd quickened my strokes, and I could feel her shock across the room. I could feel her fascination. I could feel her want, her desire, just as heavy and untamed as my own.

But she hadn't been willing to reveal herself or join in like I prayed she would while I focused on her image in the glass.

And that drove me fucking mad. Lunatic mad.

It wasn't like *I* could make the next move. I couldn't invite her to come sit on my lap without coming off as a perverted bastard. It had to be her. My cock was in my hand, but the cards were definitely in hers.

So as erotic as it was having her watch, as mind-blowing as it felt knowing that the woman I was thinking of was turned on at the sight of me hard and exposed, I was too pissed to give her any hint that she was the reason I was out there furiously beating off.

And, instead, I was an asshole. An asshole that refused to say *her* name—the name that had burst like fireworks in my head while I'd stroked myself, up and down—and instead chose to say *another* name. The one that I knew would make her turn around and walk away.

Afterward, sitting in the dark with my Elizabeth-inspired orgasm fading into memory, I'd felt like shit.

I'd wanted to run after her to tell her I was sorry for the lie, and for all the rest too—for the fighting and the pushing. I'd wanted to tell her how crazy she made me, and how crazy she was for pursuing this dream of hers, but also how fucking much I admired her for not giving up and for actively trying to be a better person than the person her father had been. Wanted to tell her how inspiring it was to know someone with integrity these days, especially in this fast-paced, rat race business world where it seemed like no one had integrity.

But I didn't.

Instead I'd tucked myself away and went to bed like the good fiancé she wanted me to be.

I hadn't expected that I would still feel so shitty in the morning. It wasn't the first or fiftieth time I'd woken regretful after having been a jerk since the beginning of our courtship. It wasn't the first morning after I'd jerked off to her, even, but it was the first morning I'd woken up and truly wished things were different between us.

Most days, we hit the building's gym together first thing, and not because I tried to go at the same time she did on purpose. It just worked out that way. Today, however, I couldn't stand to see her. If I did, the guilt would double and the knot in my stomach would tighten with the terribleness of the lie I'd told, mixed with the weight of the want I had for her.

So I skipped my workout and waited until I heard her leave the apartment before making my way out to the front room. I made my breakfast quietly and alone, drank my coffee, staring out the window at the street below, hating how silent the apartment was without her. Hating how used to her movements and noises I'd gotten in the last several weeks. She'd left a coffee mug and a spoon in the sink. Normally I'd leave those, but today I washed them out and put them away. Then I unloaded the dishwasher, thinking it might help unload some of the regret weighing on my spine.

All it did was make me late enough to still be there when she walked in after her workout. So much for slipping out without seeing her.

I picked up my briefcase and brushed past her heading toward the door. "Slept in," I said gruffly. "Running late." I couldn't even bring myself to talk in full sentences to her.

Her voice came casually from behind me. "I need a copy of your health records. Can you get that for me?"

The request was out of the blue and her tone flippant. As though she hadn't seen something so intimate the night before, as though she hadn't participated by staying in the room to watch.

I turned my body toward her and tried not to stare at the vee of her sports bra's neckline. "I don't see why you would need that."

She wiped at the sweat on her forehead with her towel then draped it around her neck. "I need to know if you're clean. A woman would want to know this about the man she was marrying."

The tension that had stretched taut between us the night before pulled tighter, as though any moment it would snap.

Shit. She was pissed.

Well, so was I. "Did you forget we are not actually sleeping together?" It hurt in my gut to say it. More than it likely hurt her to hear.

"I don't want any STDs biting me in the ass later. If someone else found out you had something and leaked it to the media and then Darrell found out, I'd be screwed." A single rivulet of sweat drew down her gorgeous neck and over her collarbone. "Besides, I should have some insurance that you aren't fucking around."

I took a step toward her, my empty hand opening and closing reflexively at my side. I wasn't sure if I wanted to wring her throat or swipe the drop of sweat off of it with my thumb and suck it off. Or watch her suck it off. "No one's finding out anything, because I'm fucking clean."

She didn't budge. "Then it will say so in your medical records."

Goddamn, I wanted to bend her over. Wanted to pull down those tight lycra yoga pants and show her all the things that she'd likely imagined while she watched me last night.

It was because of what she'd seen last night that she was demanding this now. It was because of what I'd said. I was sure of it. I considered confronting her. She couldn't deny it—I'd seen her, and God, it would be so vindicating to hear from her own lips how much she'd liked it. I'd make her admit how chickenshit she'd been not to have joined me.

But I was chickenshit too.

And stubborn.

"I'm not getting you my medical files, sweetheart," I said, staring at her one last long second. I straightened my tie, opened the door and, with more strength than I knew I had, walked out.

I HADN'T FORGOTTEN about her at the office. How could I? She was foremost on my mind as I tried to dig myself through the hectic morning.

But when Nate suggested the plan for the evening, I decided to pretend everything was cool at home and I texted Elizabeth, hoping that *she'd* forgotten our latest fight.

The office is going to Red Farm to celebrate landing Phoenix. Significant others invited. Meet at eight.

I was slammed on all sides with the new contract. Things were coming at me nonstop, but she responded immediately, so I was still holding the phone when the text came in.

No.

Goddamnit. I really didn't have time for this. I shot her a quick text back. Everyone's going. You need to go.

Wasn't that what our whole scam was supposed to be about anyway? Being seen together?

I dropped my phone on my desk and tried to catch up on the emails I was frantically sorting through. The phone buzzed less than five minutes later. Are you going to get me what I asked for? the message read.

Obviously she hadn't forgotten anything.

I'm not getting you shit, I typed back, instantly fired up.

I'm not going anywhere, she replied.

I stood up from my desk quickly, wanting to flip it. Or kick something. Or at least throw some darts, but I didn't have time for that because we had an emergency morning meeting to celebrate landing such a big account and to announce it to the staff. I gathered my things and went downstairs to the conference room.

Thankfully Nate was making the announcement to the team, so I didn't have to be friendly and boisterous. While he did his stuff, I tried once again to get Elizabeth to come with us.

It's going to seem weird if my fiancée isn't at the celebration, don't you think? *I typed.*

I made sure my phone was on silent so as not to interrupt the meeting, then stared at it, waiting for her reply. Seconds ticked by feeling like hours, but she replied not too much later. *At this short notice, I don't give a fuck. I'm not at your beck and call.*

I bit back the urge to curse loudly and stuffed my phone in my suit pocket, noticing Sabrina eyeing me from the seat at my side. I sat back in my chair wondering if she'd seen the conversation on my phone.

Probably not.

She was likely only looking at me because we'd had a Thing once. And we still might when this farce was over. If I was smart, I'd focus all my fantasies on her now, for real. She didn't drive me mad like Elizabeth did. Didn't make me want to rip my hair out. Didn't make my eye twitch.

Didn't consume my thoughts and make me want to tear off all her clothes and then mark up her creamy white skin before telling her all the ways that she made me think the world was a better place because she was in it.

Yeah. Focusing on Sabrina definitely didn't make me want to do that.

I kept thinking about the two of them through the rest of the meeting, about Elizabeth and Sabrina. Or rather, I kept thinking about Elizabeth, and wondering how I could force my thoughts to the beautiful brunette sitting next to me instead. Even when I tried to muster up memories from the weekend we'd spent together naked, it all turned into Elizabeth.

*What kinds of sounds would Elizabeth have made if I'd fucked her against the wall like that? What expression would she have made? How would she have felt around my cock when her pussy tightened and came?*

I couldn't take it anymore. I had to get her out of my head.

And the only way I knew to get a woman out of my head was to get another woman in it.

When the meeting was over, Sabrina stood quickly, eager to get back to her work.

I called after her, feeling guilty as her name crossed my lips. She was my subordinate, someone I worked with on a daily basis, and after what I'd done last night, saying her name at the worst time, for the worst reason? I'd poisoned it.

And here I was using it again for my own selfish reasons. I was such a fuckwad. But I was also unrepentant.

She turned back to me, tugging on her hair. "Yeah?"

I didn't know what I was doing.

But I gave her my widest smile and winged it. "I want to let you know that Phoenix was particularly impressed with our marketing objectives. It was one of the main reasons we landed the account." All of that had been true, and it was a good idea as her boss to praise her for it. If I were more focused on my job, I would've done that earlier.

Maybe.

"I inherited a very qualified and talented team," she said, modest as always.

I shifted my weight on my hip. "You did. I know you did. Tom Burns also let me know a few things."

"Like what?"

I looked up and saw Donovan watching us. There was nothing that I'd said that was inappropriate, but with the thoughts I'd been having about her—or rather the thoughts I *hadn't* been having about her but had been *pretending* to have about her—plus the tension I was having at home, it was seeming more and more like maybe doing something reckless was my only way out of the spell Elizabeth had over me.

And Donovan never approved of recklessness.

"We should talk about it privately," I said to her. God, I was such a dick. Was I really doing this? "Meet you upstairs in my office in fifteen?"

She blinked a couple of times, and I wondered if she understood what I was getting at. "Sure. I'll be there in fifteen."

By the time I got up to my office, I was having second thoughts about using Sabrina as a source of distraction. It was wrong on so many levels.

I needed to confront my real problem, head on.

I took a deep breath and tried once more to reason with my fiancée about the evening's plans. *It's Friday. We were going to The Sky Launch anyway. Just go to Red Farm instead.*

I sat in my chair and rocked onto its back wheels while I waited for her reply. When it came, I almost fell over. *We don't usually go to the club until later, and I already told you I didn't want to go out tonight because I have to pack and get up early for my trip with mom. Did you forget?*

Trip? What trip?

I picked up my office phone and called my assistant, Roxie, too lazy to walk out and talk to her in person.

"Do you know anything about Elizabeth going on a trip?" I could hear how terse I sounded.

Roxie's throaty Hungarian accent sounded both through the receiver and from outside my office. "It's her mother's birthday. She going on a spa trip in Connecticut with her for the week. It's been on your calendar for weeks. Did you forget?" Her echo of Elizabeth's words just riled me up more.

"I didn't forget, thank you," I snapped. I'd totally forgotten. "I just didn't know it was this week." I hung up before she could say anything else.

I bounced my foot rapidly up and down. Elizabeth still had to eat. I sent another message. We'll be home early enough. Just go to the fucking dinner.

I'll be home early enough because I'm not fucking going.

I could feel my face getting hot with anger as I read her reply. I was still staring at it when a second message came in on its tail.

And send me Clarence's phone number. Now that your phone isn't dead.

I didn't even realize how pissed I was until the growl came out of my throat. I was so angry. So frustrated.

So hard.

As angry as we'd been with each other, it was probably good that we weren't going to see each other tonight. Even better that we weren't going to see each other for an entire week. I would get my apartment to myself, wouldn't even have to stay at her place.

But . . . I *wanted* to see her.

I wanted to stay at her place. I wanted to fucking be in her arms. I wanted to be in her bed, wanted to be inside her—and since I still couldn't stand her, the whole idea had me in turmoil.

I ran my hand through my hair. Both of my hands through my hair. One after another, willing myself to settle down, but I heard Roxie's voice outside the office.

"Go on in. He's in a mood though. I warn you."

"I heard that," I yelled.

"You were meant to," she called back.

Then there was Sabrina standing in my doorway, her hands tugging at her hair like they often did, a gesture I'd found adorable when I'd first met her a decade ago.

And now?

She was striking, she really was. A natural beauty. She'd grown up to be even more sophisticated and beguiling, more sure of herself. She was serious and put together. She wasn't feisty or passionate. She wasn't late for everything.

Why did I have to remind myself that these were good things?

"Hey, what's up?" she asked tentatively. "Is there a problem?"

"Not exactly." I dropped my phone on my desk. But it sat there, staring, mocking, Elizabeth's texts shouting in my head at the mere sight of it.

I opened my desk drawer and threw my phone inside, as though that would silence the buzz buzz of my thoughts.

It was weak, but the only idea I had at the moment.

I turned my attention back to Sabrina.

"Have a seat," I said, and the world did seem a little less noisy now that my cell phone was tucked away.

She walked farther into the room somewhat cautiously, and slunk down in the chair facing me. "I'm here."

"You're here." I didn't even remember how to do this. Didn't remember how to talk to a woman.

What the hell had happened to me?

I shook my head and attempted a smile. "Anyway. As I was saying downstairs, Tom Burns spoke to me yesterday, and he had some interesting things to say about you."

"Really? Like what?" She blinked rapidly, seeming nervous.

Women were nervous when they were into a guy, right? Shit, I needed to be closer, needed to get the barriers out from between us. I stood up and circled around so I was right in front of her, then leaned back, half sitting on the desk behind me.

As soon as I sat, she bolted to a standing position, startling me.

"Whoa," I said. "You okay?"

"Yep. Just edgy today." She tugged on her hair. "Go on. Tom said . . . ?"

"That you stayed as late as anyone else, and that you provided some of the last minute additions to the project, such as the global goals message component. That was one of the selling points in the strategy."

"Really?" Her eyes were level with mine now, her focus completely on me. She was into this, then, if I was reading this right.

And I wasn't. Yet.

"Yes. Really." I kept on with my praise. I wasn't a quitter. "I wanted you to know your commitment to your team didn't go unnoticed. Everyone seems to be responding really well to you. The staff likes you. Your team likes you, and I'm really glad you came." I *was* glad she'd come. She'd done great things for the company, made my job easier. She was probably better at the work than I was.

And I was glad for other reasons. Surely.

She was still playing with her hair so I reached out and took it from her and tugged it myself, making a play of sorts.

Had coming on to a woman always felt this unnatural?

"Thank you. I appreciate that." Her cheeks grew pink. "Was that everything?"

I nodded, keeping my eyes on hers. "Yeah, that's everything." I chuckled at myself. What else was I supposed to say? *No, that's not everything, I was hoping we could meet at a hotel later so I can remember why I like you better than the woman I'm marrying.*

That wasn't smooth at all. Three months out of the game, and I'd forgotten all my moves.

"Okay, then. Thank you again." She started to leave, then hesitated. "Oh, and congratulations on the account."

She definitely wanted me. All I had to do was want her back.

Or at least try to.

"Congratulations to both of us." I put my hand up in the air to give her a high five, and when her palm met mine, I left my hand there, let it linger, and when she started to pull away, I laced my fingers through hers.

Yeah, this was how to do it. It was coming back to me now. It didn't have to be tawdry.

"You're coming tonight, aren't you?" I asked, my confidence rising incrementally along with my self-loathing.

Out of the corner of my eye, Donovan appeared in the open door frame.

Sabrina glanced over and noticed him too, but instead of pulling back, she entwined her fingers around mine. "Oh, yeah. Of course."

"Good. I'll save you a seat." We held hands, stretching our arms until she was too far away to touch, and then we let go. I watched after her, though, my heart beating hollow in my chest, my stomach feeling empty.

I sighed again and turned to my partner. "Kincaid. Whatcha got for me? Budgets for the toothpaste campaigns, I'm hoping."

He closed the door.

Which was immediately a bad sign. There was no need to have the door closed to discuss toothpaste campaigns.

"What the goddamn hell are you doing?" he hissed.

Of course. I should have seen this coming a mile away. "Oh, Christ. You're really going to be like this, aren't you?"

He paced toward me, his face looking as enraged as I'd felt all morning. "Our reputation is on the line. Our company is on the line. Elizabeth's company is on the line."

I stood up from the desk to answer him. "I know what's on the line. Trust me."

"Trust you? I walked in on you with your hands all over Sabrina," Donovan said, disgusted. "Your door was wide open. The glass is clear. Anyone could have seen you."

I circled behind my desk, putting a barrier between us so that I didn't kill him. "Because there are so many spies in our office just dying to call up Elizabeth's cousin and tell him about some harmless office flirtation? I bet he chases his own secretary's skirt. Have you seen the guy?"

Donovan's eyes narrowed to thin slits. "You're lucky it was just me," he said in a tone so quiet and controlled, it made my scalp prickle.

"*So* lucky. To think, I might've missed out on you telling me what was what and putting me in my place. Like always. Thank you. I appreciate it. Now if you don't have anything *business* related—"

He cut me off. "This isn't one of your games, Weston. You can't charm your way through this like you do everything else."

God, he sounded like my father. Not because my father had ever said words like that, but because Donovan thought he had the right to say things like that.

And he didn't. No right at all.

I leaned my palms onto the desk and bent toward him. "If you didn't think I was capable of it, then you shouldn't have insisted I be the one to do the damn job. It isn't like I wanted it." I held his intense stare for several long seconds, neither of us backing down.

Finally, I spoke again. "Look. I'll be where I'm supposed to be. I'll go through with the wedding. I'll wear the ring. I'll continue playing house—playing the part like I have been, which has been an Academy award-winning performance. But like hell do you get to keep popping in like you're directing this show. You were the casting agent, Donovan, that's all. Now step aside, and enjoy it when you get to put Reach's name on Dyson's advertising subsidiary, because that's where you get to take *your* credit. The rest of your role is done."

We stared at each other for a few more seconds, and I had a feeling he wanted to say something else, but by God, no way was I letting him have the last word. "Now, do I need to call security?" I said, acting like the total asshole that I was. "Because this is my office."

He straightened to his full height. "Technically, it's *not* your office, is it?" And he turned and left, shutting the door behind him.

Fuck him.

Fuck him for having the last word and fuck him for bringing up the money I owed him, for reminding me that I didn't have a proper stake in the company yet.

But also, *thank* Donovan. Because he reminded me why I was doing all of this. Why I was suffering day in and day out with a woman who made me question everything that I wanted and desired.

But seriously, fuck them both. Both Donovan and Elizabeth.

And if this was really how it was going to be—Donovan barking orders, Elizabeth not playing her part to the limit, not being as committed as I had been—then I was done playing by the rules. Tonight I would go to Red Farm without my fiancée, and if I flirted with Sabrina, so be it. If I had fun with Sabrina, then good for me. If anyone else was put off by it, well, maybe they shouldn't have treated me like this when all I was doing was my best.

I opened the top desk of my drawer and grabbed my phone. There was one more text I needed to send if I was going to feel completely liberated enough to do what I wanted this evening. I searched and found Clarence Sheridan's number and sent it to my wife-to-be.

I might be a dick, but fair was fair.

# CHAPTER
# TWELVE

*Elizabeth*

"I 'M PLANNING ON getting a restorative herbal massage," my mother said as I dropped a sleep mask into my suitcase. I shifted the cradle of the landline receiver so I could hold it with my chin and rifle through my dresser drawer at the same time. "Or should I get the chakra balancing massage instead?"

"What does is it say the difference is?" I grabbed a handful of panties from the drawer and dropped them in the suitcase, then shuffled toward my closet for some yoga pants. To be honest, I wasn't really paying attention to the types of services she was telling me about. She would change her mind by the time we got there.

The spa was in a resort in Connecticut—only a couple of hours away, but the driver was arriving early in the morning and I wanted to be packed tonight. I'd already spent an hour on the task, which was too long. We planned to spend most of the weeklong trip wrapped in seaweed and on massage tables, so it shouldn't have been that big of a burden to pack a bag. Problem was, I was too distracted by thoughts of Weston.

Naked thoughts of Weston.

Thoughts of Weston doing the things I saw him doing last night in the dark.

"I don't know, one's Thai style, the other one's Swedish with focus on chakras. Oh!" my mother suddenly exclaimed. "We could do the massage for two!"

I closed my eyes and pinched the bridge of my nose. "Those are for couples, mom. They're romantic and sexy-like."

"I'm sure they wouldn't mind if we did it together. There's a discount if you do it together." With the money my mother got from her divorce, she didn't need to worry about bargains. But she remembered where she came from, and she could never turn down a buy-one-get-one-free special.

"Sorry, Mom. I just don't want to see you naked." But there was that guy I *did* want to see naked.

And now I was thinking about him again. Or still. Missing his presence, trying not to notice what time it was or that he was likely out with his friends, eating dinner now. Trying not to wonder if he would show up at my house at all tonight, considering I was leaving in the morning. Our last texts had escalated in tone and tension; I had no idea whether he even wanted to be in the same room with me at the moment.

I didn't want to be in the same room with him.

But I did.

No, I didn't.

"What's Weston going to do while you're gone?" my mother asked, as though she could read my mind.

"I don't know. And I don't care." With five pairs of yoga pants and four long-sleeved T-shirts, I returned back to my suitcase and dropped them inside. "Don't you remember what it's like to live with a man, Mom? Because it's really terrible, and I'm glad I'm getting a break."

She laughed. "Of course I remember, honey. Why do you think I'm divorced? But aren't you worried that this particular man might muck up your deal while you're out of town?"

I'd been conflicted about this. He'd promised me over and over again that he was faithful to our commitment, that he wasn't going to do anything to mess up my chance at getting Dyson Media, but did I trust him?

Part of me did, actually. A deep rooted part of me trusted him when he said he would keep it in his pants. It was my head that thought otherwise, the reasonable part of me that knew what men were like and what temptation could do to a man. That was the part of me that said perhaps he was fooling around, or *would* fool around, given the opportunity.

Luckily, I had someone who had my back. "Donovan will look after him," I told my mother. "He knows how to keep Weston in line."

A muffled ringing sounded from somewhere in my bedroom—my cell phone.

"What's that? Do you need to go?"

"I won't know until I find my cell phone and check the caller ID," I said, annoyed. I had stuck my cell somewhere when I was bitter with Weston, but where?

Oh, yes. Under my pillow.

The name on the screen said, Kincaid, D. "Mom, I gotta go." I clicked off the home phone before she had a chance to say goodbye, and clicked on my cell. "What's up, Donovan?"

"What are you doing? And why aren't you here?" He was serious, straight to the point like always, but this time there was also a note of something I'd never heard in Donovan. Panic?

"I'm at home, and I'm talking to you. I am not where you are because I don't know where you are." Then I realized he was probably out with everyone else at the company, celebrating their new account. "Oh, I mean I'm not there because I don't want to be."

"You *do* want to be. Get down here. Now."

I turned to look at myself in the dresser mirror, see if my makeup had still held up from my earlier outing to the library. It had, but it didn't matter because I wasn't going anywhere. I wasn't jumping because Reach said so.

"What's the point? Why do you want me there so badly?"

"Elizabeth, I should think you would trust me enough to not have to go into a lengthy explanation. Let me just tell you this—Sabrina is here."

At the mention of her name, my stomach curdled. I had nothing against her personally; she was a nice woman. Probably. But I knew what kind of thoughts Weston had about her, and that made her dangerous.

But she was also an employee for the company, so of course she would be at the celebration dinner with the rest of the staff and higher-ups.

"Sabrina works with Weston every day," I said, not quite so sure of myself.

"Tonight, though, they aren't working."

If Donovan hadn't convinced me I should be there, the text message that waited for me when I hung up did. It had been sent earlier in the day, but I was only just seeing it now—Clarence Sheridan's contact info, forwarded from Weston.

Sure, I'd asked him to send it, but I'd asked more than once, and he'd been pissy about it. Was it reaching to think he might've sent it to relieve his guilt about whatever he was planning to do with Sabrina?

I wasn't certain, but I was damn sure going to find out.

I changed quickly into a dressy jumpsuit and heels. Instead of taking the time to wait for my driver, I went to the front desk of the apartment building and got the doorman to hail a cab. Twenty minutes after my phone call with Donovan, I was on my way to Red Farm.

It was easy to find the group I was looking for when I arrived at the restaurant. They took up most of the main room, the company staff spread out along two long tables. I spotted Weston, Nate, and Donovan immediately at the far end and headed over to them. The food had already arrived; dumplings were in the middle of the table being shared family-style. As if by fate, there was one empty seat waiting next to Donovan. Weston sat across from him, Sabrina at his side.

And Weston's hand was on her thigh.

"Elizabeth!" Weston jumped up, eyes wide, voice pitched high. "What are you doing here?" It almost sounded like he was glad I'd come, but the sting of seeing his hand on the other woman's thigh was fresh. Had he known I'd seen it? It was probable he didn't. It was possible he did.

It was possible *everyone* knew.

And that thought pissed the hell out of me.

He bent to kiss me, but just before his mouth met mine, I moved away. His lips landed on my cheek. It was only for show anyway, not like we were kissing for the fun of it.

"My *fiancé* had a celebration. Thought I should be here," I said, answering his question with the subtlest emphasis on the reminder of who he was to me. Real or not.

"I'll move so you two can sit together," Nate offered.

I waved him off. That would be the mature thing to do, but I was in battle mode. All of the people at this end of the table were in the know, and the rest of the employees didn't seem to be paying any attention to what happened down here. If my fiancé could flirt with somebody else, so could I. Weston King wasn't the only player in the world.

"Don't be silly. I don't need to sit by him. I'd much rather sit by Donovan." I slipped in next to the man, who eyed me curiously. "Now. Next time the waitress comes by, I'm going to need a drink."

Probably a double to give me enough nerve to go through with this. I put my arm around Donovan's back and ruffled the hair at the base of his neck. "So. I'm here!"

I kept my eyes pinned on Weston's, eager to see his reaction to my flirtation. He seemed annoyed, but not as annoyed as I would have preferred. It didn't help that Donovan's response was to bend forward to take a bite of his dumpling, acting as if I wasn't even there.

And it most definitely didn't help when Weston, sure I was watching, returned his hand to Sabrina's knee. Thank God, he at least was subtle enough so that only Donovan and I could see.

"You said you weren't coming," he muttered accusingly.

"I hadn't planned to. But." I turned and looked at Donovan again, slipped my eyes up and down him longingly. Or I hoped it looked longing. "Donovan called and told me I needed to be here."

Weston sneered. "Wasn't that thoughtful of him?" Then the asshole scooted his chair closer to the woman beside him. "Sabrina, you tasted the seared pork and shrimp dumplings yet?"

"No. Where are they?" She fluttered her eyes, all doe-like and naïve.

He lifted his chopsticks with a bite of dumpling on them. "Have some of mine." Then the asshole fed dumplings to his little girlfriend in front of me. She even had the nerve to groan.

I could happily have murdered them both for this rude display.

Not to be outdone—"Donovan, the pan-fried lamb—" I started for the dumpling on his plate, but before I could feed him anything, he picked it up and dumped it on my plate. "You can have it."

Obviously, he was not playing along. I consciously smoothed out my frown and smiled at him. "Guess that's better than swapping germs."

"Elizabeth's a germophobe," Weston said snidely.

"I am not." I grabbed the chopsticks next to me and attempted to pick up the dumpling, remembering too late that I'd never been very good with the things. "Just because I'm concerned about the diseases that come into my house, that doesn't qualify me as a germophobe." I chased the dumpling around my plate, growing more and more frustrated with each failed attempt to capture my food.

"She's asked for a report of clean health."

"I think that's reasonable." I'd only asked for his medical records because I knew it would rile him up. Because I'd felt riled. It was payback.

Finally, I snagged a piece of pastry and lifted it toward my mouth, but just as it reached my lips, it fell to the plate. "Goddamnit."

"Guys," Nate sounded like he was trying not to laugh while hushing us. "Lover's spats are fun and all . . ."

Weston apparently didn't get the hint. "Why do you even care when there's no way I'm sharing anything I've got with you anyway?"

It shouldn't burn like it did to hear him say that—twice in one day, no less—but it did. Especially in front of Sabrina, for some reason.

Well, fuck him.

I reached over and stole the unused fork from his setting. "Big words, King. Just remember, the thing you want out of this relationship isn't as replaceable as you are."

I stabbed the pan-fried lamb and put it in my mouth, and it tasted fucking delicious. Like redemption. It melted on my tongue.

Melted like the conversation had melted into a tense silence.

"Speaking of replacements . . ." Nate said breaking the hush. "Did I ever tell you guys about the time I needed this original painting by this Brazilian artist, Luiz Hugo Sousa?"

Weston, who'd been staring at me, moved his eyes eagerly to Nate's. "This sounds like the beginning of a good story."

"The problem was, the girl who had possession of it didn't want to sell. Fortunately, I was fucking her at the time. It wasn't even particularly valuable, but my boss wanted it, and that made it powerful. I needed it more than I wanted her, and that's saying a lot considering her oral skills."

I needed Dyson Media more than I wanted Weston. That was the lesson here. SIlently, I thanked Nate for the reminder. *Eyes on the ball, Elizabeth.*

"Skipping past the details: I got bombed on Jäger one night and decided to paint a replacement."

Weston and Sabrina laughed, and so did a couple of other staff members who were now gathering around for Nate's telling of the story.

"This is what made you stop doing Jäger?" someone asked.

"Oh, that came years and many adventures later. Long story short, there's a reason I don't paint for a living. I took the original and left a real Ecce Homo in its place. You should have seen this mess. Turns out I might have had a career as a ninja warrior, though, because the escape route I had to take to get out of her apartment that night was insane. If I hadn't been drunk enough to feel invincible, I never would have tried it. I still have the scar on my upper arm from the barbed wire." He started to pull down his shirt at the neck, searching for the mark. "It's partly covered by the tattoo."

"What did she do when she woke up and saw it?" Weston asked.

"Left me about a hundred messages threatening my life and manhood, until I tossed the burner and picked up a new phone. And then what *could* she do? She couldn't display mine, obviously, but once her friends had seen the real thing, it wasn't like she could hang any copy. It would have been glaringly obvious. Guess she has a white space on her wall now."

"Is there a moral to the story?" Donovan asked, unamused.

"I suppose if you need a moral, Kincaid, it's that there's never a replacement for the real thing." Nate looked at his partner hard. Real hard.

I glanced over at Weston, willing him to hear the point. But, surprise, surprise, he'd tuned us out and was whispering something in Sabrina's ear.

"I'm not sure the person who needed to hear you got the message," I said to Nate.

He looked from me to Donovan to Weston to Sabrina and back to me again. "There's more than one person at this table tonight who needs to hear it."

More people crowded around us from the other tables, the staff becoming looser from drinks and more jovial as the evening passed. The mood had lightened considerably since I had arrived. Weston got up from the table without a word, heading to the restroom, most likely. Someone took his seat, and another round of dumplings were set on the table.

Some nice guy from creative tried to get to know me by asking all about the wedding. It might have done my ego some good if I'd thought he was flirting, but I had a feeling he was gay.

And even if he was flirting, he wasn't nearly charming enough to make up for the stab to my heart when, five minutes after Weston left the group, Sabrina nonchalantly left the table and followed after him.

# CHAPTER
# THIRTEEN

*Weston*

I'D GONE TO the restaurant that night with every intention of flirting with Sabrina, and maybe making out with her in the back of a cab. I needed the reminder of what it felt like to have other lips on mine, needed to remember what it was like to kiss another woman, a woman who wasn't Elizabeth. And maybe, with luck, I could get her out of my head.

I had zero intention of inviting Sabrina to meet me in the back of the restaurant for a buddy bang.

But when Elizabeth showed up, everything changed.

Before she came, I had my hand on Sabrina's leg. The warmth of her, the soft silky tenderness of her skin that was supposed to get my cock going, only had me wondering what Elizabeth's skin would feel like in comparison. Were her luscious thighs as soft to the touch? Would goosebumps prickle along her skin if I rubbed my thumb on her like this?

Even with a gorgeous woman beside me, with her attention completely on me, all I could think about was pale complexion, red hair, blue eyes.

And then the woman I was dreaming of was standing in front of me, dressed in a pale gray jumpsuit with lace over the arms and décolletage. She was more covered than Sabrina was, but my cock was more interested than it had been all evening.

I'd been grateful at first—she'd shown up! She'd come to Red Farm, even after all that fighting back and forth over text, she'd come out for me.

And my gut twisted with guilt and turmoil over the way I'd been flirting, but I thought maybe all could be forgiven, that the whole day would be turned around, and we could forget everything going on between us if Elizabeth would just sit by me.

I stood up to kiss her, and I don't ever usually do that. Even for show, not since the engagement party. But it felt natural and right, and I wanted to.

And then she turned her head.

And I realized she wasn't here to make amends at all.

Especially when she started flirting with Donovan. She couldn't keep her hands off of him. What—had Clarence been busy for the night? She had to come and parade her disinterest in me *in front* of me? Every time she touched my friend, every time she glanced at him, it felt like a chess move, like she was taking out one of my pawns.

But I knew how to counterattack.

She ruffled his hair, and my hand scooted higher on Sabrina's leg. She'd sharpen her gaze on him. I'd offer a forkful of food to Sabrina. It was intense and it was tedious. I was annoyed, but more than a little turned on.

But it wasn't a game with casualties until she brought up how easily I could be replaced.

For weeks, I'd been teaching her how to be a better business woman, been bending to her rules, living in the same house, keeping it in my pants, been stifling my irrational planet-sized desire for her, been doing all of this so that she could get her hands on her company—and I could be replaced?

So I didn't know if it was to hurt her or to get over her or because *I* was hurt—probably a combination of all three, and I was too fired up to narrow down the specific motivations—but I leaned down and invited Sabrina to meet me in the back of the restaurant.

I could replace Elizabeth, too.

Five minutes later, I was slipping into the cubby by the kitchen, a

DIRTY SEXY PLAYER                    131

cut out in the wall covered by a decorative curtain, trying my hardest to turn my thoughts to the woman meeting me and away from the woman waiting back at the table.

Soon, I saw Sabrina walking past. I pulled her into the cubby with me, pushed her against the narrow wall, and pressed my lips against hers, kissing her aggressively, asking for permission with my tongue—permission to let me use her, use her to help me forget about that other woman, the woman I really wanted to be kissing.

Sabrina, sweet Sabrina, opened her mouth, her tongue meeting mine. She was familiar and safe. She was easy because I didn't have to work for her. I didn't have to second guess what she wanted or what I wanted, for that matter.

But I did need to be sure she knew what I was after.

I broke the kiss and leaned my forehead against hers. "I'm going to be completely honest, Sabrina—this is a booty call and nothing else. You have every right to slap me and walk back out there. But I'm sensing you need a release right now too."

Was it weird that I hoped that she *did* slap me? Hoped that she kneed me in the nuts and told me I was a pig before walking away, never looking back?

She opened her mouth to respond, but before she could there was a rustling outside the closet. Someone walking too closely past, and I leaned even farther away from her than I already was so I could peek out of the curtain.

*Donovan.* Fucking Donovan. Checking up on me again.

"What is it?" Sabrina asked.

I shook my head. I couldn't tell her that another one of the execs in the office knew that she was back here in the closet with me—how embarrassing for her.

And suddenly it hit me—how embarrassing for *me.*

What was I doing? I wasn't into this buddy bang. The only reason I was semi-hard was because Elizabeth had shown up. I was a fucking shitshow, and honestly, because Donovan was out there playing boss—playing *father* again—it made me wish so goddamned hard that I could go through with this, but I just couldn't. It was wrong on so many levels. Even if I could get my dick into it, my head was yards away.

"I can't do this," I said.

Sabrina's head snapped up. "I was just going to say the same thing."

I let go of her, and ran my hand through my hair instead. "I'm sorry." Then I registered what she'd said. "You were?" That was a surprise. I thought she'd been into me.

"Yeah. It's not . . ."

My mind filled in the blanks, while she tried to look for the right words. *It's not appropriate. It's sleazy. I can tell you're not feeling it.*

Eventually she said, "The timing."

"The timing," I agreed. Fucking timing. Before Elizabeth and after Elizabeth. Was my life reduced to those two time periods forever?

"I'll go out first," she said.

I waited much longer than I needed to after she left. Three minutes, four. Seven minutes. I didn't know what I was waiting for—to figure it all out, for my temper to settle down. Something.

When I finally got myself together and walked back to the table, Donovan, Sabrina, and Elizabeth were all gone.

I slumped down in the seat next to Nate. "Where did Elizabeth go?" I asked, wishing I didn't need to know. Stealing a swig of his beer because I did.

Nate shrugged. "She left when Donovan left."

I tensed. I'd been in a closet with another woman, and I had no right to ask, but I couldn't help myself. "Did she leave *with* Donovan?"

My partner eyed me strangely. "If you think that Donovan would go home with Elizabeth, you're more fucked up over this girl than I thought."

That wasn't exactly an answer. "So . . . she didn't?"

He scrubbed a hand over his face. "They left the restaurant at the same time. When I glanced out the window, Donovan was putting Elizabeth in a cab."

"Good." I was more relieved than I deserved to be. More relieved than I wanted to let on. "I mean, good someone made sure she got home okay."

He swiped his beer out of my hand and glared. "You know that I know about this kind of shit, right?"

Oh, right! Nate, the god of everything.

I leaned forward, eagerly, ready to learn. "Yeah, yeah, man. Do you know something now?"

"I do. I do." He bent in toward me, as though about to share his best-kept secret. "D. is not into your girl." He paused for effect. "And your girl is into *you*."

I let that sink in.

"You do know who your girl is, don't you?" he asked when I didn't say anything.

"Elizabeth?"

"Phew. You aren't as stupid as I thought you might be after tonight's bullshit. Now, what are you going to do with this information? Hint: the answer shouldn't include being in a closet with your ex."

I stared at him. "Nate, you don't know what you're saying. She can't stand me."

"I think you're wrong."

There *was* tension between us—sexual tension. There had been from day one. But Elizabeth had made it clear that there could be nothing between us. Because she was focused on her end goal. Because she wasn't interested in a player like me. Because she would want a guy she could be proud of.

"I don't think—"

"Weston, get the fuck out of here and find out."

I started to argue yet again and then remembered—Nate was my hero. Why the hell would I question his advice?

# CHAPTER
# FOURTEEN

*Elizabeth*

I SHUT THE door of my West Side apartment behind me and headed straight for my room. Friday nights the schedule put us at my place, but I didn't have any idea if Weston would show up.

If I were placing bets? My wager would be no.

Even though I was alone, I slammed things around as though people could hear me. Slammed the door to my closet, slammed my dresser drawer. I changed quickly into my nightgown, even though I knew I wouldn't fall asleep anytime soon. My insides were a storm of emotions—fury, jealousy, want.

God, how I wanted Weston.

That's what it all came down to. How much I wanted him to be here, rubbing his hand on *my* thigh, to be leaning into *my* ear, beckoning *me* to some secret rendezvous. How much I wanted his secret nighttime fantasies to be about *me*.

Another door slam.

But this time it wasn't me. I stomped out of my bedroom knowing it was him, yet still knocked utterly out of breath when I saw him there, his brow furrowed, his hair a mess from dragging his hand through it so many times.

He was magnificent. A goddamned hottie. A sight so pretty he almost hurt the eyes.

He dumped his keys in the bowl by the front door, his eyes on mine. Sparks shot between us. We were both wrapped up in an electrical storm, and I could feel him pulling me toward him, despite everything that happened this evening. I wanted him; I hated him.

I wanted him.

"That was fast," I said, snidely, remembering who he'd disappeared with when I'd last seen him. "I guess your reputation isn't based on your lasting power."

"I didn't fuck Sabrina," he said, toeing off his shoes, gaze pinned to me. "Ask me why."

I took a hopeful step forward. "Why not?"

He tugged his cowl neck sweater over his head and tossed it on the floor behind him, leaving his chest bare. Goosebumps sprouted down my arms and legs. "Because she wasn't the one I wanted to fuck."

My stomach flipped. My thighs started shaking.

"So, if we're in a fight," he continued, "let's hurry up and get it over with so we can get on to what's next."

It only took two steps before I crashed against him. His lips were firm and demanding, taking my mouth roughly, exploring every part of it. He kissed the way he fought—mean and hot, bordering on explosive. I wondered if he could make me come with just a kiss. The question was enough to make me realize I wanted his lips other places. On my breasts. Between my thighs.

Without any warning, he spun me around, shifting me so that I was face up against the wall. He pressed up roughly against my backside and lifted the hem of my nightgown so his hands could palm my ass.

"You've fucking teased me for so long, Elizabeth. Do you feel that?" He rubbed his erection in between my ass cheeks. "Do you feel how much I want you?"

Yes, I felt him.

But I was desperate to be sure. "Is it . . . Is it for me?"

"All for you, baby. Only you." He nipped at my neck, his hands moving upward to cup my breasts underneath my nightgown. "Three long months of watching you prance around left me with a hard-on that doesn't ever ease up." He rocked his dick against me so I could feel every bit of his painful erection. "Tell me you've wanted this too."

"I've wanted you," I confessed breathily. "From the moment you got down on your knees for my fake proposal. I wanted you then, and every day since."

He hissed as if that admission was painful. "Too long," he said. "Too long."

He drew one hand down over the flat of my stomach and slid beneath the waistband of my panties. "A landing strip," he sighed as his touch brushed over the thin column of hair above my folds. "It's been killing me, not knowing."

My knees buckled at the thought of him imagining this. Imagining it in such detail that he'd needed to know if I trimmed, if I waxed. If I was au natural.

He caught me with his arm around my waist while the other went deeper, slipping easily to find the sensitive bundle of nerves awaiting him. Swiftly, expertly, he began rubbing me toward ecstasy. Staccato gasps escaped from my lips.

"You like that? Does it feel good?" He rubbed his cock again between my ass cheeks while he massaged my clit, first slow in one direction, then quick in another. "You don't deserve this, because you've teased me for so long. You don't deserve this, but I'm going to let you come because I'm a nice guy. Tell me I'm a nice guy to let you come."

The tension was already building, I was already nearing the edge.

But even on the verge of the best orgasm of my life, I did not surrender. "No."

"You don't want to come?" His fingers kept swirling across my clit, making me dizzy.

"You're not a nice guy. You're an asshole."

Immediately, Weston took his hands off me and stepped back. I whirled around, my palms flattening back against the wall, and faced him down. He hadn't gone too far, and was rubbing at the bulge in his pants. But I worried now that he was going to give up, abandon me.

"You said you were going to fuck me." Was it a challenge? An accusation? I was too strung out on the memory of his fingers down my panties to tell, and so desperate for them to return.

He nodded. "Oh, I am. Take this off." He stepped forward and grabbed my nightie, pulling it over my head and tossing it to the ground before stepping back again to admire me.

"Jesus, you're so fucking gorgeous," he said more to himself than to me, stroking up and down over his imprisoned cock.

And then I was tired of looking. I'd been watching him, been looking for too long—*months* too long. I wanted to be touching.

I closed the distance between us and grabbed for his belt. He laughed, rough and cruel, his hands coming down flat across my back and smoothing all the way down to my ass cheeks.

"Eager to find something there?" he asked, his teeth grazing along my neck.

I was too focused on my task to answer. I had the buckle undone and now was working on his zipper.

"Didn't get enough from your peep show last night?"

I froze, my hand now on the shape of his cock outside his boxer briefs. He'd seen me?

"I saw your reflection in the window. Watched you watching me as I stroked myself." He pushed my panties down my butt cheeks so he could press his fingers between my thighs, and into the slick wetness along my crotch. "I was so pissed you didn't come and join me. I had to say someone else's name, just to punish you, even though the whole time I was thinking about you."

He'd seen me. And he'd lied.

I felt relieved and murderous all at once. Relieved and off-the-charts aroused.

"I told you you aren't a nice guy." I reached inside his boxer briefs and wrapped my fingers around the silky smooth skin of his hard erection, fulfilling my own fantasy from the night before. My blood shot hot down to my pussy.

"You're right. I'm not nice." He stuck a long finger inside me from behind, and I moaned. "I'm still going to let you come. Because I want to see you fall apart."

His words made me shiver and this time when he stroked inside me, his thumb brushed against my clit. And another shaky moan escaped my lips.

His cock jerked in my hand.

"You like making me feel good," I said, moving my hand up and down the length of him.

"I like torturing you," he corrected. He backed us up and spun me around until I was facing the kitchen island. He pressed his hand down on my upper back so that I would bend over it.

"Spread your legs," he said as he knelt down behind me. I spread my legs and stretched my arms across the island.

Weston pulled my panties the rest of the way off my legs. Then he grabbed my ankles and ran his hands up my calves, then moved them inside my knees and up my inner thighs until they were right where I wanted them. And then it wasn't his hands, but his mouth. His tongue. I jumped at the first warm swipe of his rough tongue across my slit.

He followed with a quick swat of his hand on the outside of my thigh.

"Oh," I squealed, then glared at him over my shoulder.

He dimpled at me. "Don't move, or I'll smack you again." He kept his eyes on mine as he lowered his head back to my pussy, his hand rubbing away the sting where he'd slapped me.

The thing was, the sting of the smack felt good, especially with the added rub afterwards. And the way his tongue moved along me combined with the lingering hurt to give me pleasure I didn't know I needed—so maybe I did a little more writhing on purpose.

"You liked that." He smacked me again on the other cheek, rubbing it away immediately, and I hummed as he did. He echoed my moan against my pussy and my knees nearly went out from underneath me. It was a good thing I was holding onto the island. Especially when the tip of his tongue reached out to my brush my clit with feather-like strokes.

I swear I started to purr.

He anchored his hands on my hips, his fingers digging into my flesh as his tongue made its way from my clit down to my hole in long luscious strokes. And then, just when I didn't think I could take it anymore, he pushed his tongue *inside* me, as far as his fingers had been. He was fast and strong, licking against my G spot, tongue-fucking me until I began to see spots in front of my eyes. He let go of my side and began to rub my clit with the pad of his thumb. I bucked my hips against the island, trying to get away from him, trying to get closer. Trying to get away. I couldn't tell what I wanted except that he was completely in control of giving it to me, and that scared the shit out of me.

He hooked his arms around me at my hips, though, so that I couldn't move and dove even deeper with his tongue, and that was when I finally reached the top. Unable to escape, having to stay there through the torment, having to give into his wicked attack.

"Holy shit," my teeth were chattering. "Holy shit, holy shit. I'm going to come." And I wasn't just saying it, I was actually doing it. My whole body was trembling and shaking, my legs and my arms and my knees and my insides as I groaned out a guttural sound I'd never made before.

Weston kept licking me until I was done. Until he'd coaxed the very last bit of my orgasm from my body, and I felt good everywhere.

When I was completely spent, he stood and pulled me to him, my back to his front. He still had his pants mostly on, but the warmth of his chest against my back sent shivers down my body. I could feel his cock again at the crack of my ass, but this time it was bare and begging for a warm place to nest.

"I need to be inside you," he said at my ear. I turned my face and his mouth was waiting to devour mine. I kissed him, kissed the taste of myself off of him until it mingled with whatever taste had been in my mouth before, until I couldn't distinguish what was him and what was me.

When he broke away, I was breathless.

"I need to be inside you," he said again.

"Yes," I said, because I needed that too, and because it was all I could say. "Yes."

"Should I stop for a condom?" he asked.

I didn't want to stop for anything. "Do you usually suit up?"

"Every time. Every single time." He rubbed the head of his dick up and down across my slit, so close to where I needed him. It was distracting. But I still heard what he said—heard what he *meant*.

That this was the first time he'd ever suggested not using a condom with a woman.

If he'd worn one with everyone else, there was no need for him to wear one with me. I had an implant. I couldn't get pregnant. Because of that stubborn streak I had, though, my first impulse was to say no, to tell him to go grab one.

But a bigger part of me embraced that desire I had to be different from everyone else, from every other woman he'd been with. Because I was so desperate to stand out from his crowd of women. To be the one unlike the others in his eyes.

"You're my fiancé. And I'm on birth control. I think at this point in a relationship we would not be using a condom."

It seemed to be exactly what he wanted to hear, and next thing I knew he was bending just a little bit, and I could feel his cock at my entrance. Then the tip was inside me, and then all of him was thrusting forward, in, and up.

We both grunted as he fed himself in completely.

"Holy shit, Elizabeth. You feel even better than I imagined." He bent his mouth to kiss me again, his hands gripping my breasts like handholds while he bucked into me over and over and over again. Each stroke came fast and deep, stretching and filling me.

I turned my mouth away from him to catch a breath, and he sucked down my neck, murmuring as he did. "So tight. So fucking hot."

Then he got bossy. "Touch yourself. You need to come again."

It felt so good, just having his cock rub inside me, and I was already so drained from the first orgasm. "I can't."

"You have to. I have to make you come again. Touch yourself, or I'm going to stop."

As if he didn't trust me, he took one of his hands off my breasts and used it to direct my hand down to my clit. Then he helped me touch myself, two fingers from him, two fingers from me, rubbing together in my juices, swirling around my sensitive bud. His other hand tweaked at my nipple, pulling it and tugging at it, sending sharp twinges of plea-sure-pain down to my pussy. Then there was the *slap slap slap* from the top of his thighs against the bottom of my ass, and the clink of his belt as it rattled with each thrust. I couldn't come again. But it was all so fucking hot, so goddamn sexy.

And I *was* coming again. Tightening around his cock, pulsing, and keening.

"Just like that," he coaxed. "Fall apart, just like that."

This time when I finished, he turned me toward him and lifted me up so that my legs wrapped around his waist.

"Take me to bed," I said, half begging.

He nodded once. "Whose bed do you want to go to?"

"Yours."

It wasn't just that it was closer, but also, in the midst of all the hormonal fireworks, I was able to rationalize that it would be the bed I could leave when I needed to. And I'd have to leave it eventually.

But I wasn't thinking about that now. Now, I wasn't thinking at all.

Weston's room felt like miles away as he carried me with his cock between us, rubbing against my sensitive clit. Even just after my orgasm, I wanted him back inside me. I knew it was another form of torture, and while it was torturing him as well, it had to be pleasing him more to know what it was doing to me.

We kissed as we walked, little mewling sounds escaping from the back of my throat, sounds of need. Sounds of begging. I begged for mercy. Mercy that I didn't deserve, mercy I prayed he'd give me.

Once in his room, he tossed me onto the mattress and turned on the bedside lamp so I could see him, so he could see me. The bed frame in his room was high off the ground, and after he finished undressing, when he tugged my thighs to bring me to the edge of the bed, we were nearly lined up. I only had to lift my hips slightly to be able to reach him.

I bucked up before he even asked, impatient, greedy.

He chuckled, his dimples mocking me. "More?" he taunted, grazing his fingers across my wet slit. "You already need more?"

I propped myself up on my elbows and stared at him, my eyes saying what my voice was unwilling to. *Please, please. More, more.*

He rubbed the head of his cock against my entrance, teasing me by sticking it just barely inside before pulling out. I lurched forward, trying to get what I craved.

"You can't have it until you ask. Until you tell me what you want. Until you tell me *I'm* what you want." With his hand, he continued to rub up and down my slit, making wide circles around my electric bundle of nerves.

Goddamnit, he was going to make me do it. Why was I so stubborn?

"Give it to me," I uttered. Would that be enough? I put my hand down to where I wanted him, landing on the spot he was purposefully avoiding, but he quickly swatted me away.

"Not good enough. Tell me it's me. Tell me it's my cock you want." He pushed just the tip in again, circling his hips so that I could feel him everywhere around the mouth of my entrance. I gasped, and he pulled out again.

"Fuck," I cried at his absence, my resolve crumbling in the face of my need. "It's you. Your fucking cock, Weston. Goddamnit fucking asshole. Your fucking cock is what I want. Now get it in me."

With a satisfied grunt, he wrapped his arms around my thighs and thrust in hard, deep. He drove into me over and over and over again, showing me how magnificent his body was, how much he wanted me, needed me. I was mesmerized in the moment and swept away at once with waves of pleasure, swept away in watching him, in knowing how much he enjoyed being watched.

He lifted me higher, and my breasts began to bounce uncontrollably with his thrusts. I had the self-conscious urge to cover them up until I realized that Weston's gaze was trained on them, his eyelids half-closed like he was drugged from the erotic sight.

And he had other plans for my hands.

"Play with yourself," he gritted out, directing me to move my fingers to my pussy. "You need to come before I do."

I was already close to the brink; it wouldn't take long. I moved my hand down and only a couple of brushes of my two fingers—up and down, up and down—and then I was exploding, the tightening in my pelvis and my thighs transforming into strong bursts of cold-hot pleasure soaring down my legs into my toes, through my belly and torso, escaping up my throat in a hoarse, raspy cry of murmured curses and words that meant nothing mixed with words that meant everything—Weston's name and God's.

Weston sweetly coaxed me through my total abandonment. "You're so gorgeous when you come apart. So beautiful, baby. Let go. Just like that. You turn me on so much. Just like that." His fingers were digging into my thighs. And he was lifting up my legs higher until his body stuttered, his pelvis stilling against mine, as his face twisted into a new expression of anguish and delight. His orgasm was accompanied with a long wrenching groan that made me shake, its sound so erotic and primal.

Then he was finished.

He collapsed onto the bed beside me. We laid there for several minutes, me half off the bed, both of us on top of the bedspread. Though my body was finally still, my thoughts were now racing, circling so fast I couldn't keep any one thread in view. So I focused on my lungs and air and the in and the out of breathing.

After a few silent minutes, when my heart rate was beginning to settle, he sat, and I sat up with him. Then he stood, and I followed suit, awkward, not knowing how I was supposed to act. He pulled down the bedspread and the sheet, and I turned to leave. What else was there to do? He hadn't said a word to me, and I hadn't said a word to him. I'd never done this before. Never done casual sex. How did it work?

Running away was the easiest solution.

But before I could get too far, he wrapped his arm around my waist and tugged me back. "Where do you think you're going?"

I shrugged, unable to look at his eyes. His beautiful eyes that could always see right into me. "To my room?"

He pulled me closer until I was flush against him, his body warming mine, which was cooling with the sweat that had glistened all over me from our fucking. He kissed the top of my head, wrapping both arms around me now. "But if you go to your room, then I can't fuck you when I wake up in the middle of the night."

I relaxed, leaning into him. Then he wanted me again, as much as I wanted him. I cautiously lifted my gaze to his. "I don't know how to do this," I confessed.

He raised a brow, questioning.

"I've only ever slept with guys who were my boyfriend."

His mouth curled up ever so slightly, and he rubbed his thumb along my bottom lip. "And what would you do with your boyfriend, after you had amazing mind-blowing sex?"

Well, I'd never had amazing mind-blowing sex before. Just regular sex. But I let my mind wander back to those occasions, trying to remember the usual pattern after making love. "I guess . . . whoever would usually just hold me."

Weston let go of me.

I thought for a moment I'd scared him off, but he climbed in the bed and scooted over enough so that there was room for me. Then he reached his arm out inviting me into it. "Come on then. If that's what your boyfriend would do, I imagine that's what your fiancé would do, too."

My breath caught somewhere in my chest, trapped under the sudden expansion of my heart. I managed a quiet, "Okay." Then I turned off the bedside lamp, crawled into his arms, laid my head on his chest, let him wrap himself around me, and fell quickly asleep.

HE WOKE ME in the early hours, climbing on top of me in the dark and easily slipping his cock into my entrance, as though he'd already memorized the way. We spoke no words, the only sounds the quiet gasps and moans of pleasure as he moved inside me, less furious, but still driven. I traced my fingers along his chest and shoulders, admiring every part of his solid form above me. Wanting him even as I had him. Wanting more of him. Wanting all of him.

After we'd both come, he drifted quickly back to sleep, spooning me from behind. I reached out and set the alarm on his bedside table, then lay awake for quite some time listening to the gentle even pattern of his breaths, wondering what all this would mean for us *after*. Wondering what would change.

Realizing nothing would change.

We'd had sex. That was all. But we were still two people tied to each other only through a business arrangement, nothing else, and even though his body felt good inside mine, even though he turned me on, even though he pushed all my buttons in the best ways—and the worst ways—we had no commitment to each other. Not really. And Weston was definitely not the kind of guy who was interested in more than a tumble or two. I wasn't naïve. I couldn't be stupid about him because he'd stuck his dick in me. I'd learned about men like him from my mother.

I'd learned about men like him from my father.

I barely slept after that.

When the alarm went off in the morning, I quickly turned it off, hoping not to wake him, and started to slip out of bed.

But Weston snagged my wrist and tugged me back down.

"Where you going?" he asked like he had last night, his voice rougher with sleep this time.

"I have to take a shower and get ready. My mom's driver will be here in an hour."

He lifted his head from the bed, his brows knit in confusion. "Driver? Are you going somewhere?"

I sighed in exasperation. No, nothing had changed. "My mother's birthday trip. You never listen to me."

He laid his head back down on the pillow. "I remember, I remember. I just forgot." He stroked his fingers along the length of my arm, up and down. "When will you be back? Friday?"

I nodded, trying to ignore how much I loved the feel of his fingers on my skin, how this simple touch could make my insides twist and my pussy slick.

"Let's have dinner then. Friday night." He sat up, simultaneously pulling me to him and kissed me. Briefly, but sweetly. "Okay?"

"Okay. Friday." That meant I had one week to get my head together. One week to try and forget how incredible our night had been.

But how did you forget a night that was unforgettable?

# CHAPTER
# FIFTEEN

*Weston*

**W**HEN I WOKE up later that morning, I could still smell her in my bed.

I could smell her in my room. My room that wasn't even my room—a guest room in her apartment that felt lonely and bare without her. It was an excuse to go to my own place for the weekend, a chance I didn't get often these days.

But without her, it would feel just as empty.

It was fucked up. *I* was fucked up. I'd slept with her, we'd done the deed, we had the sex. She was supposed to be out of my system by now. This wasn't how things were supposed to go.

I went down to the gym in her apartment building and did twice my usual number of everything—twice the arm workout, twice the back workout, double the time on the treadmill. When I headed back up to the apartment, her fancy maid had come in and changed the sheets, made the bed, and sprayed some kind of scented spray around. It no longer smelled like Elizabeth, which made it better. And worse.

Maybe it would just take a couple days to get her worked through my bloodstream. It had been so long since I'd had good sex—sex at all, even—that maybe my body needed time to metabolize the endorphins. I gathered my stuff from her place and went home to bury myself in work for the rest of the weekend. There, I put my own glasses in the sink, and tried not to notice how quiet it was.

Monday morning wasn't any better. She was still in my head, but in new ways. In the past, everything had been my imagination, which had been frustrating because all I could do was fantasize about what it would feel like to touch her skin and hear her moan and see her face when she completely let go.

Finally, I'd gotten to enjoy it all, and that was exhilarating. But I felt like a man who'd been to the moon, and was now trying to readjust to life on earth. It was satisfying and unsatisfying all at once. I found myself equally happy and confused. Jubilant and aching. Longing for what, I couldn't even begin to know.

It wasn't until I was in the elevator headed up to the offices at Reach, and other people were filing in, that I realized I had another dilemma that I hadn't considered yet.

And she was now standing next to me riding up to my floor.

"Morning," Sabrina said, her eyes shifting, looking everywhere but at me.

Now this was awkward.

She was probably embarrassed because of what happened in the closet on Friday night. She'd said it was okay, but it had to be embarrassing, to be standing next to me today. To still have to work with me when I'd rejected her.

And I hadn't only rejected her, I'd gone and slept with another woman the same night. An incredible, sexy, amazing, outspoken woman.

Was this something I needed to tell Sabrina about?

Considering how I'd told her I wasn't going to sleep with Elizabeth, and that I'd suggested we could get together when this whole charade was over—yeah, I probably needed to tell her.

Others got off the elevator on lower floors, and soon we were the only two people left. My gaze focused on the dial as we climbed closer to our destination, wondering if I should do this now or later.

Finally, I burst out, "We need to talk."

She side-eyed me. "If this is about Friday . . ." She gathered her thoughts and started again. "If this is about the restaurant, I don't think there's anything else that needs to be said."

Damn, I'd really stung her hard.

I had to sting her again. It sucked, but it had to be done. "This isn't about the restaurant."

"Oh." She rubbed her hands on her skirt. "Okay."

We arrived on our floor, and I stepped out of the elevator with her, assuming she would follow me to my office. But she lingered behind me.

"If you're free . . . is right now good?"

Sabrina's shoulders slumped. I would have to try to be gentle with her, as she was obviously upset already. "I'm free. I'll just drop off my bag and be there in a few."

I headed to my office, checked in with Roxie, put my briefcase down, unbuttoned my suit jacket, got settled in at my desk. It was about ten minutes later when Sabrina arrived.

"He's more relaxed than he was the other day, but something has him on edge. Good luck."

"I still hear you," I called out to my assistant, while simultaneously admiring how she'd correctly assessed my mood, and in such little time.

I stood up from my desk and walked toward her as Sabrina came in, so that I could close the door. The door was for Donovan—because he'd screamed at me about leaving it open while I'd been with her on Friday. But I was aware that Sabrina might think it was for other reasons, so I made sure to keep the windows clear. I invited her to take a seat and then returned to sit behind my desk.

She sat down and crossed one leg over the other and seemed to be as nervous about this conversation as I was. And no wonder. She was probably expecting that I would give her some consolation, a bunch of reasons why I hadn't been into her, and she'd have to relive the awkward moment all over again.

She hadn't realized yet that it was much, much worse.

She sighed.

I inhaled. "Friday night, after you left the restaurant . . ." I trailed off, not sure quite how to finish that sentence.

God, I didn't know how to fix this.

My silence seemed to urge words out of Sabrina. "Things change, you know, Weston. Things don't always happen the way we plan and—"

"I slept with Elizabeth," I blurted out. Ripping off the Band-Aid. That was the best way to do it.

She sat stunned. "Uh, what?"

I straightened my shoulders and met her eyes. "I slept with Elizabeth. I didn't mean to. I don't know where things are headed in the future, but I thought you deserved the truth."

"I see."

I studied her face, seeking a change in expression, finding none. It wasn't quite the reaction I'd expected. It was too calm. Too controlled.

"Are you upset?"

"No! Not in the least."

Huh.

Shouldn't she be at least a *little* disappointed that I hadn't held out for her? Or perhaps she was just very good at hiding her emotions.

She went on. "We didn't have an arrangement between us. I didn't expect anything from you."

Man, Sabrina was really letting me off the hook here, and I was grateful.

I grabbed the stapler from the corner of my desk, needing something for my hands to do. "I realize that, but I gave you the impression that we had something together when you moved here." I pushed the stapler down several times, wasting a bunch of staples. "It's unfair to you that Elizabeth and I. . . ."

I searched for the right words to untangle the mess I'd made. Of my desk. Of the situation. Of my life.

Sabrina narrowed her gaze, watching me closely as I returned the stapler to its original position. "So you and Elizabeth . . . ?"

It was obvious she was asking if we were a thing now.

"No. God, no." I'd answered too quickly. I needed to think about it. I picked up my pen and started flipping it back and forth between my fingers. "I mean." *Were* we a thing? We were engaged. We had an arrangement. "I don't know. It's complicated."

*Complicated.* That was too simple of a word. It was more than complicated, actually. It was knotty. It was convoluted. It was all I could think about.

Sabrina sat back in her chair and folded her arms across her chest. "So . . . What does this mean for the pool? I had good money on you holding out."

"You . . . you what?"

She shrugged, then grinned. "I'm joking. Any bet I would have placed seemed to be against my better interest."

I dropped the pen and put both palms flat on the desk. "But you're really okay with this situation?"

She smiled again. "I am." Her smile faded, and I tensed. "Actually, I slept with someone this weekend too."

I sat up straighter. This was . . . unexpected.

She paused to take a breath. "I slept with Donovan."

The air suddenly felt thick between us, my eyes squinting at her, my blood feeling hot, and not in the sexy way.

"Uh. Say something?" she prodded.

"I'm trying to decide if I'm jealous or if this relieves me of my guilt." I was also trying to decide if sleeping with a girl I was still entangled with made Donovan a giant douchecanoe. Well, more giant than I already gave him credit for.

She reached across the desk and playfully punched my lower arm. "It relieves you of your guilt. Jerk."

I nodded. "Donovan, huh?" I inhaled, trying to calm whatever fury was stirring inside me and nodded again. "I have to admit—I didn't see that coming."

But I hadn't seen much of anything besides Elizabeth in the last several weeks. Correction, last several months. Time was flying by, and I was spending all of it with the woman I was soon going to marry.

So I couldn't really say if Donovan was being a bad friend or a good friend. Was he looking after Sabrina? Helping her feel more at home in the city, less lonely, less rejected? Was he really interested in her? Or was he being a fucking prick, telling me I couldn't have her, and then banging her to prove it?

Whatever it was, I was cool with it on Sabrina's end. She was content with her one-night stand, which she insisted it was, as we talked more. And she couldn't know about all the layers of baggage between me and Donovan.

So good for her. And maybe even good for them.

Definitely good for me and Sabrina. It felt like whatever we'd had was resolved and done. It was probably the most grown-up way I'd ever ended a relationship in my life, much more mature than the dodge and delete method I'd perfected over the years.

If only dealing with the other woman in my life could be as easy.

THE REST OF the week sauntered by in a state of unease. Each minute ticked by slowly; each hour seemed agonizingly long. Before I'd slept with Elizabeth, she'd been a distraction at work, creeping into my thoughts while I tried to concentrate on what I needed to at the office. I'd often been consumed with my anger, my irritation, and my desire.

After I'd slept with her?

I was twice as consumed. Twice as agonized. Each night now, I tossed and turned, unable to sleep, even after jerking off. It was like before I'd been so horny and filled with lust, and now I was in need of something else. Something that no amount of alcohol or work or time in the gym or staring at my graphic novels could fill or replace. I just wanted to talk to her, to fight with her.

I missed her.

Jesus, I'd never missed a woman in my life. What the hell had she done to me?

By Friday I was so wrapped up in this new amazing-terrible-wonderful-irritating emotion inside of me that I was anxious for her to return that night. Nervous to see her again, but anxious for it nonetheless.

In desperation, I stormed into Nate's office over lunch.

"You said it would make it better," I said accusingly as I walked in.

He cocked his head at me, setting his deli sandwich onto his desk, which was set at standing position. He gestured at the chairs stationed by the windows, indicating that I should take a seat. I strolled over and sat down in one of them, my foot bouncing as I unbuttoned my suit jacket.

He strolled over and sat down in the seat opposite of me. "I take it you and Elizabeth . . ." He let the silence fill in the blank.

"I thought you could tell. You said you'd be able to tell." I was feeling grumpy, grumpy at Nate specifically since he was the one who'd suggested that sleeping with Elizabeth was the right thing to do, and though I didn't regret it, it really hadn't seemed to fix anything.

"Oh, I can tell. You've been much happier." He reconsidered. "Or, you were earlier in the week. Now it seems you've gotten yourself riled up again. Want to tell me what's going on?"

I bent over and leaned my elbows on my knees, noticing they were both bouncing now, and tried to put this problem into words. "Well, we did it, like you said we should. It was supposed to get her out of my system. It was supposed to get me over her. But it hasn't changed anything. I'm still just as fucked up about this. She's been out of town all week long, and I'm still thinking about her. She's everywhere. I can't get her out of my damn head."

"Uh huh."

"I'm miserable." I shook my head. "Except at the same time, I'm not, because I keep remembering that night and all the . . . things . . . and the . . . ways . . ." I could dish about sex as well as the next guy, but it didn't seem appropriate to dish about Elizabeth. "And remembering it makes me feel all weird and . . . good. And shit."

Nate nodded. "Right."

"I know what I have to do, though," I said, the idea coming to me suddenly.

"Of course you do. What is it?" Nate asked patiently, and it didn't escape me that this felt an awful lot like the therapy sessions I'd tried a couple of times a few years back when I'd first realized my father was an asshat. Minus the rage and the overpriced bill.

And I'd just had a bigger breakthrough in Nate's office than anything I could have discovered from that stuffy psychiatrist.

"I have to have sex with her again." I jumped up and started pacing the room. This was brilliant, and obviously the right answer. We had to continue to be together through the engagement anyway, and of course, this had been why I had been worked up all week. Because I didn't know how to deal with the after-things, with women I wouldn't bang again after we'd had sex once.

So the solution here was to just keep doing it. That hadn't really occurred to me as an option for some reason.

Perhaps because living together and sleeping together with the same woman—a woman who was wearing a ring that I put on her finger—felt an awful lot like a real relationship, the kind I'd always managed to avoid.

"All right," Nate laughed harder than I thought he needed to. "How does Elizabeth feel about this? Do you think she's open to continuing?"

I shrugged, not really seeing why she *wouldn't* be open to it. It had been pretty damn good sex. "I haven't talked to her since."

Nate's jaw went slack, his eyes wide. "You haven't talked to her since you slept with her? Not at *all*? Not even a text message?"

My pacing slowed and I began to feel a new sense of dread. Shit. Had I fucked this up already?

"Look, I don't usually talk to the girls afterwards. They are usually texting *me*." Which begged the question—why *hadn't* she texted me? Had it not been as good for her as I'd thought? Had I done something wrong? Did she . . . regret it somehow?

Nate frowned and shook his head. "I don't know, man. Women really like to be reassured after that kind of thing. Especially if you want to have another shot with them."

I sank back down in the seat across from him. "Shit, Nate." I ran a hand through my hair. "Is it too late now? She comes back tonight. We're supposed to have dinner. What do I do?"

Nate nodded, thinking. "Your best plan is to make it seem like the space was part of your strategy. And then reassure her. *Reassure her, Weston*," he repeated. "Make sure she knows she's special to you."

It was my turn to frown. Special to me? I didn't like that. To be certain, I'd never wanted to continue sleeping with a woman like I wanted to continue sleeping with her, so that made her special in a way. But I didn't want to give her the wrong idea or anything.

This was still a business arrangement.

Nate seemed to sense my train of thought. "You don't have to tell her you're in love with her. Just let her know that you had a good time with her. That you're not just using her for her body. Are you using her for her body?"

In the week that she been gone, I had thought about Elizabeth's body a whole hell of a lot. The things I wanted to do to it, the things I'd already done to it, the things I wanted her body to do to mine. But I'd also thought about conversations I wanted to have with her. Things I wished I'd said, things I was sure she'd argue with, but I'd made up counter-arguments, and then made up fascinating ways to make up after we argued about it.

"No. I can honestly say I'm not just using her for her body." Why did that feel like such a gut-wrenching admission?

"I know," Nate said, again. The therapist who saw all. "Just making sure *you* knew. Now make sure *she* knows."

I left Nate's office and immediately started composing a text message as I walked back to my own corner of the floor, worried I was already too late. Still on for dinner tonight? We could meet at Gaston's at seven.

Nervous, I hit SEND, regretting it immediately. Elizabeth liked making decisions. I should have given her the choice of restaurant.

I stopped in the middle of the hall, halfway between Nate's office and mine, and sent another message. Or we can go somewhere else. Tell me where and I'll make the reservation.

I sent it, shaking my head at myself for not taking care of this earlier in the week. Donovan owned Gaston's—I could always get in there last minute. Finding reservations last minute elsewhere was going to be tough. There were only a few strings I could pull through some clients. Some other strings I could pull if I called my father.

I didn't want to call my father.

But she responded before I had to get too worked up about other options. Gaston's is fine. I'll see you then.

Immediately I felt better.

Except then another text came through. Could you give me Elizabeth's number?

Clarence Sheridan.

Why the fuck did he want her number? Was he still into her? If I gave it to him, would he call her? Would they get back together?

"You're setting a great example for the staff," Donovan said sarcastically, startling my gaze up from my screen. "Maybe if you were more focused on your work than your phone, we'd actually get some stuff done around here."

It was a typical snide Donovan remark, one that I would usually let roll off my back, but I was stressed about this latest text, and he'd pushed me to my limit. He'd been playing me like I was his puppet, telling me what to do and when to do it, telling me who I could sleep with and who I couldn't, treating me like I was a pawn on his chessboard. That was annoying enough, but to get razzed about it too was pushing me over the edge.

On top of that, he still hadn't told me about sleeping with Sabrina, and that pushed a bunch of emotional buttons that I had yet to face. Not the least of which was—why hadn't he confided in me about it? Why did I have to find out about it from her?

I'd been so irked by his lack of disclosure, I'd purposefully not told him about sleeping with Elizabeth.

And I was still irked. More than irked.

So instead of shrugging off his asshole comment like I normally would, I looked him right in the eye. "So, you and Sabrina, huh? Maybe it's *your* distraction that's compromising office production."

I left him in the hall before he could reply, knowing Donovan hated it when he didn't get the last word.

Back in my office, I made a decision. I'd waited too long to take control of my own life. I'd let others run the show while I'd sat back playing whatever cards I was dealt.

Well, no more.

It was time for me to be the dealer.

Starting with Elizabeth.

I would take Nate's advice—make a plan, find the words, let her know that I wanted things to go on.

And I dealt with Clarence's text the same way I dealt with all annoying messages that came in on my phone, usually from *my* ex-lovers, not someone else's—I deleted it and never thought about it again.

# CHAPTER
# SIXTEEN

*Elizabeth*

I RETURNED TO Manhattan, feeling cool and calm and confident. Relaxed. A week without Weston had cleared my head. I was
a new woman, pampered and refreshed.

At least, that's what I'd told myself through the entire car ride home.

All of it was bullshit. It was evident even in the way that I had dressed
for tonight's dinner with Weston. My dress was a load of mixed messages.
I'd intended to wear something smart and modest. Instead, here I was
in a low-cut black sexy mid-length. It cinched in my waist and hugged
my hips, creating a perfect hourglass. While it didn't scream seductress,
it was definitely one of the more provocative outfits I owned.

Maybe I just wanted to remind Weston what he'd had. What he
couldn't have again. That's what I said to my reflection in the mirror by
the coat check at Gaston's as I double-checked my appearance.

I turned to the host, already fifteen minutes late. "Are you ready to
be seated, Ms. Dyson?" he asked. "Mr. King is waiting for you."

I wasn't ready. I would never be ready. "Yes, please."

He took me inside the restaurant, toward the tables near the windows. Gaston's was fine dining, and the view was spectacular, since the
restaurant was located at the top of the building on Fifty-Ninth Street,
just across from Central Park which was framed by the city itself. It was
a romantic spot, and as we approached the table, Weston stood for me,

handsome in his business suit, his dimpled grin greeting me.

Butterflies took off in my stomach at the sight of that smile; it wasn't a reaction I could control. So I smiled back. As the host pulled out my chair, Weston leaned forward and kissed me.

"Now that's a way to say hello," the host teased.

"I haven't seen my fiancée in a week," Weston said, his eyes never leaving me. "I've missed her."

The butterflies turned into an avalanche of snow at his words. His endearment wasn't just intoxicating, it didn't just make me feel fluttery inside—it made me feel overwhelmed, like I was being crushed with the weight of something bigger than I could handle.

Was it even real? Had he really missed me? Or was this part of the show we were putting on?

I was trembling as I took my seat, grateful there was already wine on the table. Weston reached to pour me a glass before the host could offer, so with no other task to complete, the man left, and we were alone.

I smoothed my napkin on my lap and grabbed a hunk of bread, eager to keep my hands busy as Weston finished filling my glass.

"How was Connecticut?" he asked, setting the bottle down as I took a sip of my wine. It was white and crisp, like the autumn air had been outside.

But here inside, the air was warm, and the chardonnay felt good going down. "It was relaxing. We did a lot of relaxing." And a lot of thinking. A lot of thinking about Weston and his lips and his tongue and his body. His body inside mine.

"I didn't reach out, because I thought you might want space."

"I still had to share the suite with my mother. And she's messier than you. Though we had housekeeping every day, so that made it bearable."

"That's not what I meant by needing space."

I swallowed and glanced up at him. "You mean because we had sex." I'd wondered if my phone wasn't getting texts initially when I hadn't heard from him, but then I'd gotten one from Marie asking about my mother, and another from a college friend.

I shook my head. I couldn't feel that bad about his silence, because

I didn't try to reach out to Weston either. Then I recited the words I'd said over and over and over again to myself this last week. "Nothing's changed."

At the same time, he said, "Everything's changed."

We stared at each other, both of us caught off-guard by the other's answer. *Everything's changed.* My heart began to race for no reason except for those two words.

Weston looked almost hurt by what I'd said. "What do you mean nothing's changed?" he asked, his brows furrowed.

I looked around to make sure that we were in a private enough section that no one could hear us. We were. "Because nothing has. We're still just pretending for the sake of our respective businesses. We're still only in a *fake* relationship. You still don't want to live in my apartment all the time. You're still insistent that you want to split our time between the two places. You still won't get a damn maid."

I looked at him as though I had proven my point, which I felt I had, and yet I went on. "You still have yet to tell me what's going on with your family."

He waved his hand, stopping me from going on. "My family has nothing to do with anything. They are not a part of this. And it's irritating that you keep bringing it up."

"And *I'm* still going to be irritated every time you mention Sabrina's name."

He glared at me. "I was a dick about that, and I admitted it. But she works with me. I'm going to mention her name—"

"Look, we're still fighting, even." Nothing had changed.

"This isn't fighting," he said.

"What is this, then?"

"Foreplay?" He grinned, his eyes gleaming mischievously.

"It's bickering, like we always bicker," I said, trying to ignore the images that last comment brought up and how they made my legs shake. "How can you say things are different?"

"Yes, yes. All that. Still the same." I was suddenly moving closer to him and realized he was pulling me nearer with his foot wrapped around the leg of my chair. He didn't stop until we were side-by-side instead of angled toward each other, until we were looking out the window into the quiet darkness that was Central Park.

He put his arm on the back of my chair, his mouth near my ear. "But now," he said, his breath tickling my neck, sending electric shocks through my veins. "We can fuck."

I was suddenly hot everywhere, and it wasn't from the wine. My cheeks felt red and flushed. I turned my face toward him and our mouths were so close we could kiss.

"You want to . . . ? Again . . . ?" I tightened my glutes and thighs as I asked, as though that could hold the want and desire inside me, as though that could keep my panties from getting wet. I'd tried so hard in the week I'd been away from him not to imagine another night of passion. Tried not to relive the one night we'd had.

But every time the lights had gone out and my eyes had closed, he was all I could see, and I swear I had his touch memorized. Goose pimples would sprout up just by thinking of him. By remembering his mouth on my collarbone, his lips along my shoulders, on my breasts. It was absolute torture to share a room with my mother. All my masturbation had to be done in the shower, and with the insane amount of lust that was inspired by my daydreams of Weston, I'd found myself making excuses to take more than one a day.

But in no time during any of that fantasizing had I ever thought he would want to do it again. He was a player. Weren't those guys only into one-time-per-woman deals?

I felt his fingers on my shoulder now, on the opposite side from where my head was turned. Felt his touch grazing down my bare arm. He looked me directly in my eyes.

"Do you *not* want to do it again?" he asked, curiously, as though he hadn't even considered that was a possibility.

"I didn't think *you* would want to do it again," I informed him honestly.

"Oh, I want to do it again, Elizabeth. I really, really want to do it again. It's all I can think about."

My breath caught, and I pulled my head back, studying his face to be sure he was telling the truth. Everything in his expression said he was sincere. "I didn't know."

He moved in closer, his lips brushing against mine. "I'm sorry I didn't make it clear. I should have texted you. I should've called."

I really hadn't expected that from him, but now that he'd suggested it, I wanted to know more. "What would you have said?"

He brushed his nose against my skin down to my earlobe and said in a hushed voice. "I would've told you how much I thought about you all week. How blue my balls were over you." His hand was on my knee, moving higher onto my bare thigh. "I would've told you how I couldn't stop thinking about touching you. I would've told you how hard you make me. I'm hard right now. I need to know if you're wet."

I was, and his hand was sliding higher on the inside of my thigh, about to find out the answer for himself. It was so fucking hot and so amazing and I wanted him to keep going, wanted his fingers to touch me and find out . . . but—

"Wait. Stop." I recognized the feeling of panic before I could even understand the reasons why.

Fortunately, Weston was a decent man and he pulled away, immediately taking his hand off of me, and setting it back in his own lap. He left his other hand on the chair behind me, but he gave me space. Too much space. I missed how close he had been just a moment before.

But now the waiter was here asking if we were ready to order, and I couldn't even think—I was still wanting Weston's hands on me and wishing he was inside me—I couldn't be bothered with the daily soup and fish specials.

"We're going to need a moment," Weston said, reading me. "In fact, I'll signal you when we're ready."

The waiter nodded and shuffled off to his other tables. There was a beat of silence, and I took a swallow of wine, trying to figure out what I was going to say to Weston to get him to touch me again. Also, how not to panic this time when he did.

How was I going to explain to him what was going on inside my head when I couldn't even explain it to myself?

Thankfully, he asked the right questions, the kinds of questions that helped me think, helped me sort myself out.

"Can I ask why? No judgment. Are you not into me? Or is it that we're in public? Because it's okay if you're not into that like I am. Just because it turns me on, doesn't mean it has to turn you on."

I swiveled my face toward him. "That's just it. It *does* turn me on. A lot. I think I kind of made fun of you at first when I realized that was something you're into, and then I realized that it was really awesome."

He nodded. "Really awesome." He paused, and his face changed. "Then it's me. You don't want me touching you."

"Weston, I can't . . . I don't even know how to put into words how much I want you to touch me." I looked down at my hands, too embarrassed to face him for this. "This doesn't make any sense to you, I'm sure. I wish I knew how to explain. See, it's one thing if Darrell thinks all I'm good for is spreading my legs. If he thinks I'm slutty it doesn't matter. And it really doesn't matter if most of the Internet thinks I'm slutty, either, though. I mean it kind of does. Since I'm trying to build a reputation of being a classy woman and everything. One step at a time, I guess."

I snuck a glance up at him and saw he was listening to me carefully. "I know the Internet isn't here right now, that it's just me and you. And that's the problem, because I really do care what *you* think of me. It really matters to me that you respect me and that you think that I'm capable of being this thing that I'm trying to be."

Out of the blue, tears stung my eyes, and my throat got tight.

"You're the one who's been teaching me and building me up for this, and if you don't think I'm a classy person, if you only think that I'm worthy of spreading my legs, then—"

He cut me off. "I respect the fuck out of you." His hand was back on my knee, but comforting this time, not attempting to make a move. "Are you saying you're worried that having sex with me takes that away? That if I find out you're into kinky things, I'll think you're less brainy?"

It *was* what I was saying, but I couldn't trust my voice. So I just stared at my hands, twisting them around each other.

"Did you know the minute I saw you, I couldn't breathe? I lost all ability to speak. I didn't even know words anymore. It wasn't even because you looked amazing, which you did, by the way. It was because I could tell you were the smartest person in the room. Do you know how hot that was? I am *so* attracted to you, Elizabeth. I have been from the minute you walked into that Reach lounge, because I could tell you were a woman who knew what she was after, a confident woman, a smart woman. And the way you could just bulldoze Donovan? That took some serious skill. I have mad respect for you. I spent that entire meeting hiding my boner."

Air stuttered into my lungs. I burned with the relief of it.

"And every time you speak, every time you argue with me—I wouldn't put up a fight if I didn't enjoy hearing what you had to say." He leaned in close again, his lips brushing my neck. "The only reason I want to touch you right now so fucking bad is because I respect you."

Under the table, I took his hand and guided it up under my dress toward the damp spot on the crotch of my panties. I let go of his hand once he was where I wanted him, and grabbed on tight to the chair edge while he slipped his fingers inside my panties to find my clit under the hood of skin where it was hiding, plump and aroused from his words.

I could feel him smile at my ear. "So wet. You want this so bad." He massaged expertly in fine circles, small and then wide, clockwise then counter. "You're so disciplined and strong, your eyes on the goal. Not even giving in to your own pleasure when you think it might take you away from what you want in the end. If you had any idea how much this stuff fucking turns me on, Lizzie . . . I wish I had half your ambition. Your drive." I opened my legs wider, making it easier for him to dip his fingers down my slit and back up. "I wish I had your brain. You're the total package—sex and smarts all in one. The sexiest thing I've ever had underneath me. The sexiest thing I've ever had in my bed, in my mouth, around my cock."

I focused on the cars driving through the park, the dots of light beneath us as my orgasm built. Each compliment, each line of praise was as much of a turn on, as arousing as what he was doing with his hands, and it wasn't long before I was exploding, right there in the restaurant, coming from just his whispered words in my ear and his thumb on my clit. I tried to swallow my gasps, tried not to make a single noise. Weston took his free hand and covered my mouth to help stifle the sound, and I turned my face toward his, locked my eyes on his baby-blue gaze, and for the first time in my twenty-five years—as I was climaxing in a French restaurant owned by Donovan Kincaid—it occurred to me that maybe men didn't just hurt women after all.

"Can we go home now? I'm not really in the mood to eat anything," I said, when I'd come down, desperate for another orgasm with him inside me.

"The only thing I'm hungry for is you."

And for the second Friday in a row, we skipped The Sky Launch and stayed in.

# CHAPTER
## SEVENTEEN

*Weston*

"YOU GREW UP out here, not in the city." Elizabeth made it sound more like a statement than a question as I pulled into the driveway at my parent's house in Larchmont, probably because I'd told her this already.

"Yep." It was Thursday, nearly a week after she'd come back from her spa vacation, and we were taking another trip, this time together and just for a day. I'd borrowed one of Donovan's cars to make the ninety-minute drive out here to the suburbs. It seemed stupid to use Elizabeth's driver to come to my childhood home, and even more stupid to take a train, especially if we planned to lug a bunch of crap back with us.

"And your dad did that commute every day of your life?" she asked as I put the Tesla into park in the circle drive.

"Ten hour work days, five days a week. He had a driver so he worked in the car both to and from. He still does it. Mom says his days are shorter now." I turned off the car and looked over at my fiancée. "Mom wanted the house. It was the price she had to pay. At least that's what she always said to me."

For all her talk of sacrifice, I'd learned it had a limit.

But we hadn't come out here to get worked up about the past.

"Let's do this," I said to myself more than to Elizabeth, then opened the door of the car and ran around to her side to open hers. Together, we walked up to the front of the Georgian-style house. I pulled out my spare key—it was strange that I had one, and not strange, too. After all, I'd grown up in this house. And yet now it felt like it belonged to somebody else, like I was an intruder sneaking up on it.

With sweaty hands, I entered my code into the security pad, praying it still worked, and when the light went green, I put my key in the door, and we slipped inside.

Once we were both in the house, I took Elizabeth's coat, then peeled off my own and hung them both in the hall closet. I couldn't shake how nervous and uncomfortable I felt being here. Being here with *her*. There were so many ghosts from the past, memories of a lifetime spent in these rooms. Thankfully, we didn't need to take a tour of the grounds and visit them. It was a straight shot to where I was headed today—through the gallery, past the living room, into the library.

I grabbed Elizabeth's hand and started tugging her in the direction I wanted to go, when Linda, our housekeeper and my former nanny, appeared in the archway coming from the dining room.

"Weston," she greeted me affectionately, her Swedish accent still lingering after all these years. I let go of Elizabeth's hand so she could hug me. "What are you doing here? It's been so long. You nearly gave me a heart attack. I heard someone walking through the house. I thought we had a prowler."

I kissed her on the cheek. "Just me. I didn't tell anyone I was coming. It was last minute. Needed to grab some things from the library." I turned toward Elizabeth. "Linda, this is my—" I paused. I'd introduced her as my fiancée to everyone in town, including my parents, but in some ways I was closer to Linda than I was to them. It felt weird to tell this lie to the woman who had gotten me through both AP European history and my first wet dream.

My former caretaker finished the sentence for me. "I've heard much about your fiancée, Elizabeth. I'm right to assume that you're her?"

"That's me," Elizabeth said, smiling nervously. She held her hand out to shake, but Linda drew her in for a hug that Elizabeth did well in tolerating.

"I'm so glad to meet you. A little heartbroken that it hasn't happened sooner." Linda glared at me in the way she always had when I was younger, the glare she used when she wanted me to know she was disappointed in me without actually saying the words.

"Well, you've met her now. You can stop with the guilt trips." I snagged Elizabeth's hand again and started toward the library. We were already going to be here all day, and I didn't want to risk staying any later than we had to. "I don't mean to cut this short, but we have, you know . . ."

"Always busy, that one," Linda said, sticking her tongue out. "Go on into your library, and I'll bring you some coffee and cookies."

"Thank you, Linda. You're the best." I turned forward, pulling Elizabeth closer to me as we headed to the library.

"She seems nice. Pretty, too," she said, looking back to where Linda had just disappeared into the kitchen.

"Oh, you can't even imagine how many times I spanked off to her when I was growing up." Confessions of a former horny teenager.

And then we were in the library, the reason for our trip to Larchmont and my day off from Reach.

"This is it," I announced.

It wasn't that the library was so spectacular. It was that all my books from school were still here, including all my textbooks, complete with the notes I'd taken in business school. That wasn't the kind of thing that you could just buy on Amazon and have shipped to you. I'd tried to keep her out of this piece of my life, but so much of the stuff I wanted to teach Elizabeth was here on these shelves.

And the more time I spent with her, the weirder she found that separation, so this seemed like a good idea.

My parents had always believed that sharing was what you did with books. And I did rightfully own a lot of the ones that were here already, so it wasn't like I was doing something wrong by showing up and grabbing what I wanted. But I had purposefully not announced my intentions, afraid my mother would have skipped her weekly bridge game, or worse—that she would've told my father, and he would be here when we arrived.

No, this was perfect. A quiet house, with no one but me and Elizabeth and Linda.

"This is really nice," she said, trailing her fingers along the spines of books that lined the bookshelves as she walked along them. "My father had a library like this in his château in France. He never let me touch those, though."

She drew a book out of the section dedicated to Peter Drucker and flipped through the pages. "And you're serious that I can take whatever I want? Your parents won't miss them?"

"My father will only be pissed if you take any of his Steve Berry's or Dan Brown's. Other than that, he won't even notice." I headed toward the wall that I knew contained my textbooks from college and started pulling the books I wanted to take. *Business Ethics: Concepts and Cases*, *Consumer Behavior*, *Anatomy of a Ponzi Scheme*. I laughed to myself, finding the last one on the shelf.

My father could've written that book.

I flipped open my old earmarked copy of *Business Law* and sunk down in the oversized leather armchair while Elizabeth collected books she was interested in. Thirty minutes went by, then forty, and soon I found I was not reading at all, but staring out the window at the bay in the backyard. It was a beautiful house to grow up in, a beautiful life that I had taken for granted.

It was the kind of place I liked taking girls home to, to impress them, the kind of place that Elizabeth was already accustomed to. The kind of place where she deserved to live. I felt an ache between my ribs because I couldn't give it to her, which was dumb, because I wasn't trying to give her any life at all.

And even if I were, I hated the kind of sacrifices this house had required. Yes, my mother loved her maid and her groundskeepers and her water view—at the cost of only seeing her husband two days a week. At the cost of everything he did during his time away from this house.

Reach would one day be that successful, as big as King–Kincaid had been for my father and Donovan's father. I believed it, not just because I believed in myself and our company, but because Donovan had the skill of not letting anything go any way except exactly how he'd planned. And he planned for us to be successful. So it would happen.

But even when it did, I didn't want to only come home to see Elizabeth on the weekend, only see our children from the doorway of the bedroom while they slept in their beds every night.

Why this fantasy had Elizabeth's name in it, I had no idea. Except that she was the one currently wearing my ring and playing my bride-to-be.

Anyway, I guessed I'd rather live in the city. I could raise kids in the city, as tricky as that was. Donovan had grown up that way, and he'd turned out . . . well, he'd turned out.

And I was a long way away from having kids, so all of this was ridiculous overthinking, inspired by being in my childhood home with someone who had me talking about weddings all the time.

There was a bustle in the house all of a sudden, voices coming from the vicinity of the kitchen. Linda had already brought us the coffee and snacks, and a glance at the clock on the wall said it was about time for my mother to be home.

Elizabeth heard it too, and looked over at me expectantly.

"I'll go tell my mother we're here," I said, getting up before she could offer to join me.

I left the room, closing the library doors behind me, afraid that whatever conversation I had with my mother might escalate quickly, and I didn't want to disturb Elizabeth and her studying.

As I'd suspected, I found my mom in the kitchen, filling up a glass of ice water from the dispenser in the refrigerator. She looked over her shoulder at me, then back to the task at hand.

"Linda said you were here," she said crisply, obviously upset. "If you'd told me you were coming I would have had lunch prepared."

"Lunch wasn't necessary, Mom. We didn't come for food. We came for books." I stuck my hands in my jean pockets, avoiding the temptation to reach out to her physically.

She turned around toward me and took a swallow of her water, then put it down on the counter between us. I'd left that barrier on purpose.

"Books. You came for books?" It seemed like she was sorting through a lot of thoughts in her head, a lot more than she was speaking out loud.

"I'm helping Elizabeth brush up on her business skills, and there's a lot of textbooks I left here."

She nodded. "Your father's not going to be happy he missed you. Are you coming home for Thanksgiving at least?"

I hadn't spent a holiday in this house for more than three years. It was amazing that she kept asking. Amazing how I still got choked up when I told her, "No."

"Your father won't be happy about that either," she said, sharply.

I looked out the window and caught a heron flying, tracked its flight with my gaze. It was easier than watching her when I said, "Yep. I'm sure he'll be disappointed."

I knew she wanted me to offer her more, but I didn't have more to give her. It was hard enough being on her turf. Couldn't she see that?

When I turned my head back to her, she was patting the kitchen counter with her hand, soundlessly. Our eyes met, and hers were brimming with tears.

*Jesus. Not today, Mom. Please.*

But I didn't say it. I didn't say anything. I let her talk instead. Let her say the things pressing against her heart, pushing those tears to the surface.

"I understand why you're upset, Weston. I do. I didn't for a long time, but I do now. I just don't understand why you're so upset with *me*."

"I'm almost *more* upset with you than with him," I said, exasperated. She *didn't* understand. She didn't understand at all.

"Why? What did I ever do except—"

I lurched forward and placed my hands on the counter. "You encouraged him, Mom. You *begged* him to do the wrong thing. You could have convinced him—"

"I couldn't live without him! We would've lost everything. Our house. Your trust fund. The company, Weston. Everything. Don't you get it?"

The sacrifice was too great to pay. That's what she was saying.

Too great for *her* to pay, anyway. She didn't care that someone else had to pay it for her.

Well, I did.

"I came for the books, Mom," I said, pushing off the counter, stepping away. "I didn't come for this conversation."

I headed back into the library and shut the doors behind me when I was inside. Then I locked them, afraid my mother would come in after us. I didn't need any more of her tears and her heartache. Her excuses.

Elizabeth looked up from her book, but the look I gave her said I wasn't in the mood to talk, and she went right back to reading.

My mother did try the door handles, but she didn't knock when she was unable to open them. Ten minutes later, though, a text came across my phone from my sister, Noelle. Mom says you're not coming home for Thanksgiving.

I'm spending it with Elizabeth's family, I texted back quickly. It was manipulative of my mother to get my little sister involved.

I was really hoping to meet her!

You'll meet her at the wedding.

I felt bad about not telling Noelle the truth about my arrangement with Elizabeth. I knew I'd tell her eventually, maybe even at the wedding if I got a moment alone with her. If not, sometime later. There was a decade between us, but I liked the kid. And if she told my parents, I guess I'd have to live with that. It didn't really matter if they knew.

"You're texting Sabrina, aren't you?" Elizabeth said from where she was curled up on the couch.

I let my gaze shift over to her, a grin playing on my lips. I hadn't told her about the shift in my relationship with Sabrina to just friends yet. It was too fun to let her stew with jealousy.

"It was my sister," I said.

"Oh. I was sure it was Sabrina because of the way your face got all broody. She's usually the one who has you riled up."

No, it was usually Elizabeth who had me riled up, and she knew it. She was taunting me. Even after a week of sex every night, it still seemed poking and prodding was our foreplay.

I didn't mind at all.

But we were still in this house and my head was still in the other room with my mother, and I needed to untangle the knots in my psyche before I could play naughty with her.

"I have a business ethics question to pose to you," I said, suddenly wanting to tackle this from another angle.

"Should companies have a no-fraternization rule amongst managers and their employees?"

She stretched her legs out on the ground in front of her. "I do think that would be a good policy. I'm surprised Reach doesn't have such a rule in place."

I laughed. "Donovan and I are co-CEOs and all three vice presidents are dirty, filthy men. The only one of them who might have suggested a no-fraternization policy just banged my next-in-command." Maybe I wasn't too interested in keeping the information to myself after all.

Elizabeth's brows rose in shock as she figured out who I must be talking about. "Donovan slept with Sabrina? That's surprising." She twisted her lip in that awkward cute way she often did. "Were you jealous?"

"As far as I know, it was only a one-night thing. Don't get too excited." She'd kicked her shoes off earlier, and her toenails, crimson from her trip to the spa the week before, tempted me. I reached down and grabbed one of her feet and set it in my lap, massaging her sole. "Anyway, that wasn't the ethics question I wanted to pose."

"You can ask me anything as long as you're doing that," she said, sinking into my massage. She closed the book she'd been reading and tossed it aside. "Hit me."

"So let's say you're a major shareholder of Dyson media, and you also participate on the Board of Directors. And then the board votes for you to take a role as an officer. You're responsible for maintaining the best interest of the corporation. Not only are you actively involved in the day-to-day operations, but you also report to the shareholders."

"Once I inherit, I'll hold seventy-five percent of the ownership. The majority of the shareholders will be *me*."

"Right, but even if you are the majority, you're still responsible to everyone."

"I know, I know," she said defensively. "Do you think I don't listen to anything you say in these little lessons of yours the last few months? Sure doesn't seem like *Darrell* acts like he's responsible to one-hundred percent of the owners. But go on."

"There's a company scandal. Something that goes deep on many levels. It's maybe not illegal, but definitely unethical." I tried to be vague in the scenario. I didn't want her to assume I had any reason for being specific.

She ticked her head to the side. "Do I know about the scandalous behavior as it's going on? Or only after it's discovered?"

"You know from the very beginning," I said moving on to her other foot.

"Well, that doesn't sound like me. I would've nipped it in the bud as soon as I knew about this terrible behavior." She moaned at the end of her sentence as I found a particularly sensitive spot on her foot, and my dick went semi-hard.

And that was the problem with this proposed situation—Elizabeth never would be involved with a scandal like this to begin with.

"But just say you were. For whatever reason, you were convinced it was the right way to go, and then it becomes not the right way to go. Someone's going to have to take the fall for it, because the news gets out and everyone knows Dyson Media is involved with this really terrible scandal."

"So is that the question? If I take the fall for it?" She stared up at me with her big beautiful eyes blinking, so brilliant she could see to the end of my scenario.

"Yeah. That's the question. Do you take the fall or do you let some-one within the company take the fall?" My heart started pounding in my chest, my hands felt sweaty as they rubbed the inside sole of Elizabeth's foot. It was a stupid, silly example of a question, and I was placing all this weight on it. I was desperate for Elizabeth's answer to give me some sort of absolution, and I didn't even need absolution. I felt good in my decision. Felt good in my stance.

I did want to hear *her* stance, though.

She tilted her head again, her eyes lifting upward and to the left as she considered. "I suppose I'd have to let somebody in the company take the fall for me. Which is terrible. And I feel god-awful about saying that." She wrapped her hands around her belly as though it gave her an ache.

I stared at her hard. "Why?" Did my voice tremble when I asked? "Why would you let someone else take the fall?" That didn't seem like her character at all.

"I'd want to do the right thing. And the problem is the right thing would've been to never be involved in the scandal in the first place. But as an officer and a board member, you told me that my main responsibility is to protect the best interests of the shareholders. *All* of the shareholders. I would imagine that if a major officer went down in a big scandal, that wouldn't be good for the best interests of the shareholders. So wouldn't the right thing, wouldn't the most ethical thing, be to uphold my responsibility to the people counting on me? Protecting the shareholders would protect the integrity of the company, which would protect the majority of the employees. It's the best answer for everyone."

It was the right answer. It was the answer that would keep Dyson Media afloat if it was ever embroiled in the kind of scandal we were talking about. The answer that a wise, business minded person would give.

But it was also the wrong answer.

Because I wanted her to say something else, wanted her to change the decisions of other people with what she'd said.

It was stupid, but it made me upset, made me mad all over again at my mom and my dad and all the other people who did stupid things.

I pushed her feet off of my lap, and then pulled her roughly into it instead.

I brushed her hair to the side, kissing along her neck, biting her fair skin, until it turned red and angry.

"Did I say the wrong thing?" she asked in between gasps.

"Nope," I said shortly.

"But you're upset."

"Yep. I'm upset. And now I'm going to fuck you." I quickly unbuttoned her blouse and pulled down the cup of her bra, so I could get her nipple in my mouth, so I could tug it between my teeth until she whined.

"But you *are* upset?" she asked again, even as she rubbed her trouser-clad pussy against the rock hard bulge in my jeans. "At *me?*"

"Not at you." I sucked on her nipple some more and then took over pinching it with my fingers between my thumb and forefinger. "And at you, too, maybe. It doesn't matter. We're going to fuck it out and everything's going to be fine."

I tangled my other hand in the back of her hair and yanked her head back so I could lick along her neck up to her mouth. Then I kissed her wildly, aggressively, as though I could wipe out everything she'd said with my tongue, and replace it with my own saliva.

We moved fast, and urgently, and she didn't ask again about my mood or where it came from or who it was pointed at; she just seemed to understand that she could fix it and was intent on fixing it fast. We only undressed as much as needed to fit ourselves together, moving as quickly as possible. While I worked on getting my cock out of my jeans, she stood up right there on the chair, placing a leg on either side of me as she pulled her trousers all the way down below her knees until they bunched at her ankles.

Then she sat down on me, taking my cock inside her expertly after only—what had it been? A week plus the one night before she went on her trip. She knew how to line me up, knew how to swallow me in, and she was still so new at this—new at me. Damn, she was a quick learner. Sharp and astute and fun to challenge.

Even more fun to let her ride.

When she was seated on top of me, and I was so deep, so snug in her tight pussy, I wondered for half a second if I should wait for her to stretch and get used to me before plowing into her the way I needed to.

But before I could make up my mind, she took over, bouncing on me exactly the right way, up and down, fast, hard, fucking herself with my cock like she needed it as much as I did. Like it hurt her as much as it hurt me not to be completely inside her over and over and over again.

And when she began to wear out, and her rhythm slowed, I put my hands on her hips and did the lifting for her, forcing her up and down, up and down, up and down, making her take all of me, take all of this rage and anger and betrayal.

She came without me once even touching her clit, just from the position, just from her body rubbing against my pelvis in the right way. And when she threw her head back and cried out my name, I lifted my hips up and bucked into her from below, thrusting wildly as though I were driving away the nightmare that had become my life in the last seven years. Chasing it chasing it chasing it away until finally my own orgasm came and there was light and bliss and warmth and a life that was almost in my grasp if I could just hold onto it somehow, somehow.

And then it was over. Gone.

I wrapped my arms tightly around Elizabeth, pulling her to my chest, kissing her forehead and her face, any part of her my lips could reach, my eyes still half blind from the spots my climax had spattered in front of them. I didn't feel angry anymore, or upset, or even disappointed.

I just wanted to go home. To my *real* home, in the city. The place I'd built for myself with my own sweat and hard work and—yes, Mom— sacrifice.

So we gathered up our stack of books, loaded up the car, and Elizabeth and I headed back toward my apartment in Manhattan. And, for the first time since we'd started the schedule of living together, I was really glad I had someone to go home with me.

# CHAPTER
# EIGHTEEN

*Elizabeth*

I COULD FEEL the blood run to my face as I read the Google alert that had come through on my email. The headline had to be wrong. I clicked through to scan the entire article, my jaw dropping with each new word.

"What's wrong?" Weston asked from the seat next to me in the back of the car. It was Sunday, and we were driving to get Weston fitted for his tux. I didn't need to go along with him, but there was a fundraiser ballet afterward that we planned to attend together—part of playing the role of a couple, of course—and it was just easier if we went to the fitting together first.

Or maybe that was an excuse.

I also found that I liked being near him a lot lately. And not just because of the sex.

Right now I was especially glad he was around, because I couldn't deal with the shock of this article on my own.

I looked up from my phone and over at him, shaking my head. So many thoughts were rushing through my mind, and I couldn't figure out which one to hold onto. I searched his face, as if he could read my mind and find the thoughts that needed to be spoken, bring them to my lips.

He studied me right back, then realizing the source of my anguish was my phone, took it from me and quickly read the article on the screen.

The statement said that Dyson Media was selling off the advertising portion of the company, the very subsidiary that I intended to let Reach buy at a very reasonable cost after I got my hands on my inheritance.

When he was done reading, he frowned, but he didn't seem quite as upset as I would be in his shoes.

"I won't let him go through with it," I promised aimlessly. "I'll find a way to stop Darrell from selling." *I'll find a way to make this—us—worth it for you.*

I didn't know how, but I had to.

"I'm not worried about that part," Weston said. "What worries me is him trying to start a sale at *this* point in time, only a month away from our wedding—" He broke off as he handed the phone back to me.

"It's as though he isn't factoring me in at all. Does that mean that he's so confident he can prove we're a fraud that he doesn't think I'll actually get my hands on the company? Or is this a head game, and he's trying to freak me out? Because it's working." I twisted the ring on my third finger, wondering how long it would be there if this deal went through.

In the few short months I'd worn it, I'd become accustomed to it and often found myself playing with it, especially when I was nervous or worried.

Like now.

Weston glanced down at me, noticed me fidgeting and pulled his own phone from inside his suit jacket, scrolled through to find the contact he wanted, and put it on speaker. As the phone rang, he said, "I'm sure it will be fine, but D will know what to do. He probably has—"

He was cut off by Donovan's voice coming clear and loud from the phone. "I already know, and I'm on it."

"What does 'on it' mean?" I asked, sitting forward so he could hear me.

"Oh, you're there too?" He sounded irritated, snappier than usual, which only made my anxiety worse. If Donovan was in a bad mood about the situation, surely there really was something to worry about.

"We're both here," Weston said. "I have you on speaker. Tell us what you're doing."

"Donovan, if I'd thought for even one second that Darrell would try to sell the advertising portion of Dyson Media, I would never have offered that as a bargaining chip. Darrell barely blinks at the advertising company. I didn't even think he knew it existed from as much attention as he normally gives it." I couldn't explain my guilt. My cousin's actions weren't my own, but I did feel responsible for the predicament we were in now.

"Of course you wouldn't," Donovan said, possibly trying to be reassuring. "And I approached *you* with the idea, not the other way around. But there's no way the sale can go through before your wedding. At which time your lawyers will step in and halt all major deals from proceeding. I've already sent your team to work on the matter."

I could practically hear the quotations around the word *your*.

"Meanwhile, I'll need to send someone over to France to make sure your cousin isn't trying to overhaul things at the firm in preparation for the sale. I'll reach out as a potential competing buyer, and slow things down that way."

"He won't sell to you," I said. "He knows Weston is one of the owners of Reach."

"And I'm sure all of this is just a scare tactic because of that. I don't need him to actually sell to me anyway. I just need to be a speed bump. I imagine I have a contact or two that can help with this."

Weston gave a shrug of his shoulders that said the plan was better than anything else we had.

And truthfully, it *was* a pretty good plan. I probably didn't need to worry about it, and everything would go exactly as Donovan said.

But it did scare me that Darrell had made this move. It meant he either felt threatened, or he knew somehow. Knew that I was using this small piece of Dyson Media as the ace in my hand. And the only reason he would know that would be if someone had talked.

But that was impossible. Wasn't it?

"I'll need to get some papers signed by you for the lawyers," Donovan said. "Where can I find you today?"

"We'll be at Coletti's Tuxedos in about two minutes," Weston said.

"And our afternoon is already booked."

"Then I better hurry and get the papers together so I can meet you there." Donovan hung up without even saying goodbye.

Weston pocketed his phone and shifted to look at me. "He's calling your bluff. He doesn't know anything. He's guessing that I would want that company. If anything, this means he believes in our marriage, and he knows that when we get married and you take over the company, I would want to take the ad company and give it to Reach."

I nodded. It made sense, what he was saying. More sense than Darrell having a mole inside Reach.

"Okay. Maybe that's right. But why would he do this now, if the sale can't possibly go through before our wedding date?"

"He might not think you pay enough attention. He might hope you're too busy with the wedding and the honeymoon to even notice the sale go through. And," Weston said, his eyes sparking a little, "he might've even tried to get the sale to go through earlier and been delayed. For this reason or that."

I relaxed just slightly, and noticed the whole side of my body was touching his when I did. He put his arm around me and brought me in closer. "Thanks for talking me down."

It felt so secure in his arms. He smelled so good, and his body was so warm. I wanted to take his strength and believe in it, but I reminded myself for the hundredth time that it wouldn't last. "I'm just so afraid he's going to find out this is a fake wedding, a fake marriage—"

"Hey," Weston pushed me away just enough so that he could meet my eyes. "You need to stop calling this a fake wedding. This is a real wedding. I am *really* getting married to you, Lizzie. You are really going to be my bride. In one month, you are going to be Mrs. King."

I took a deep breath in, and thought about that for a moment. I was *really* getting married to the man whose arms were holding me. I was going to stand up in front of all our friends, family, and business associates in a white dress and walk down the aisle toward *him*. Toward Weston.

And when everything was over, when the marriage had been dissolved and the final papers signed, that memory would still be real.

I realized my heart was pounding, racing faster than it usually did.

"You're going to be Mrs. King," he repeated as the car pulled over to the curb in front of Coletti's Tuxedos. "Which means you need to start acting like a queen."

I shivered a little at the thought of ruling by his side.

*Married.*

I was getting married.

We checked in at the counter for Weston's appointment, then he perused accessories on the wall while I watched a handful of men parading around in matching tuxes nearby. A few women were with them, critiquing the fits of their suits, laughing and having a good time. One of them was obviously the bride, deciding how she wanted her party to look, giving her attention to every detail of what would be the best day of her life. Certainly the most expensive. She went up to the one that had to be the groom and brushed lint from his shoulder before kissing him on the lips. "You look so sexy, baby," she said, flirting.

Was that the role I was supposed to play here today?

When her fiancé left for the fitting room with the tailor, she went back to giggling with her girlfriends and scrolling through her phone.

Perhaps that was how a normal bride acted, but it wasn't how this bride was going to act. It wasn't how Mrs. King would act.

It wasn't how this *queen* would act.

When Weston's tailor called him forward, I stood up and followed. Weston glanced over his shoulder at me and cocked his head, slightly confused.

"I'm just playing my part," I said.

That seemed to mollify him, and we walked into his assigned fitting room together.

The tailor didn't seem bothered at all by my presence and pointed to a chair where I could sit while Weston went into the dressing room to get into the tuxedo. It was his second appointment. The first time he'd come in on his own to be measured for the initial suit. This time, the outfit was being fitted to his body in particular. It was all about adjustments and hemming. He'd said it wouldn't take too long, but I'd never been to a tux or suit fitting, so I didn't know exactly what to expect.

I *had* expected that Weston would be drop dead sexy when he walked out of the dressing room—I just didn't expect to actually drop dead from his sexiness.

The tuxedo he'd worn the night of the engagement party had been a traditional fit, and he looked suave and hot, but this one was an ultraslim fit with a vest, and it hugged every part of his body, as though it had been molded to him.

I trailed my teeth along my lower lip, trying to manage the breath that was desperately trying to escape my body at the sight of him.

One thing was for sure, I couldn't sit through this. I had to stand, stand and watch while the tailor did his work. The gentleman who was working with Weston—Colletti himself, I soon learned—frowned at the sight of Weston. I couldn't understand that—what was there to frown at? But I stepped closer, trying to see the same flaws in the fit as he did.

The man bent down to kneel at Weston's feet and tugged at the pant leg. "These are the shoes you'll wear?" he asked.

"Yes," I answered before Weston could answer. Colletti glanced at me. I nodded. "He needs to wear suspenders to keep the pants in the right place."

Weston growled. "I hate suspenders. I'll be fine without suspenders."

I looked from Weston to Colletti. Colletti shrugged. "If you want the classic flare to last through the whole event, you wear the suspenders."

I could see what Colletti was saying now, about where the pant hit on the shoes. Without a belt to keep them properly at Weston's waist, and everyone knew you didn't wear a belt with tuxedo pants, the pants drooped and the leg fell too far onto the shoe. "He'll wear the suspenders."

Weston moved his eyes toward mine, and I could see the challenge behind them, but there was something else too. Admiration? Respect, maybe.

He didn't argue, which was good, since I was the one picking up the tab for this whole wedding thing. Was this what it was like to act like a queen?

It sure did feel pretty good.

Colletti went on to examine the jacket sleeves that were slightly too long—the shirt didn't show a half inch beyond the cuff. He made some markings, then turned Weston around to look at his back. He pulled me over for this.

"The shoulders fit good, see? And through here." Colletti gestured at the middle of Weston's torso. Then he tugged at the bottom of the jacket. "But this—this length was okay twenty years ago. Today we tend to keep it shorter, just below the behind." He lifted the back of the jacket for a second so he could figure out where to adjust it higher, and there was Weston's perfect ass, molded into the slim tuxedo pants.

Damn, those pants fit well.

"So what you want to do about the length?"

"Shorter," I answered, feeling like a billionaire asking for the clerk to bring the skimpiest dress out for his secretary. But, seriously. It was a shame to cover up so much of that backside.

When I circled back around to face Weston, the gleam in his eyes said he didn't only find this highly entertaining. He also found it kind of arousing.

I glanced down at the front of his jacket where the break—which was perfectly split, according to Colletti—displayed a slight bulge.

"Don't give it any attention," Weston said quietly while Colletti fussed at the back of his collar. "That's certainly not going to help."

It didn't help the dampness of my panties, that was for sure.

Colletti finished up his measurements, wrote out a receipt, and handed it to me. "Okay. Final adjustments will be ready in three weeks. Make an appointment for pickup at the front desk." He shuffled out of the room.

"I guess you're allowed to change now," I said, suddenly aware that we were alone.

"Yep." Apparently also aware of our aloneness, Weston grabbed me at my elbow and escorted me into the dressing room with him.

"I said *you* could get dressed now." I meant to sound authoritative, but my voice came out flustered and breathy. My heart was racing, and I could hardly pretend I didn't know what he was after.

"But you've been so helpful with the rest of this fitting. Surely you're not going to abandon me now." He clicked the door shut behind me and began working on undoing his pants. I was already excited, already ready for whatever he wanted. Even though we were in public, even though this was inappropriate.

*Especially* because we were in public. *Especially* because it wasn't appropriate.

When his cock was out—fully hard, his tip dripping—he pushed me to my knees. "How about you measure that?"

I glanced at the dressing room door. From a standing position, the two feet that it rose off the floor didn't seem so revealing. Down here was a whole other story.

"If anyone walked into the fitting room and saw me on my knees, they'd know exactly what I was doing."

It was kind of hot.

"Then you better hurry and get measuring," Weston said, rubbing his crown along my mouth, painting my lips with his pre-cum.

I hesitated only half a second before circling my fingers around the base of his cock and slipping my mouth around his hot, soft, tight skin. Because that's what I wanted to do.

And even queens bowed down to their kings.

We were quiet and fast, Weston whispering instructions and praise, one hand wrapped in my hair, the other braced on the dressing room door. I sucked him all the way in until he hit the back of my throat before drawing back, bobbing at a rapid speed while I massaged his balls, and when I looked up at him, he was watching us in the mirror, his expression fascinated and hypnotized, and so turned on.

I was going to get off to that sight for years to come.

It was only a few minutes later that I ducked out of the dressing room so that Weston could finish changing. Luckily no one else had come in and caught us.

Well, almost no one.

Donovan was waiting for me in the fitting area where Colletti had made the adjustments to the tuxedo.

I had no idea how long he'd been waiting there, or if he'd paid any attention to what was going on in the dressing room, so I acted like he knew nothing, brushing my likely messy hair behind my ear as I crossed over to him.

"You have those papers?" I asked, loudly enough so that Weston could hear that we were no longer alone.

"I do. Why don't we take these outside, so we have some place to lay these all out."

I followed Donovan out into the main part of the store to a display counter that showcased cufflinks. He spread some papers across the glass and handed me a pen. I quickly found the places to initial and scratch my signature, then handed him the pen back after he gathered the papers together.

"Thank you for this," I said. "Thank you for always being on the ball. I really am sorry that this—"

He cut me off. "How did it fit?"

He had to mean the suit, not the cock. It wasn't some terrible, dirty, sexual reference, but my cheeks went red anyway, and I stammered, "What?"

"How did Weston's tux fit?" He asked, his voice cold, his eyes hard.

It hadn't been what he'd said the first time, though. And it seemed that even though he'd corrected himself, there was something hidden or manipulative in the way he was looking at me. This was the Donovan Kincaid people whispered about. The ruthless emperor of the New York business world.

I didn't know what to do except answer. "It looks good."

He smiled tightly. "Weston does always wear a tuxedo well."

"Yes. He does."

He opened his jacket and put his pen in the inside pocket, then turned his gaze back to me, his expression serious. "It's not for keeps, you know." There was no question in his statement. It was very definitive, very final, and very confusing, because I wasn't sure what he meant about keeping anything.

Did he mean the tux? I'd paid for it, but of course I would give it to Weston. Why would I have any use for a tux? A tux that fit Weston so perfectly.

And then it clicked, and I knew what he'd meant. I knew because I was so like Donovan in so many ways, and because Weston fit me in so many ways. I realized he was talking about *him*.

Donovan was talking about Weston.

Telling me that I couldn't keep Weston.

My chest pinched like I was wearing a corset and somebody had tightened the straps much, much too tight. Which was crazy because I hadn't even considered keeping Weston, but for someone to say that I couldn't, for Donovan to say that I couldn't . . .

"I don't gather that it's really any of your business," I managed to say. Not at all queenly. More like a woman who had been gaslit and underestimated and harassed and was still trying to find her confidence in this man's world.

"Oh, my dear, but it *is* my business. This whole arrangement has been my business. And the arrangement we made was that you would have Weston temporarily. I'm sure you know by now that he's expecting to end up with Sabrina. She's rather suited to him, isn't she?"

My cheeks went redder, this time from rage. "That seems odd when you're the one currently banging her."

He didn't bat an eye. "I'm just doing a friend a favor, keeping her entertained until Weston's not so tied up."

My backbone crumpled, the little that I had anyway. Had Weston asked Donovan to be with Sabrina? Was he planning on being with her when our divorce was final?

It wasn't like I could ask him. He wouldn't even tell me about his family. Why would I expect him to tell me about his love life? The only arrangement we had was to wed and divorce. We had no arrangement that we would mean anything to each other in between.

I felt my eyes get watery, and I blinked extra hard, trying to make the tears go away.

Weston came out of the fitting room then, chipper and upbeat, likely from his recent orgasm. I, on the other hand, was a smashed bug on the bottom of Donovan's shoe.

"Did you get everything you needed, D? Damn, whatever you said has Elizabeth all worked up again." His tone was concerned and compassionate, and I had to swallow and look at my shoes.

"I'm okay," I lied. "Really. Donovan was just reminding me of Reach's commitment to our agreement, and it made me a bit emotional." I was stupid for defending someone who'd just made me feel like shit, but it wasn't fair to be angry at him. He'd only spoken the truth. The truth I'd reminded myself of so many times before. It just hurt to hear it spoken out loud.

And wasn't it the job of a good businesswoman—and a good queen— to act in the best interests of her company? Not herself.

"Good," Weston said, putting an arm around me and rubbing his hand up and down along my skin. "We are committed. All of us."

Right. Committed right up until we said I do. The marriage *was* real—but the feelings were not.

# CHAPTER
# NINETEEN

*Weston*

"**D**ID YOU GET in okay?" I asked, stretching out on my bed, fully clothed. Elizabeth had only been gone half a day and I already missed her—missed her in my bones, and in my blood. And not even the kind of missing her that meant I wanted to jerk off, though I'd probably end up doing that too.

"Yeah, I did." She sounded so far away, but she *was* far away. Utah might as well have been a million miles from here. She'd gone early for Thanksgiving, and I was set to meet her in two days, on Wednesday night.

Two days and it felt like a lifetime.

But even though she was physically far away, I couldn't help the feeling she was far away in other ways too. She had been for a couple of weeks now, or maybe it was me who was feeling closer to her than I should.

Ever since the day at my parents' when I'd realized that she was a form of home to me, I'd started to cling to her, started to think of her in a new light. I started to think of her as more of an anchor than an obstacle, and instead of counting the days toward our wedding with anticipation, excited for the day when I would finally be rid of her, I hated the fact that our moment at the altar was just another step toward our demise.

Was this what love felt like?

And if so, how could I get her to look at me, to feel for me the way

I was feeling for her?

There had been moments before when I was certain she did, but lately I wasn't so sure.

"Is the rest of your family there yet?" It was small talk, but I didn't want to let her go just yet.

"The house is too small to hold everyone. They'll come for dinner on Thursday. Right now it's just me and Nana and my great-grandmother." She paused, seeming to stifle a yawn. "What did you do tonight?"

"I worked. Then had dinner with Dylan—he's in town from the UK visiting his son. We went to Gaston's with Sabrina and her sister." I'd gotten tipsy and spent half the conversation debating with Dylan about whether love was real.

Me—arguing for the side of love.

It was Elizabeth's fault. And if I was under her spell, I didn't ever want it to be broken.

"Oh," Elizabeth said, her voice suddenly tighter. "That sounds fun. Hey, I've been thinking. There really isn't any reason for you to come and join me here. It's already awkward pretending we're a real item to Nana, and you're not even here yet. It's not like there's going to be anyone who sees us together in Utah. The whole point is to be seen, right?"

The buzz I'd felt from the wine suddenly wore off and soberness hit me like a brick wall. I moved the phone to my other ear and ran my hand through my hair, thinking fast. I needed to see her. Needed to be with her.

"But . . . There are still people who could see me here. And it would look wrong if I was here for the holiday without you. No, it's better if I'm where you are. What if Darrell tracked our flights? Hired a PI? Let's just stick to the plan. It keeps our asses covered." Which *was* true, I just didn't mention that I wanted to spend the week with her. Wanted to sit at a table over a meal where we expressed our gratitude and, at least in my heart, know that I was grateful for meeting her.

"I guess I'll see you Wednesday then." She sounded resigned. Maybe she was just tired from her flight. "Call me when—"

"Are you done with me already?" God, I was so desperate. I'd never been desperate. This was a new one for me.

"I was. Do you have more to discuss?"

"Well, we've never had phone sex."

She laughed lightly, and just the sound of her giggle got me semi-hard. "Weston, I can't. Not here. Nana's just in the other room."

"Where's your sense of adventure?"

"I guess I left it in New York," she said with finality. "Goodnight. I'll talk to you Wednesday."

She hung up, and I tossed my phone to the bed, giving up on jerking off. It wasn't an orgasm that I wanted. It wasn't a business arrangement I wanted. I just wanted her.

⌒∽

IT WAS EARLY evening and the sun was just setting when I arrived in Salt Lake City. I picked up my rental car and followed the directions to Elizabeth's grandmother's place in Bountiful, amazed at how little traffic there was on the short drive. The airport was only twenty minutes from her house. Elizabeth and I were staying in a hotel, but we'd agreed to meet here, where she'd been staying the last couple of days, so she wouldn't have to take a taxi.

I pulled into the long driveway of the single-family house around six-thirty p.m. It was simple and small—white siding, no front porch, probably no more than two bedrooms if I guessed from the outside. My father would refer to it as a shack. I knew that Angela, Elizabeth's mother, hadn't come from money, but I still double checked the address to be sure I was in the right place before knocking on the door.

A blonde-and-gray haired woman who looked very much like Elizabeth's mother greeted me, an exuberant smile on her face. "You must be Weston. Come in, come in."

I set my bag down, and Elizabeth suddenly appeared behind her.

My chest got warm and tingly just at the sight of her. It was weird, because usually my emotions for women originated much lower. And when she slipped into my arms and kissed me hello, the tingly feeling expanded through my limbs into my fingers and my toes, and all I wanted to say when she stopped kissing me was, "I'm home."

But I got ahold of myself somehow and said the more appropriate thing. "I'm here."

She formally introduced me to the woman who answered the door, Nana, Angela's mother. She was in her mid-seventies, spry for her age—spry for a woman twenty years younger, even—but though she looked like her daughter in her features, she dressed much more plainly, wearing no makeup, her hair just towel-dried instead of the perfect grooming her daughter preferred.

Next, Elizabeth showed me in and introduced me to a woman sitting in a recliner in the living room. Grandmama, Nana's mother, had turned ninety-five this year, Elizabeth boasted proudly. She had white frizzy hair, what was left of it, anyway. There were several spots where her scalp could be seen, patches of dry skin showing through which matched the red, angry splotches that dotted her arms. Psoriasis, most likely. Or just age. She was stout, not one of those frail old women that comes to mind when someone says 'geriatric.' And her face was radiant, her eyes bright, her cheeks rosy, as she stood to greet me.

"No, no, please," I said, trying to stop her from getting up. "I can come over there. No need to stand."

"Oh, we're about ready to have supper anyway. It's time for me to get on my feet." Her voice was cheery, her whole persona delightful.

"Then at least let me help you stand up." I moved toward the chair, but she stopped me again.

"It's actually easier if I do it myself," she said, and I suddenly began to rethink the notion that Elizabeth got her gumption from her father. "See, I rock back and then rock forward, and the chair just sort of lifts me up." She demonstrated the motion as she spoke.

I exchanged a glance with Elizabeth, who was grinning just as widely as her grandmama. When she'd made it to her feet, Elizabeth was there with her arm offered. "I'll help you to the table, but then Weston and I are headed to our hotel."

"You aren't staying for supper?" She looked to Nana as if asking permission. "I'm sure there's plenty to go around."

"I did make enough for everyone," Nana confirmed.

"I'm sure after the long flight and everything . . ." Elizabeth began.

"We'd love to stay," I finished for her. Because there was nothing in the world I would rather do than stay and soak up the warmth of these happy people, so honest and real. So different from my own family.

There was a dining room, but supper was served in the kitchen around a small table that barely fit four chairs, and we had to pull the table out from the wall to accommodate all of us. The meal was simple—soup and homemade bread and canned pears that I learned came from a tree in the backyard. There was prayer before we ate. It wasn't scripted, and we didn't hold hands—just a short, simple grace, words of gratitude and a request for blessings.

Grandmama's words came quickly to her tongue, and I could tell her mind was still sharp as she made these personal requests to a God she sincerely believed in.

When she finished, and the food began to be distributed around the table, Elizabeth looked over at me covertly and mouthed the word "sorry." As though I would've been bothered by a prayer when it had been my favorite thing about the day so far, especially the part where Grandmama had thanked God for her great-granddaughter's visit and the man she'd chosen to share her life with. Even if it was a lie, God knew, it was the intention of this woman that meant so much. It made my throat tight and dry.

It was funny how these women were so surprising when I thought I knew all about them. I'd already learned so much about this branch of the family—about all of Elizabeth's family—in the months we'd been together. She wasn't guarded about the people around her the way I was. It shamed me when I thought about it, how she could be so transparent and giving when I was closed off and embarrassed.

She didn't seem to be worried that I would associate her with her family members, that I would blame her for anything they had done or who they were, whereas I was scared to death she would discover things in my family's past, and would never again look at me the way I sometimes caught her looking at me now.

The way I wanted her to look at me all the time.

During dinner, I got Nana and Grandmama's version of the family history. Grandmama had lived in the tiny white house since she'd gotten married in the forties, had raised all seven of her children here, somehow stuffing most of them into two rooms in the basement. Nana, her middle child, had three children of her own, two who lived in Utah still, and her baby, Angela, who had run away from home at an early age to explore the world. She'd met Dell Dyson and found the world was more interesting with dollars in her bank account. Nana had spent a lot of time in New York with Angela and Elizabeth in place of a nanny before she grew too old to need one. Then, when her father got sick, she moved in to take care of her parents.

"So she's the black sheep," I said, after Grandmama added that Elizabeth's mother's line was one of the few that no longer practiced the Mormon religion.

"She's not a black sheep," Nana said, offended. "She's welcome here anytime. She just prefers I come visit *her*. She likes her fancy things. Even tried to buy us a fancier house time and time again, but we're happy with what we have. Doesn't stop her from sending us all sorts of New Age technology, though I do admit to enjoying my TVR."

Elizabeth tried to hide her giggle. "It's DVR, Nana. It's part of your cable subscription." She turned to me to explain. "I helped them get it figured out last time I was here."

"Angela is so kind with her money. She sends it all the time. But we have no need for anything," Grandmama said, her finger pointing at the table as though she really wanted me to hear that point. "Besides occasional repairs to the house, we just put the rest in savings. It can pay for my medical bills when I need it down the road."

"I don't think that's coming anytime soon," Nana said. "Your mother lived to be one hundred and five."

Grandmama sighed as if that was the last thing she wanted to be reminded of. "Well. We'll see."

When dinner was over, Nana started to gather the empty plates and stack them in a pile until Elizabeth stopped her. "We'll get that. Go watch your shows with Grandmama."

I stepped into line, gathering items and carrying them to the sink alongside her. We put leftovers in Tupperware and made room in a fridge already crowded with pre-Thanksgiving cooking, and soon we were side-by-side at the sink, loading it to wash the dishes by hand.

"I don't hear you bothering *them* about hiring a maid," I teased.

Elizabeth narrowed her eyes at me, but she had a smile playing on her lips. "They don't want a maid. They don't even want a dishwasher." She handed me a sudsy plate to rinse off and put in the dish rack.

"Why do we need a dishwasher?" Nana asked coming in behind us. "What would we do with our days if we didn't at least clean up after ourselves?"

"But at least you *do* clean up after yourselves. This one," Elizabeth gestured to me, "does not. He needs a maid so I don't have to be the one who does it."

Nana put a hand on my shoulder, warm and friendly, as though she'd already welcomed me into her life. "This one works hard all day. He's earning the money. He doesn't need to clean up after himself."

I could practically hear Elizabeth choke on her shock.

"Yeah," I teased. "I'm earning all the money."

"Oh, you do not," she said, but Nana had already walked away. Elizabeth flicked at me with her fingers, spattering water on my shirt and face. I flicked water at her right back, and then we were both laughing, and I vowed right then I would never, ever get a maid if it meant that I could do dishes with Elizabeth Dyson forever.

AFTER DINNER, WE stayed to watch TV for a bit with the older women. "Their shows" turned out to be murder mysteries on PBS, British detectives from the 1920s era. There was lots of talking and everyone was glued to the screen. I mostly nodded and kept my arm around Elizabeth, and tried not to stare at her profile and how her skin glowed from the light shining off the TV screen.

"We'll have twenty-eight here for dinner tomorrow," Grandmama said with a sigh when the show was over. "Better get to bed. We're going to have to get up early to start the turkey."

"Twenty-eight," I gasped. "Where are you going to fit them all?" There was only the TV room and a large master bedroom upstairs plus the living room, dining room, and kitchen.

"It's tight, but we've done it," Nana said. "You'll just have to see how it works out tomorrow. We'll be stuffed in more ways than one."

Everyone laughed and it was our cue to leave for the night. "I'll just run out to the camper and get my suitcase. But I can be back here as early as you need me to help cook, Nana."

"You stayed in a camper?" I supposed that made sense. There was only one bedroom in the basement now, the big dorm room having been turned into a playroom for the grandkids when they visited.

"Yeah, it's in back."

"Then why don't we just stay there?" I'd thought the whole reason she and I weren't staying here was because it would be awkward having sex in the same house with her grandmothers. Because we both knew we couldn't sleep in the same room and keep our hands off each other. But an unattached room next door? That sounded like it would work just fine.

"There's no room service in the camper," Elizabeth said. "And no plumbing, so we have to use the bathroom in here."

"I don't need room service, Princess."

She rolled her eyes and huffed. "Obviously I don't either. Since I've been staying there myself for two days." She wandered into the living room where I'd left my bag and hoisted it onto her shoulder. "If we're going to stay, then you'd better go take your turn with the toilet."

I chuckled to myself and did as she'd told me as she let Nana know about the new arrangements, then I took my bag from her, and she led the way to the backyard.

If Elizabeth's room service remark had been meant to warn me about the state of the camper, I didn't pick up on it. It was old, beat up, well used. It was definitely from Grandmama's era, and as we climbed inside the rickety thing, I almost wondered if it would fall apart on us. Inside, there was a dining table surrounded by two benches, a kitchen, which consisted of a sink, counter and range top that looked a hundred years old and a bedroom in the back with a mattress that took up the total width of the trailer. A long, thick cord ran underneath the door behind us and led to a space heater on the floor in front of the bed.

"I'm guessing this is what they call vintage," I said, setting my bag down. It was cute despite the weathering with it's wood-paneled walls and the benches wrapped in teal pleather—the kind easily wiped down and probably highly toxic.

"Vintage is one way to put it," Elizabeth said, walking over to the space heater and turning it on. She sat on the bed and began pulling off her shoes. "*Well-loved* is another. My mother bought her a new one about twenty years ago when Papa was still alive, and they turned around and gave it to my uncle. They said this one was still good. They didn't need a new one."

"I suppose it still does what it's supposed to." I followed her into the bedroom, eager to touch her now that we were alone.

Eager just to be with her.

"Nowadays it's just used as an extra room when family visits, but it's here at least as long as Grandmama is alive. My great-grandfather inherited it from someone before they got married. It was pretty much all he had to his name when they wed. He'd grown up a poor farmboy. He was super smart though so he was able to become a schoolteacher. And she was . . ."

I sat on the bed beside Elizabeth, tilting my body toward her. "She was—what?"

She let out a sigh. "She had money. Her dad was a lawyer. She married down, so to say."

Like how Elizabeth was marrying down by marrying me.

Sweat suddenly gathered at the back of my neck. "And then what?"

She waited a beat before breaking into a smile. "And they lived happily ever after." She laid back on the bed, her body turned toward me.

I followed suit, stretching out and facing her.

"They didn't have much money," she went on. "They took their honeymoon in this camper. They raised seven kids in that tiny house.

They grew a lot of their own food, relied on goods they canned themselves, had a newspaper route for extra money, and camped for every vacation they took, but they were super fucking happy."

Her expression was soft as she talked about these people she was so fond of.

And I was anything but soft.

When I reached for her, it wasn't out of anger or lust or a need to satisfy something within myself. I simply reached for her, and she reached for me, lips meeting gently, kissing without frenzy, without bruising intentions.

We undressed each other slowly, and it felt like I was discovering her body for the first time, feasting on something new. I spent time on every inch of her skin, licking and sucking, learning her landscape like it was a place I'd never been. I was grateful for every part of her that she let me see, thankful for her trust and the honor, and I showed her in every way I knew. I made up ways just for her, watching her closely to gauge what she liked. What she loved.

So many times I'd prided myself on giving a woman pleasure, but it had always been for my own satisfaction. So I could take the glory. So I could bask in the title of best lover. But with every kiss, with every graze of her skin, tonight I truly wanted *her* to feel good. Wanted her to know how beautiful she was, how fucking incredible.

I wanted to please her.

I wanted to love her.

And when we were completely naked, shivering from the way that we moved across each other, I slid inside her, thrust deep, deeper, deeper still, my eyes locked on hers, wanting nothing but to give her everything I felt inside. Wanting to give her this crazy, insane, turbulent feeling racing through my blood, skittering across my nerves. The same thrill that I felt when I got a beautiful woman in my bed, that high that always disappeared when the orgasms died down, but which with Elizabeth, lingered and grew and exploded, even when our clothes were on, our bodies not quite touching. I wanted to share that with her. Wanted to ask her with each thrust, *do you feel this, do you feel this, do you feel this?*

And not mean my cock, but that crazy fucking shit going on inside me. That bizarre, wonderful magic love stuff circulating through my veins.

*Do you feel this? Do you feel it, too?*

I held her close against me when we were finished, our bodies sticking to each other as our sweat dried. I thought of her great-grandfather in this camper almost eighty years ago, how he held the woman he'd loved in his arms, how it was all he'd had and it had been enough.

And I got it. Because this could be enough for me too.

All that was left was for me to find out if Elizabeth felt the same.

# CHAPTER
# TWENTY

*Elizabeth*

I SLIPPED OUT of the camper early Thanksgiving morning while the sky was still dark and frost still tipped the grass in the backyard, not because I was worried about Nana getting the cooking underway without me, but because I was worried that if I stayed too long in the paradise of Weston's arms, I wouldn't be able to leave.

In the two plus weeks since Donovan had reminded me of the business arrangement—of Weston's loyalties—I'd tried to stay true to myself and my own goals. Tried to remember first and foremost that this charade was just that—a charade. I hadn't stopped sleeping with Weston because I only had so much self-restraint, but also because it was easier than a complicated discussion of why we *shouldn't* keep sleeping together. And the *why* was that I was falling for him. And I was worried about my heart.

How embarrassing that confession would be.

And it wasn't like I needed another man to reject me in my life.

But every day in his presence, and his arms, and his bed made the next day harder to get through without wanting more, more, more. Without dreaming that there wasn't an expiration date on us, without fantasizing that the inheritance of Dyson Media wasn't the cherry on top of my nuptials, rather than the whole reason for them.

And last night had been especially hard.

Whereas our usual tense and fraught living situation led to rough, wild sex, this time it felt as though he were making love to me. As though he were giving himself to me in ways he never had.

I'd been right there with him too, receiving all he had to offer, letting him take from me too, pretending I wasn't a wreck over it.

God, I'd gotten so good at pretending.

But there were only nine more days until our official wedding date, and then we were flying to a remote island where we could ignore each other for the two weeks of our honeymoon and begin the process of moving on. I just had to be strong, had to keep my head clear. Remember that this was all a game and play it like I had nothing to lose.

Nana was already up when I got inside the house, thankfully. She set me right to work peeling potatoes and it was a much-needed distraction. Cooking overtook the morning and by the time Weston awoke and joined us, my aunt Becky had arrived, instrumental Christmas music was playing in the background, and there was enough hubbub to keep me from having to deal with him one on one.

Dinner preparations took the rest of the day and early afternoon. Weston jumped in, helping as soon as he got himself showered and dressed by setting up extra tables, bringing up the dining table leaves from the basement, pulling the metal folding chairs out of the carport. By the time we were finished, there was a large round table set up in the master bedroom for the kids, a long banquet set up in the living room, and the dining room was stretched to max capacity.

At two o'clock more family began arriving. Aunt Nora brought the pumpkin pies that everybody hated but no one would admit, Aunt Debbie brought the pecan pies that everybody fought over. A can of olives was set out for early nibbles on the dining room table. The younger cousins quickly discovered them and walked around with black fingertips until Aunt Becky admonished them and swapped out for a fresh can that she supervised until dinner was served. Finally, each table was loaded with portions of all the sides. Green bean casserole, stuffing, mashed potatoes and gravy, rolls, glazed carrots, yams. And in the middle of each table sat a plate of turkey, already carved and dished up from the birds in the kitchen.

Everyone gathered in the living room for prayer which was given by Nana's younger brother. Then the room burst into a fit of joyful noise as everyone dispersed to their designated seats, ready to enjoy the amazing feast.

Weston and I were seated at the long table in the living room with most of the spillover adults, as I liked to call them. The oldest adults were the ones who got to sit in the dining room with grandma; those included Nana and her siblings. With most of the people around us being our age, the conversation was lively. Weston had plenty of opportunities to show off his business knowledge as the men began discussing their recent investments, and the latest trends in stocks. With his connections to King-Kincaid, they were quite eager to hear his opinion.

"I'm not really one to give advice on investments," he said. He placed his hand over mine on the table. "But I do recommend investing in Dyson Media. I hear it's about to go through some management changes that are going to be quite excellent for the company."

I smiled tightly around my mashed potatoes, trying not to blush. The majority of women in my mother's family were homemakers. It felt odd for me to discuss business.

"We'll invest," my cousin's wife, Sheila, said. "I'm looking forward to you taking over. You're going to be amazing. Go women!" She gave me a wink and I winked back.

"Unless she has a baby," her husband Jeff said.

My body tensed, my chewing paused, and Weston's hand suddenly felt stiff over mine. This was not a conversation we'd prepared for.

"Women can't have babies and jobs these days?" Sheila's tone seemed to indicate this was a discussion that had been had before in her household.

Jeff didn't seem fazed. "Every family needs to make the decision that's right for them. What decision have you made? Will you quit working when you have children?"

I coughed, choking on my turkey. Weston handed me my water goblet, and I gulped half of it down.

"Uh, we haven't talked about it," he said while rubbing my back.

"You're getting married and you haven't talked about it?" Katie, another cousin, asked, her expression aghast.

"No, we've talked about it," I said, trying to recover. What kind of engaged couple hadn't discussed children? "Weston meant we haven't *decided*. Haven't decided when we're having them. Not if I'm quitting. I'm not quitting."

"Right. That's what I meant," he said, and from the way he looked at me, I could almost believe he was imagining the same thing I was— beautiful, blue-eyed babies with red-hair and deep dimples. Smart and playful and independent.

But of course he wasn't imagining that. I wasn't even sure Weston liked kids.

I wasn't even sure Weston liked me, most days.

"Will you be joining in at Dyson Media?" Jeff asked Weston, changing the subject. I'd never been so grateful to my cousin in my life.

"I'll be staying with Reach. It keeps my hands busy," Weston said. "Of course, any time Elizabeth needs my advice, I'm happy to give her my input."

"Oh, that's right," Jeff said. "You have your advertising business. Wasn't there some sort of a scandal a few years back with King-Kincaid? Some banking thing? I hope that didn't affect your own business."

Scandal? I raised a brow and looked at Weston.

He shook his head definitively. "There were rumors when the house financing bubble burst. Nothing really stuck. It was before my business got started, but luckily I had no problems."

Weston moved his attention back to eating, and while he'd brushed off the comment, I noticed his body had stiffened, and I suddenly wondered if there was something there, something I had missed, something I hadn't thought to look at.

Then someone was asking me to pass the mashed potatoes and

someone else began a story, and I forgot all about it again.

AFTER DINNER, WESTON and the men got the tables torn down and put away within ten minutes then chilled out while the women cleared dishes and washed them in the kitchen. I ignored the sexist division of tasks that resulted in more work for the women. Everyone seemed happy, and that was what mattered, I supposed.

When the last plate was dried and put away, I went to the door of the living room and waited for my uncle John to finish his story. As I waited, I watched my cousin's baby playing, recalling the earlier dinner conversation. Was this something I wanted?

She had a toy car she was trying to roll back and forth but kept getting frustrated when it didn't roll smoothly over the shag carpet. She started to fuss, her cry escalating in the crowded room.

Her father was already soothing a toddler on his lap, and her mother was in the kitchen whipping cream, so I stepped forward to soothe her when Weston, whose back was to me, beat me to it. He slipped from the couch to the floor, then laid down and showed her how she could roll the car on him, allowing her to make a race track of his torso and legs.

She squealed, delighted, and he was sexier than I'd ever seen him.

But it wasn't just sex appeal. Yes, the feelings I had watching him with this baby were primal and base. Some sort of innate need to produce offspring was set off at the sight of him, the same feelings I'd had at the question of us having kids.

But there was heart appeal, too. Like, this was the kind of guy I wanted to be a parent with. The kind of guy who would wear a suit all week, do the dishes with me at night, fuck my brains out in the bedroom, then lay down on the floor and play with his child. The kind of guy who could be in it all the way. Not just for me, but for everything that came with.

I could picture Weston as that guy. I could picture it so well that I had to swallow twice before asking the room who was ready for pie.

After everyone was full of dessert, the games began. Some went to the back room to watch football on the big TV, the youngest kids went downstairs to play their own board games. A group of adults sat around the dining room table and began a vicious game of Uno. Aunt Becky won several rounds, as always, but the trickiest hands, the most draw-fours and surprise reverse cards were placed by Grandmama.

Weston played a good hand, too, and I hated myself for being impressed with how savagely he played against me even while he played footsie under the table. It was the same game we always played—the push and pull. The I hate you/I want you. The poke and prod.

It was getting harder and harder for me to play this game.

At eight o'clock, when families started to clean up and announce they were going home, I let out a deep sigh of relief.

Not much for goodbyes, I busied myself with cleaning up while various cousins made their farewells. I tied up the bag of trash from the kitchen and pulled it out of the trashcan. I'd just started to open the door to take it to the backyard when all of a sudden Weston was at my side.

"Let me help you with that," he said.

He was the one I needed to be away from the most. Reluctantly, I said, "You can grab the recycling," and nodded to the blue can next to the trash.

He collected and tied that bag, and a minute later we were heading out together into the chilly, crisp night air toward the large cans that were in the back of the carport outside.

"That baby Nicola," Weston said, as we walked. "She is just the cutest. I could gobble her up. She's so happy!"

"She does seem to love everyone." I was glad that I was ahead of him, and he couldn't see my frown. Even though I'd loved watching him play with her, it irritated me to hear him talk about her, for some reason.

Maybe I was just irritated with him in general.

"And, man. Aunt Becky," he went on, and I had to bite my tongue because that struck a nerve too. "She's a killer at Uno. Grandmama needs to watch her back with that one. Though, really, Grandmama can probably handle herself. Hey, do think we should invite cousin Jeff to the wedding? And his wife seemed super cool too. Maybe we could go in with them on a gift for—"

I dropped the trash bag in the outside garbage can with a grunt and cut him off at the same time. "Stop it."

He looked at me curiously, cautiously, as though he wasn't sure if I meant the talking or the recycling.

I grabbed the recycling bag out of his hand and put it where it belonged, then turned to face him. "Stop it," I said again, more harshly. "They're not your family. We are not going in on gifts for anybody together. He's not *your* cousin Jeff. She's not *your* aunt Becky. And it's not *your* Grandmama, either. They're *my* family. Mine. Not yours."

He stood there with his mouth open for several seconds. Then I thought I caught a flash of pain behind his eyes, but it was dark and the carport light cast shadows across his face, so I couldn't be sure. It was enough, though, to cause a sharp stab of doubt.

"You're right," he said softly, sincerely. "I got too into the role and crossed a line. Sorry about that."

He turned to go back toward the house, his shoulders low.

"Weston—?" I called after him, suddenly worried I'd been wrong about everything. That he'd felt it too—that strange, real connection between us, pulling us to be something more than just an arrangement—and I'd just fucked it all up by not giving those feelings a chance.

But when he stopped and swung his head back at me, he was smiling. "Everyone's leaving," he said, as though I hadn't just snapped at him. "That means all the leftover pie is ours. We got to beat your Grandmas to it, though, so come on."

So it was like he'd said—he'd gotten into the role. With the estrangement between him and his own family, it was probably natural that he soaked up the warmth of one that was so ready to give it.

Regardless, it was still true that he'd crossed a line.

And so had I, by imagining a life with him. I needed to stop with the daydreaming and wishful thinking. Needed to harden myself. Needed to learn how to ignore these feelings before they got out of hand.

For all my father's flaws, I couldn't forget the most valuable lesson he'd taught me—there was no room for emotion in business.

# CHAPTER
# TWENTY-ONE

*Weston*

"**A**RE YOU NERVOUS?" Nate asked from behind me.

I met his eyes in the mirror, then moved my focus back to my own image as I finished knotting my tie. Elizabeth had chosen a standard tie rather than a bow in a deep midnight blue that matched my pocket square. It was a perfect color for December. Moody and wintry, and it brought out the blue in my eyes.

Brought out the blue in my mood.

"Why would I be nervous? It's not as if this wedding means anything to me."

"Yeah, but the girl means something to you."

I glanced at his reflection once again, frowning. I knew Nate was the one to talk to about sex and women and good times, but I wasn't so sure he was the one to confide in when it came to heartache. And though I'd never felt this feeling before, that was the best description I had for it—heartache—the pain, tightness, and anguish in the general vicinity of my heart.

It had been there ever since that day in Utah when Elizabeth had reminded me so bluntly that her family was not mine—that *she* was not mine. She would never be mine. And there was no longer any reason to ask how she felt about me because she had made it plain and clear then.

After the trip and in the week that we'd been home, I'd barely seen her. Between preparing for the wedding and getting things wrapped up at the office before I left for our honeymoon, there was just no time. And that was a good thing. Because these days when I saw her, I didn't want to fight and I didn't want to just fuck, and yet those were the only two things I was allowed to have.

Thankfully Nate was the only one who knew she'd become such a weakness of mine.

"I do like her," I admitted, turning to him. "I'll be disappointed when she goes. But it's the circle of life, right?"

He chuckled. "That's the spirit. By my watch you have thirty minutes. Do you need anything?"

"I could use a drink." And another week before this was over. Another month. Another lifetime.

Nate slapped me on the back. "Save it for after the ceremony. Then you can have all the drinks you want." He headed for the door of the dressing room. "Speaking of drinks, I have a date waiting for me in the bar. I've got to get down there to her. Oh, your mother was saying she wanted to see you. Should I send her to your dressing room?"

"God, no. She can see me after. When I have that drink in hand."

He laughed again, but then grew serious. "It's worth the pain," he said. "Trust me."

"My mother isn't worth any amount of pain," I said, wishing he would just go and give me the alone time I needed before going through with this.

"I'm not talking about your mother, Weston."

"Yeah. I think I knew that."

He laughed as he left, and I was alone, which I had wanted. I could finally take a moment to consider whether it really was worth the pain. It wasn't like I'd never been sorry to lose a girl before. When I was a teenager, it seemed I'd been sorry to lose *every* girl. Every one of them, back then, I'd wanted to keep forever. Wanted to love forever. Was devastated when they stepped out of my car, snuck out of my room.

It was nothing more than my desire to have something of my very own. Eventually I learned that if I didn't get attached, I didn't experience the stab of pain that accompanied their departure.

At least once this particular heartache was done, I'd have Reach. Debt-free, something that belonged to me.

So Nate was right—the pain would be worth it. Eventually.

Still wishing I could have a shot of hard liquor instead, I walked over to the fridge to get a water bottle when there was a knock on the door. I'd already seen everyone I was expecting to see for the afternoon.

Which meant . . . fuck. It was probably Mom.

I girded myself for an encounter with her that I absolutely wasn't in the mood to have when I already had so much emotional baggage to deal with.

But when I opened the door, it wasn't my mother standing there.

"Kelly?" She was the last person on earth I expected to see. A senator's daughter I'd spent some time with about three years ago in Colorado. Mostly naked time. She must've made it onto the guest list somehow.

"Callie," she corrected, seeming mildly irritated. And deservedly so considering all that we'd done. It was a slap in the face that I didn't get her name right. This was why I didn't do reunions.

"Callie. I'm sorry. I have a lot on my mind today." I opened the door farther. "Come in. I'm glad to see you. Come in."

She hesitated a moment, seeming to consider, then with a deep breath she crossed the threshold into the dressing room, and I shut the door behind her.

I didn't remember much about Callie, but I tried to recall what I could. I'd met her on the slopes of Aspen and the week that we'd spent together had been a combination of daredevil skiing and acrobatic sex. She was attractive, more petite than Elizabeth, more athletic. Her eyes were a soft brown and her hair a light chocolate. She was one of those natural kinds of girls, the kind that didn't wear makeup and liked adventure. She'd been a fun time that I hadn't thought about in, well, years.

But here she was, standing in front of me, clutching the strap of her purse like she was nervous, or excited to see me.

Either was possible.

I was suddenly nervous as well, awkward. I hated confrontations with women from my past. At least I had an excuse now for why there would be no further confrontations—a.k.a. I was getting married in less than an hour. It almost seemed fitting to see her, out of the blue as it was, since it was the last day of my bachelorhood and all.

Or temporarily, anyway.

"I really didn't want to bother you today," she said before I could ask her why she was here.

"No. No bother. I'm ready to go and just twiddling my thumbs. Are you here for the ceremony?" Now that I looked her over, she wasn't at all dressed for a wedding. She wore leggings and a cotton dress over it. A scarf was wrapped around her neck and she still had her coat on and open, as though she'd come directly to my room, not bothering to stop at the coat check or find a seat first.

"No. I'm. Well," she chuckled. "I wasn't invited. Which is fine. I didn't come for the wedding, is what I mean. Congratulations and all. I just came today because I knew I could find you here."

She was definitely nervous.

Which definitely made me more nervous.

"Look, Weston, I know this is a terrible time to talk to you, so I thought I could just see you and make an arrangement to meet with you again some other time—a more appropriate time. I tried texting you a few times this summer, but you never responded, so I wasn't sure it was still your number. And then I tried calling your office, but your assistant is really good, actually. She doesn't let anyone through to you without a specific agenda, and I wasn't going to share my reasons for talking to you with her. I didn't think it was a good idea just to show up at your place of business either. I imagined it would be the same scenario. Not that this is any better." She seemed to rethink her actions then shook her head. "Anyway I'm here now because I didn't know how to find you without getting lawyers involved and that was definitely not the way I wanted to go—"

The hair on the back of my neck stood up. "Callie. Why would you need to get lawyers involved?"

She took another deep breath. "I'm doing this wrong. I don't want to do this on your wedding day. I promise. Just tell me when I can meet you again, and I'll leave."

But I knew it in my gut, the way she was acting. I felt an innate sense of psychic dread. The kind that made my skin prickle and the air hum.

"I think you need to tell me what you have to say *because* I'm getting married today, Callie." I said her name like it was a weapon. The only one I had.

She paused a moment. Then dug into her purse and pulled out a photograph and handed it to me.

My hand was shaking as I took it from her, because I already knew what I would see. Blue eyes, deep dimples, hair darker than mine, but the features could've been a twin for any picture in my baby book.

My voice was scratchy when I spoke, my eyes never looking away from the little boy in the image. "What's his name?"

"Sebastian," she said, equally choked up.

And then it hit me, full force, like a basketball thrown while I wasn't looking and landing squarely in my gut—*I had a son.*

I staggered back to the arm chair and sat down, one hand over my mouth as I studied the toddler, memorizing every detail of him. His smile, his chubby cheeks, his squishy hands. The adorable overalls he wore. The shoes on his feet that looked too small to be real.

I had a son.

I already knew he was mine—it was evident just from looking at him. Anyone would be able to see it. There wouldn't need to be a paternity test with the proof he wore on his little face. And Callie had money—as much as I did, if not more—so her reasons for being here weren't likely monetary.

There was no reason to doubt her, but plenty of reason to ask, "Why are you just telling me about him now?"

"I made a bad decision. I should've told you sooner."

I tore my eyes from the picture and looked at her, anger quickly filling me. This—this tiny *person* had been brought into the world without any thought at all of me, and she'd summed it up in the same words she might use to describe ordering a second dessert.

"You made a *bad decision*? What the hell is that supposed to mean?"

She took a step closer. "Look. I really didn't want to talk about this today. There's not enough time to go through everything—"

"Try," I demanded.

She searched the room as if searching for her answers, then resolutely sunk into the chair opposite me. "I didn't know if I *wanted* to tell you. That's the honest truth, and its terrible. Go ahead and hate me for it, but I didn't know you. I didn't know what kind of a father you would be. We only spent five days together."

"You didn't know me so you decided that I didn't get a chance to prove myself? That's not the way that paternity works. That's not fair. That's not even legal." My voice was too loud, and I knew it.

"I know. Don't you think I know that? But you have a reputation of being a ladies' man and that's not the kind of person who usually wants to be a father."

"I didn't even get a chance to decide that." A bit quieter now but still just as intense. Just as pissed off.

"You didn't. I made a bad decision. I said that. But I was trying to do what was best for our son."

The phrase *our son* froze me, and I couldn't speak for several moments because I couldn't deny that I didn't know what kind of decisions I would make if I was making them for *our son.*

"This is probably more information than you want to know," she continued, "but my dad was never really around. He was a full-time senator—a career politician, and we don't get along. I thought that maybe instead of a sometimes father, Sebastian would be happier without one at all. That it would be less disappointing for him than the way I felt, always watching my father leave. Recently I've reconsidered and decided I should have given you the chance to be a different dad than my dad was to me. Because I haven't changed my mind about that, Weston. I can't have an unreliable father in his life. I can't let him be hurt like that. I won't let you do that to him."

I tilted my chin up, ready to argue because of her tone, but how could I argue with those words?

She knew I couldn't, and she went on. "I screwed up by not telling you about him before now but—here he is. He turned two in October. He's never had a dad. Here's your chance. If you want to be a father and actually be in his life, I welcome you."

The same sort of deep and long emotions I felt for Elizabeth stirred in me at Callie's words. Her invitation was long overdue, and I was pissed and hurt, and both were emotions I didn't have time to deal with at the moment—she was right about that.

On top of that there was recognition in her words. I understood what she meant about not wanting a sometimes dad. My father had probably been in my life more than hers, and I already knew, having never really thought about what kind of parent I wanted to be, that I wanted to be a better dad than him.

"I have to get married," I said to Callie, not trying to dismiss her, but cognizant of the other woman—the one who was waiting for me to say 'I do.'

Her birthright was the one I was here for.

"I know," Callie said. "That's why I'd wanted to wait. Please, let's talk more. Be angry at me. Be pissed. But, please, don't make any rash decisions about this. Let's talk first before you decide whether or not you're going to claim Sebastian. Because if you can't really be there, really commit to being in his life, then I don't think you should be there at all."

She didn't have a legal right to make that plea. Though, with the strings her father could pull in his office, it wasn't a battle I would ever want to take up.

And she was right, if I did want to be this little boy's dad—Sebastian's dad—*my* little boy's dad, it had to be all or nothing.

If I made this decision, it wouldn't be for sometimes. It would be forever.

I thought as quickly as I could with my head buzzing like it was. "I don't leave for my honeymoon until Monday. Can I see you tomorrow?"

We exchanged information, made a plan to meet, and then I escorted the woman who had changed my entire life out the door.

When I was alone again I only had five minutes left before I was due to line up for the ceremony. Five minutes to get my thoughts together after this bombshell that Callie had laid on me. It wasn't enough time.

And yet I already knew what I wanted to do.

I felt it in my bones. In the way my heart sang at the memory of those tiny dimples, perfect replicas of my own. In the way this was finally something of my own, something I could do right—of course I would be there for Sebastian. Even if it changed everything. Even if I wasn't ready to be a father. I was ready to try.

I wanted to try.

And he wasn't the only one I wanted to try with. If I was making long plans now, laying out a future, I couldn't pretend anymore that this day-to-day shit was gonna work. I had to set anchors, had to plant roots. And maybe Elizabeth really didn't want to be mine, but before I let her walk away, I had to try one more time to fight for her for real, fight like it mattered, starting today.

Because if I was going to give my child a home, I wanted it to be perfect. And for me, perfect was the home I already had.

# CHAPTER
# TWENTY-TWO

*Elizabeth*

I TILTED MY face up as Marie put the finishing touches of gloss along my lips.

"And Nana is already seated?" I asked my mother, who was fussing with the bow at my back.

"Yes," she said, losing patience with me. "I already told you Nana is seated. Along with Aunt Becky. And Grandmama already called and wished you a happy day."

"What about Weston's parents?"

"You know this would be easier if you would stop talking." Marie gave me a stern look.

I let my expression deliver my apology and parted my lips exactly the way she'd asked so she could finish her application. "All done," she said after a minute. She dropped the gloss into her makeup bag and stood back, wiping her hands on a paper towel.

"Oh, Elizabeth, you look gorgeous," Melissa, my maid of honor exclaimed. She looked beautiful herself, in a midnight blue gown, simple and classic, exactly the style I preferred. Mirabelle had been a genius at finding the particular details she'd noticed I liked.

And all for a wedding that didn't even count.

My mother came around from behind me and stepped back with Marie and Melissa to take me in. Tears sprang to her eyes. "Baby, you are stunning. Absolutely stunning." She took my hand and pulled me over to the mirror so I could see for myself.

My breath caught when I saw myself in the high-necked ivory Vera Wang gown. It was simple, with a halter bodice and an elongated silhouette. I'd elected for no train and no veil, the one unique detail the T-strap razor-back which I turned to admire now.

I really did look stunning. Like a bride. Like a *queen*. A lump gathered at the back of my throat, and I had to swallow hard past it.

"It's too bad . . ." I trailed off remembering that Melissa didn't know the truth and just squeezed my mother's hand instead.

"Yes," my mother said, before Melissa could ask. "It's too bad your father couldn't have been here. He would've been really proud of you."

My mother's cover-up only made the knot in my stomach tighten more, but I appreciated her effort.

There was a knock on the door, and Melissa opened it to find Lee-Ann Gregori. "Places," she said. "It's almost showtime."

Funny how she'd chosen exactly the right word—showtime.

I hugged Marie and my mother, and they went off to take their seats. Then Melissa embraced me and slipped into the hall to line up, not as worried about being seen since she wasn't the bride. I stayed behind the door, waiting and wishing for something impossible.

The next knock, I assumed, was my cue, but when I opened it, Donovan was standing there.

"Just came to check in."

I sighed, not really interested in seeing him. After he'd warned me off at the tux shop, Donovan had ended up going to France himself to work on halting the sale of Dyson Media's advertising subsidiary and prepare for the upcoming merger with Reach. I hadn't seen him since then, and I was grateful for what he'd done, apparently having slowed Darrell's plans down. But it didn't override my irritation that he'd said the things he'd said to me before he'd left.

"I'm good," I said. "It's about time for me to go, so . . ."

"I know. I just caught you. There's something else I wanted to tell you," he added, as though he was unsure how to say it.

I looked up, my curiosity piqued. "Yes?"

"I came here today with Sabrina."

My eyes rolled, and if I didn't need it I would have thrown my bouquet at him. "More entertaining for a friend?"

"No," he said. "I'm keeping her for myself."

Keeping her for himself? As though she were property. As though she were an object passed between friends.

But never mind that chauvinistic choice of words that Donovan had used—did that mean Sabrina wasn't Weston's?

I didn't have to speak the question out loud, it was written all over my face, and Donovan answered it unprompted.

"I led you to believe that Weston was planning to end up with Sabrina," he said, seeming uncomfortable with his admission. "And that may have been more of what my plans had been than his. I thought you should know that."

"Oh," I said digesting this information. That was quite a lot to take in and I only had a couple of minutes now until I was set to meet my groom face-to-face and exchange wedding vows. "It would've been nice to have known this, I don't know, before today."

Before I'd written off any possibility of exploring the feelings Weston had sparked in me.

"I'm sure it would have been. The main message isn't any different, Elizabeth. I would still give the same warning, if you'd like to hear it. Weston has never settled down with a woman for more than two weeks. I appreciate that you've felt a connection between the two of you, but I don't recommend you put any faith in that lasting. If you do, it'll only get messy. There's already a pool set up on how soon the divorce will go through. That's advice given as a business partner who doesn't like messes. But it's also given as a friend."

"A friend?" I scoffed. "A friend would have told me the whole truth sooner and let me decide how to think and feel for myself. You just assumed you knew what was best for me." *Just like my father*, I mentally added.

I took a slow breath through gritted teeth and let it out before speaking again. "I appreciate what you've done for me and Dyson Media, Donovan. But if you don't mind, I think maybe you aren't qualified to step in as Weston's protector anymore." I stepped closer and put my hand on his arm. "That's *my* advice, as a friend."

For a moment he looked like he might argue, but then he simply said, "Advice taken."

LeeAnn peeked in then and gave the signal.

"Walk me out?" I asked Donovan, and with a nod, he led me to the foyer outside the Onyx Ball where the opening strains of Appalachia Waltz could be heard, my chosen processional just beginning to play. He left me standing behind my maid of honor where she waited, still hidden from view. And after she took her trip down the aisle, it was my turn.

No going back now, even if I wanted to. My future was waiting.

With my shoulders thrown back and my head held high, I stepped into the doorway of the ballroom, and the entire audience stood to face me.

It was nerve-racking, and threw me for a moment to see an entire room standing at my presence, to have so many people looking toward me. It was a feeling I had intended to embrace, as I wanted to be the officer of a company that was so much larger than this simple ballroom could hold.

It was more intimidating than I had counted on.

But even with all eyes on me and the wave of anxiety that produced, the thing that made my knees buckle and the breath stutter from me so that I had to try to catch it in large gulps was the sight of Weston standing at the end of the aisle, waiting for me.

And everyone else in the room disappeared.

What had felt like an overwhelming number of footsteps between us became simple and easy, like crossing a well-worn path, one I could travel blindfolded. I set him as an anchor and he reeled me in, and there was no way I was imagining the look on his face as I neared him. As though he'd never seen anyone more beautiful, as though he'd never wanted to look at anyone but me.

As if I were his queen.

When I finally slipped into place next to him he took my hand in his, and I could feel that he was trembling, or maybe it was me. I was glad that it wasn't a time for us to speak, because there weren't words that I could say in that moment. Nothing seemed to sum up the feeling in my chest. And whatever wisdom there was in remembering that all of this was a performance, that every bit of this was going to have an end, I couldn't listen to any of that right now.

There was just this. Now. Our hands joined together.

Whatever happened after didn't matter.

The officiant welcomed everyone, the words he said already a blur even as they came out of his mouth, my head whirring too much to focus on any one particular phrase or sentiment. He did a reading, something we'd chosen early in the planning process, and then his speech began where he talked about the definition of marriage, where he imagined the life that we were creating together, and the future that we could bring to the earth as Mr. and Mrs. King.

I let his speech go by, background noise to the pressure of Weston's palm against mine. The way the warmth from his body traveled into mine was biology, I supposed, but right then it was mysterious and magical.

For the rest of my life, if this was all I had to hold onto, just this, this moment and this connection—this connection that Donovan said not to make too much of—it would be enough. This magical, fascinating spark that ebbed and flowed and never broke. I couldn't buy that anywhere. I couldn't barter it from anyone else. How lucky that I'd managed to discover it and grow it with this man whom I never would have met if it weren't for my father and his old-fashioned notions.

Maybe there was something wondrous about that too. How things came around. How karma turned the tables.

Then it was time for us to speak, for us to say our vows.

The officiant instructed us to turn to each other and Weston took both of my hands in his, and I realized I'd been wrong about needing something special and original because even hearing the traditional vows I'd settled for come from Weston's lips today, spoken while he looked at me the way he was looking at me, was going to be incredible.

Even if he didn't mean them, there was enough to build a fantasy around.

But when he started speaking, I didn't recognize the words that came from his lips.

"I didn't know what I was getting into when I met you, Elizabeth," he said, and my heart started hammering so hard against my rib cage that I was sure that he and every person in the room could hear it. "I had no idea that my house would be cleaner or that I would be late to every event that we attended together. I certainly didn't have any idea that you would change me so much. Not just me but the world that I live in, the world around me. How I think, how I feel, how I breathe. You're in my heart, now. You're my home."

His voice caught, and he had to pause. "You're my home, and for as much of your life that you let me, it would be my honor to be that for you."

And then it was my turn, which wasn't fair, because I was tearing up, and if he'd done this, if he'd made up these vows on the spot just to get a reaction from me, then it worked. Everyone in the room would be fooled—including me.

But if he really meant them . . .

God, I *hoped* he meant them.

"Elizabeth," the officiant prodded.

"Yeah, I got this," I said, and the audience laughed. I took a deep breath and tried to find words that would equal his. "Weston, you knock me off my feet, every time I walk into a room. You frazzle my head and you make my insides do somersaults and somehow you make me braver than anyone I've ever known. I've never felt more wanted and important and worthy than I do when I look at myself through your eyes. And how you make me feel about myself is only a fraction of how I feel about you. I don't want you to ever let me go. I want to serve all my days beside you as your queen."

The rest of the ceremony went by in a daze. We exchanged rings and it didn't feel awkward or pretend—it felt real.

It *was* real.

And when it came time to kiss the bride, we reached for each other like we were starving and a kiss was the only thing that would nourish and bring us back to life.

Afterward, there was chaos and confusion and hubbub, and LeeAnn was rushing us along to our next destination. The ballroom was being changed over to fit our reception in the very same space, and we were hurried out to take photographs. Some of these were to be alone and some with family, including Darrell, and I knew there wasn't time for chatting or trying to figure out what had just happened on that podium in front of everybody.

Nevertheless, Weston pulled me into the event room across the foyer, an area we had reserved for breakfast earlier in the day, and when LeeAnn scolded him, saying she needed us right then, he said, "One minute with my wife," with such finality that she backed off.

And a shiver ran through my entire body because I was his *wife*.

He closed the door and I wanted to jump into his arms and kiss him some more, wanted to tear him out of his so carefully fitted clothes and ravage his body, but even more I wanted to ask him, needed to know, "Did you mean it?"

"I meant it. Every word," he said practically speaking over me.

Just like the ceremony, we were standing face to face, our hands held in each others, this time with new matching rings on our left hands.

"I meant it too, Weston, I meant it too. I want to be with you."

"I want to be with you, too," he said kissing my face everywhere, quick and urgent. "I want my home with you. I want a life with you."

"I do too. I was so scared that you didn't. I thought—"

"I know. I should've—"

"No, I should've told *you*."

We were talking at the same time, kissing and laughing and apologizing. And everything inside me threatened to burst. I wanted to throw open the door and yell to the whole room, *Everyone, it's real. Weston and I are real!*

"You make me so happy," I told him instead, knowing I only had a second, and I couldn't say anything out there.

"When you don't want to kill me that is," he added, joking.

I nodded and laughed. Another explosion of joy went off inside of me as I imagined our life ahead, us living together, taking over my father's company. "You're going to love life in France."

"Sure," he said. "I've been there before. When are we going to France?"

"Well, we'll live there. To run the company."

Weston chuckled. "What do you mean, *we'll live in France*?"

It was my turn to chuckle. His forgetfulness was becoming legendary. "You're kidding, right? It's always been the plan that I'll live in France. Dyson Media is headquartered in France. My father lived in France."

He took a cautious step back from me, dropping my hands, and sticking one of his in his pocket. "No, no. You can be a shareholder without having to live in the country."

"But you know that I want to be more than a shareholder. I want to be on the board. I want to be an officer." His expression didn't budge. "Weston, you *know* that was always the plan. That's what you've been training me for all these months."

He shook his head slowly.

"You'll have the subsidiary. You'll merge with Reach and you can still have the business there. Is that what this is about? We can still live there and you can still have your company." We'd just found each other. And he was saying we couldn't be together already?

No, I wouldn't lose him this fast.

"Elizabeth, I can't. I—"

LeeAnn knocked on the door, and came in without being invited. "You guys, the photographer is waiting! And your guests! We have to go!"

"Weston?" I asked, not caring that LeeAnn was still standing there. I was begging, pleading with everything I had, by saying just his name.

He looked at our wedding planner and back to me, and shook his head one final time. "I'm sorry, Elizabeth. I can't go with you."

The photographer was waiting to capture my heartbreak; there was no more time left for this. No more time left for *us*.

We walked as one out of the room and into our separate lives.

HIS PAST WAS SUPPOSED TO BE BEHIND THEM.

*Hudson Pierce-*

*You act so high and mighty, you and your perfect pregnant wife Alayna.*
*With your perfect child and your perfect home.*

*You weren't always perfect. Your past is filled with misdeeds.*
*Does your wife know all your secrets?*
*Would she stand behind you if she did?*

*You think because she's on bedrest you can protect her? How sweet.*

*Sleep tight, you two.*

*-An Old Friend.*

# Also by
# Laurelin Paige

## THE DIRTY UNIVERSE
*Dirty Filthy Rich Men* (Dirty Duet #1)
*Dirty Filthy Rich Love* (Dirty Duet #2)
*Dirty Filthy Fix* (a spinoff novella)
*Dirty Sexy Player* (Dirty Games Duet #1)
*Dirty Sexy Games* (Dirty Games Duet #2, November 2018)

## THE FIXED UNIVERSE
*Fixed on You* (Fixed #1)
*Found in You* (Fixed #2)
*Forever with You* (Fixed #3)
*Hudson* (Fixed #4)
*Fixed Forever* (Fixed #5)
*Free Me* (Found Duet #1)
*Find Me* (Found Duet #2)
*Chandler* (a spinoff novel)
*Falling Under You* (a spinoff novella)

## FIRST AND LAST
*First Touch*
*Last Kiss*

## HOLLYWOOD HEAT
*Sex Symbol*
*Star Struck*
*One More Time*

Written with Kayti McGee
under the name LAURELIN MCGEE
*Hot Alphas*

*Miss Match*

*Love Struck*


Written with SIERRA SIMONE
*Porn Star*

*Hot Cop*

# ABOUT LAURELIN PAIGE

WITH OVER 1 million books sold, Laurelin Paige is the *NY Times*, *Wall Street Journal*, and *USA Today* Bestselling Author of the Fixed Trilogy. She's a sucker for a good romance and gets giddy anytime there's kissing, much to the embarrassment of her three daughters. Her husband doesn't seem to complain, however. When she isn't reading or writing sexy stories, she's probably singing, watching *Game of Thrones* and *the Walking Dead*, or dreaming of Michael Fassbender. She's also a proud member of Mensa International though she doesn't do anything with the organization except use it as material for her bio.

*www.laurelinpaige.com*
*laurelinpaigeauthor@gmail.com*

CPSIA information can be obtained
at www.ICGtesting.com
Printed in the USA
BVHW032040110721
611675BV00005B/27